The Hungarian Cemetery: Secrets Within

The Muddy Waters Series

Joshua Banks

Copyright © 2024 by Joshua R. Banks
First published in 2024 by Marauder's Row
ISBN 979-8-9850847-4-0
All rights reserved. No part of the book may be produced in any form or by any electronic or mechanical means, including information storage and retrieval systems, without permission in writing from the publisher, except by a reviewer who may use brief quotations in a book review.

The characters and events in this book are fictitious. Any similarity to real persons, living or dead, is coincidental and not intended by the author.

Interior & Cover Design by Joshua R. Banks
First Printing, 2024
Edited by: Joshua R. Banks

Dedication

I wanted to dedicate this novel to Erik Nelson. You have been my brother, best friend, and support system since junior high. I miss and think of you every day. The world lost one of the good ones. When you passed, a part of me died I will never get back. This new series is in your memory. Until we meet in the hereafter, I will carry your memory and influence into my novels, where you can live forever in this world.

In memory of my grandma, Mildred Banks who always listened, loved, and supported my choices, always. Mom and Dad, your support over the years has meant more to me than you could ever realize. It doesn't matter how old I get, I will always need your love and guidance. What a journey we find ourselves in life? It never turns out quite the way we planned it. I've learned the destination is not remotely as satisfying as the journey itself.

AND FINALLY…to all those who influenced my characters in the story, I hope you smile a little when you read this novel; especially if you were in my 2021 Freshmen English classes.

Acknowledgment

Shana, to whom I got the pleasure to work with over the last year. You have been a wonderful mentor and support system to my learning curve. Without your guidance and insight, I would not have been able to succeed in this undertaking alone. I will take your constructive criticism all week long and twice on Sundays! If ever you need my help with anything, simply ask.

Chapter 1: A New Break

"Look there," Kayden said, pointing towards the turkeys roaming the open field.

"Whoa," exclaimed her younger brother, sitting beside her, "there's at least six of them."

"Seven, moron," Kayden retorted, "I thought you were supposed to be smart, Jackson."

"That is more than enough from you, Kayden," her mom responded quickly from the driver's seat.

Kayden sat back in her seat, no longer interested in looking out the SUV's window. Kayden's jet black hair fell a little over her face from the motion. Kayden had entered her sophomore year of school, riding the wave of starting on her volleyball team. True, she didn't have a boyfriend, but who had time for those anyway when playing sports and fitting in with friends? Her emerald eyes looked back out the window of their SUV. She was already upset over the fact her family was moving smack dab in the middle of the school year. She had to quit the team right when they were getting ready for districts.

What a punch in the damn gut, she thought. *I worked so hard to break into the starting varsity line-up and then mom yanks the rug out from under me.*

It was the start of October and upon coming home from school; she found her mom packing up their stuff.

So freakin' unfair, mom didn't even give any of us warning, just ups and leaves, she thought.

"Look Kayden, I know you're upset over our leaving Nebraska..." started her mom, only to be immediately cut off by the fuming teen.

"Upset, Mom," Kayden interrupted, her voice gaining volume in the small confined space of the SUV.

"When I get a poor grade, I'm upset. If I lose a volleyball game, I'm upset. If I drop a slice of my favorite pizza because I tripped over Jackson's stupid shoes he leaves on the floor, I get upset. What I feel right now isn't upset. It's anger, and I direct it at you. You didn't even tell us we were leaving. You didn't even give us a chance to say goodbye. It was just us coming home and 'oh by the way guys, we're moving tomorrow. Pack your things...' La, La, La, La," Kayden spat sarcastically.

Kayden's mom quieted almost immediately and focused on the road. Kailynn had inherited her Raven colored hair and bright green eyes. Truth be told, they could have passed for sisters. The family had been driving for over ten hours, barring any quick stops for gas or bathroom breaks. The family had spoken little.

They just selected podcasts on Pandora's app from their mom's phone during the ride. They'd stop every time Kayden's stupid brother's bladder was about to explode. Kayden didn't really have much of an appetite, nor was thirsty. Her frustrations over the family situation were causing nothing but stress and depression in her.

Jackson had been playing almost non-stop games on his phone. It was difficult to see any resemblance between the two siblings. Unlike his sister and mother, Jackson sported sandy brown hair and dark brown eyes. A trait he inherited from his father's side of the family. The two things either of the siblings had in common were they had athletic frames for sports and both were intelligent. However, neither of them had very much in common. These two similarities were the catalyst for most of their arguments.

He was a 13-year-old eighth grader who loved Sony Play Station, the Oculus, and his phone apps. Oddly enough, he liked to read, or at least listen to, stories on podcasts while playing games. The debate in their family (mainly his mom and sister) was what 'defined' reading.

His sister felt that if he didn't actually read the words from a book or an online document, she did not consider it reading. His mom argued he was an auditory learner, so listening to it was the same as reading. Jackson could remember any story or piece of information he heard just like anyone else who read it. Therefore, if he has the information they have from the same piece of literature, how is that not reading? They went in as far as researching actual documented sources online to argue their points. The damn fight had last two weeks.

In case no one knew, his mom and sister butted

heads like those rams on the discovery channel vying for territory. Neither one of them would give an inch for their argument. This argument had finally ended once outside viable sources had weighed in. While at school, every teacher Kayden had interviewed for their opinion on the subject had sided with her mom on technicality. They also agreed with Kayden that she was right. When arguing the point about physically reading with one's eyes to get the information; it was reading. However, when her friends asked how a deaf person or blind person read when nothing in brail was available, well, it negated her argument.

Reading is reading, is reading it would appear, but who gives a dead rat's fart? thought Jackson. *Girls were dumb and illogical.* A natural frown appeared on his face at the thought.

Their sense of structure was aloof to him. Probably why girls didn't talk to him. *Again, who cares? he* continued to ponder.

Still, it alluded to the young lad why they were moving. It bothered him, obviously; but his mom was in charge and if she said they needed to leave, guess it was important. It pulled at his logical brain, though, so he decided he'd try to engage his mom a little differently than his confrontational sister.

"Mom," he innocently inquired.

"Yeah," she automatically responded.

"I suppose you lost your job or something? You never really told us specifically where we were going except to Illinois. So, any chance you might tell us a little more than what you have?"

Their mom considered her son's question understandable. She herself was a little more than frustrated as well. She didn't know how much to really tell them up front. She didn't want to scare or worry them more than she had already. Since their departure from Norfolk, she had been thinking about how to deal with the issue. They had lived in a semi-large city as far as Nebraska was concerned. The city had a population which spanned a little over twenty-four thousand, give or take. Now, she was moving her children to a place where it was under ten-thousand in a rural area of Southern Illinois. In fact, the actual population of the little area they were driving towards had around one-hundred people. The surrounding towns were tiny; all over sporadic distances. The nearest large city was St. Louis, but it was at least two-hours from there.

"Well," she started slowly, "I didn't lose my job, Jackson. Aunt Hollyn called and things have been very difficult for her as of late. She's been having health concerns and lives alone now that Grand-pa died."

"Don't tell me we're going to live at Aunt Hollyns' mom?" interjected Kayden immediately.

"Shut up Kayden and let mom talk," defended Jackson. "Do you have to yell, argue, and fight about everything?" His dark brown eyes met her bright emerald ones and both knew a new argument between them was about to ensue.

"Hey you little dip shit, this affects you as well," spat Kayden vehemently.

"Kayden Lynn Toth, what did I tell you about your mouth?" her mom scorned. "Since you turned 15, your attitude and mouth have gotten ten times worse. What is it with you?"

"Oh, I don't know, mom. Maybe it's because dad left us a year ago, without so much as a goodbye. Just came home after work one day and 'later-on'. You couldn't really give us a reason for that. How can you not see any of that coming, huh? No warning? Nope... Now we're up and moving on a whim. We had to downsize our stuff, so we sold a bunch of it and our house to pay bills. You quit your job, we move from our new apartment, bye. Just a lot to absorb right now, but hey, my attitude has gotten worse. Let's just blame it on puberty and my hormones are going wild. Oh, almost forgot, I just started getting my period two months ago, so yeah, there's that wonderful genetic fun I now deal with as well." Kayden's furrowed brow was completely turned down, like a frown.

"Gross," exclaimed Jackson. He made a disgusting face towards his sister, who just rolled her eyes at him.

"Honey, I totally get your frustrations. I couldn't help anything to do with your dad. He had some agenda which didn't include us. No one knows where he is. He just left. How do you think I feel? My husband not only abandoned me, but our children. I hurt on both fronts for you and Jackson, while trying to be the sole provider for our family."

Kailynn was barely keeping it together herself and the kids were just about the only thing allowing her to focus on survival as a parent. Her need to focus on her personal relationship had turned upside down and left her bereft of her usual happy-go-luck self.

"It's okay, mom," Jackson chimed in, immediately seeing his mom's vulnerability. "Kayden is going to blame you no matter what, because the one she should blame isn't here. She still makes excuses for him by making you the bad guy," Jackson said, goading his sister.

"Shut up, you little shit," Kayden blasted towards

her brother.

Jackson just gave one of his patented shoulder-shrugs with a lip sticking out sarcastically. The kind that says, *if the shoe fits, wear it.*

Just when Kayden was going to really lay into her brother, her mom jerked the wheel of the car hard. She had enough.

Kailynn Toth was a loving, compassionate mother, however, even she had her limits and once she lost her temper, step back fast. She had always been innately protective of her children and always put their needs before her own. She had not come from a rich family, nor had a very strong education in college. She had only graduated from a junior college with an associate's degree, but far be it for her not to have inherited her father's strong work ethic. When her husband had left, she instantly took over the full responsibilities of her family. She had two jobs and ran herself ragged to make sure her children's lives weren't up heaved even more with the loss of one parent. One parent, who, for better lack of a word, didn't give a 'shit' about any of them.

Now all of this was coming to a head, and she'd heard enough from her entitled, yet albeit emotionally hurting, daughter. She pulled over to the side of the highway, slamming on the brakes to add a little more effect. Shifting the car into park, she turned off the engine. Undoing her belt buckle, she immediately turned around and placed her upper body in-between the front chairs.

Without preamble, she went straight at her daughter.

"Here's the facts, Kayden, so we mistake nothing or there's no misperceived notions. Your father left because he either wanted to be rid of us, which he probably considered us baggage, or he left us for someone or something else. Either way, his actions should have been more than enough for you to get the picture. He wanted nothing to do with any of us." Kailynn's face had turned blood red with all the pent up resentment she had been holding inside for months now.

Jackson's eyes moved to the floorboard of the SUV and Kayden stared back at her mother, but with a face expressing emotional pain, not anger. There it was, stated clearly and with no pleasantries. A simply fact no one in the family, flat out, wanted to say.

"If he had left me, fine, at least he would have been able to get visitation with you guys and he'd still be a dad in your lives. However, he couldn't even come to the divorce proceedings because no one can find him. He jumped town, our state, maybe even the country. No one knows the reasoning behind his choices, which is another reason I took my maiden name back. You two also felt the same way and took my name as well because of the pain he had caused us."

Kayden looked away from her mother, down at her lap. Her mom continued.

"I have been busting my ass for a year, working two jobs to keep our family afloat. I am worn out. We have no family in Nebraska; it is just a place your dad moved us to for his job a long time ago when you were just a baby. I get it, you have friends there and it is where both of you have grown up. The fact is, our genuine family that's left is from Southern Illinois. To be more specific, we were from a little area called Ledford."

Jackson's facial expression took on an old man's

wrinkled face. "Ledford? Who has ever heard of Ledford? It sounds like a bad sitcom on TV."

Kayden just rolled her eyes at her brother's statement. She looked up at her mom, "never even heard of a place like that mom."

"That's because we always told you Aunt Hollyn lived in the Chicago area with grandpa. You know of my sister and dad from cards and pictures, but you've never met them. Your dad always made excuses for not traveling to visit them. He knew they couldn't really travel to us, so it was a nice convenience for him to make sure you never met part of your family. I can only say I'm really sorry I didn't do something more about the situation. My love for your dad blinded me."

Kayden made a sour face. "Let me get this straight, mom. We never met your sister or dad because our dad wouldn't let us?" she said skeptically.

"Pretty much, yeah," responded her mother.

Jackson chimed in, "why exactly didn't dad want us to meet them, mom?"

Kailynn looked at both children while Jackson's question hung in the air like an anchor around their mom's neck. She didn't really have a great explanation other than her ex-husband had feared where she grew up and never wanted to see the place again, nor her family. An unspoken event from the past had plagued their relationship and made the murky topic of her family difficult for him to address. Kailynn couldn't tell the kids the truth about the past, at least not yet. She needed more time to think about it. They also needed to grow up a little more. What she knew was she needed her family.

She answered the question by side-stepping it indirectly.

"Dad didn't like my father or sister much, guys. They had a falling out a long time ago. We never mentioned it because we didn't want to include you in our past issues. Your dad thought if we just ignored what happened, it just wouldn't be a problem for us. So we moved to Nebraska to get a fresh start."

"So Aunt Hollyn and grandpa were bad guys?" questioned Kayden.

"No," Kailynn responded immediately, "they were not bad people. Your dad and them just couldn't see eye to eye about things in life. He felt they never would. He didn't want conflict at home. So... we left."

Their mom continued, "I guess the longer we were away from where I grew up, the less and less inclined I was to rekindle things. I know now that was a big mistake. Grandpa died just recently, and I didn't even get to say goodbye."

Genuine sadness spread across Kailynn's face, which quieted down the kids. Seeing their mom in emotional pain, struggling with things, was a rare event. Kailynn kept those types of problems away from her children. She simply didn't want to burden them with things out of their control.

"So there's the whole of it. We're going back to where I grew up and helping Aunt Hollyn. I need some helping too. Your dad did a number on me emotionally. I know Kayden," she said, centering directly on her daughter.

"You think I should have seen things coming and been more prepared or forthcoming with you and Jackson? The fact is, I was blind-sided by your dad. We all were and if there was ever a time to start over fresh, it is now. The area of Ledford has a small population, but its fair share of history. There are neighboring towns around as well."

Jackson responded, "how big is the school in Ledford, mom?"

Kailynn looked at Jackson and smiled. "Actually, there is no school in Ledford. Kids who live there go to either Harrisburg or Carrier Mills school district. Ledford is almost smack dab in the middle of both towns. I figured you would probably like Harrisburg. It is a bigger school and wouldn't be a tremendous change from your Nebraska school."

"How long before we enroll?" Kayden interrupted.

Kailynn's eyes turned back toward her stubborn daughter.

Letting out a large, exhaustive sigh, "We'll see Kayden. I know it seems like things suck right now and I'm a terrible person for up heaving you. Just as you were getting comfortable over the school year, but things have been tough financially, emotionally, and a little spiritually for me. If the truth be told, I've seen both of you struggling too."

Both of the siblings looked at each other and kind of acknowledged that what their mother had just said wasn't too far off the mark. It had been hard without their dad and now another change of pace was occurring.

Jackson just shrugged his shoulders, and a gave kind of 'okay' grunt. He always was one to just roll with the punches. It was in his personality. Kayden wasn't as easygoing nor open to change. In fact, change felt almost impossible, and she usually dug in tooth and nail to keep things on an even keel with nothing rocking her boat. Unfortunately, this was a situation she simply couldn't run or hide from.

She looked away from her mom out the window and said with finality, "Still sucks, though."

Her mom looked them both over, gave a brief nod, and got back into her seat. She fired up the car and put it into drive. As she started back onto the highway, she looked in the rear-view mirror and made eye contact with her daughter. In that instant connection, Kailynn said, "such is life."

Chapter Two: Aunt Hollyn

    The drive was over 12 hours and that wasn't counting stops. Kailynn knew it was a bit of a trek, and it would take all day to get there. Once they hit St. Louis, the trio passed by the Arch and crossed the bridge covering the Mississippi River. The Arch was huge and right there along the riverfront. It was white and lit up. She wondered how long it took to get to the top of it inside. It was something she never did when she lived close to St. Louis, but had secretly always wanted to.

    Crossing over into Illinois flooded her mind into the past. When she was younger, she attended Southeastern Illinois College. A small junior college which catered mostly to the surrounding counties. It actually pulled students from two other states besides

Illinois. It was so close to the borders of Kentucky and Indiana that the school allowed those students to attend with in-state tuition outside a sixty-mile radius.

Harrisburg was located so far south that Kentucky and Indiana were less than an hour's drive from there. It wasn't uncommon for a few graduates near those locations to choose to attend Southeastern to "get away" from home. After junior college, many Illinois students went to Murray State University or University of Southern Indiana.

Kailynn didn't really have too many options for college because of finances and, if truth be told, she didn't really care about going to college either; but she had a few opinions on the subject. As a compromise, she would go to SIC and at least get a two-year degree.

Kailynn and some of her high school friends who also attended SIC liked to go out of town to party venues on weekends or Thursdays; such was college life. Someone always knew of a good place to hit. They engaged in typical older teen behaviors. Find a bar, club or party; bring a fake ID, then dress enticingly while drinking and dancing to have fun. If you were lucky, you might get someone's digits.

Digits? Do they even use that phrase anymore?

There were colleges in Illinois as well. Adventures at SIU (Southern Illinois University) was an excellent location to hit. Carbondale used to be one of the best party college places around. If they were feeling especially rowdy, they made their way over to the Belleville area. It was closer to St. Louis. There was a club called Stages Nightclub.

Kaitlynn smiled to herself. *That place was a loose operation for sure, but of course back then it was exactly the place a college kid would love.*

She knew it had eventually got shut down. Someone else probably has bought almost all of her old haunts from the past, converting them to whatever business they had in mind now.

Change happens. Unfortunately, she pondered, *places like Southern Illinois were slight exceptions to that thinking. Folks there hold the past close to their chest and pass down to new generations the issues of their elders; in other words, generational grudges.*

"How much further, mom?" whined Kayden.

Her question snapped her mom out of her thoughts. Kailynn rubbed her tired eyes and actually looked around at the landscaping they were passing on the road. She had turned off the highway at Marion and hit Route 13. Her mind did the estimated math in her head, using the experiences of her youth to determine how much further they were out from Ledford.

"Well, mom?" badgered her daughter again.

"It's not like I have an exact watch or measurement tool, Kayden," her mom responded, irritated by Kayden's bored voice.

"Yes we do mom, it's called Google Maps," her daughter returned sarcastically.

"Kayden, I'm driving, not screwing around on the car's map."

"All you have to do is look," she sassed back.

"Why don't you look, yourself? I know it's hard having to move your head to a logical line of sight on the map. That way, you wouldn't have to ask and annoy all of us with your sarcasm. It gets old," bellowed her little brother.

She turned and punched him hard in the arm. Kayden wasn't a starter on the volleyball team because she was pretty. She was a hard hitter and explosive on the court.

"Ow!" exclaimed her little brother, dropping his phone to the floorboard of the car.

"Oh, sorry," Kayden sneered unapologetically.

"Kayden! That is IT!" her mom yelled back at her daughter. "That little stunt is going to cost you one week without your phone."

"What!?" cried her daughter. "He's the one who made the smart-ass comment."

"Your entire existence on this drive has been one big smart-ass comment," retorted Jackson.

"Jackson, I'm handling this," his mom returned. "Kayden, you have done nothing but complain and smack off to anyone who tries to talk. You've earned the punishment."

Kayden grimaced and looked at her mom through the rear-view mirror.

"I'm not giving you my phone," she declared snidely to her mom.

"No problem," her mom replied unconcernedly. "I'll call our service provider tomorrow and shut your line down."

This caught Kayden off guard. The reality of checkmate just hit her.

"Y-you can't do that, mom," she said in disbelief.

"Oh yes, I can, and maybe taking away screen time will help improve your disposition."

Her brother smiled at her conspiratorially. It irritated Kayden beyond belief. Just when she was going to go ballistic, her mom beat her to the punch.

"Harrisburg is up ahead. It's a miracle we haven't seen a ton of deer on the road," she said, looking around the perimeter of the highway where her car lights shined.

Both of the kids perked up. Finally, the place where they would go to school.

As the car came into the outskirts of town, they hit their first stop light. The area was new and unfamiliar at the same time to Kailynn.

There had never been a stoplight here before, she rationalized.

She looked around while the light was red.

Well, Route 13 had changed. It used to be a longer, one-lane road when I was in school. There were two major twists: Jordan's and Dead Man's.

Many wrecks had occurred at those two locations over the years. Luckily, the state of Illinois seemed to have added a new two-lane road, which was as much of a straight shot as it came.

She looked over to her right and saw the Juvenile detention standing where it had been since she was a little girl. It still had its patented tall barb-wired fence wrapped around the facility.

Well, she thought, *I sort of have my bearings.*

She knew there would be some more changes in the town she had grown up in, though. Fifteen years away does that. With the light changing, she continued on a little further. It was too dark to see anything beyond her headlight's vision. Coming to the next set of lights, she saw a familiar sight.

The BBQ Barn with its red exterior. She stopped at another red light and realized the Route 13 had extended into town now, which went past the old mom and pop restaurant. It looked like they had added on to the restaurant since she last saw it. The BBQ Barn looked originally just like the exterior of a barn with extensions in the front. Now it looked to have expanded on the side with a much larger parking lot available.

Damn, I loved those barbecue sandwiches. Oh, and don't get me started on the dessert.

Looking to her right, she saw where the road went right through, where the old Knights of Columbus Hall had been. They had actually celebrated her after-Prom party there. Many nights of bingo flashed through her mind. Her dad used to take her and Hollyn there to gamble on those games. The smoke inside the place back then was just a normal night out. The building was just a simple meeting hall with tables and chairs everywhere, but it was huge to a kid back then. A tinge of sadness reached out to her, remembering a propitious time with her family when she had been younger.

Pushing past the light, she came to another four-way stop. A gas station on her right had popped up and looking across to her left she recognized what used to be the old Walmart. She now had her bearings straight. She took a right when the light turned green, right into the heart of town. They were on Commercial Street.

Now tons of businesses lined both sides of the streets. On the right, they passed a newer building with a big sign that said Speakeasy. It was a liquor store that had a Roaring 20s kind of vibe going for it. It was kind of big for such a small town, but Kailynn assumed they sold many types of alcohol there.

"Whoa, cool name," Jackson muttered, looking at the building. He saw it sold alcohol, cigars and other drinking paraphernalia upon getting closer to it.

"Why is that a cool name?" Kayden asked in response to Jackson's barely audible comment.

"Speakeasies were businesses back during the

prohibition era which sold illegal alcohol. You had to say the password to get in. They did that to hide it from nosy police officers trying to bust them," he curtly responded.

Kayden continued to act uninterested, but the fact was she absorbed everything they passed. She had a small check-list of things; she wanted the town to have, so it didn't seem like living in a farm community with one bank, grocery store, and nowhere to hang out as a teen.

As Kailynn continued to drive on Commercial St, lots of businesses passed by her. The area was stranger than the last time she had seen it. It now had a Walgreen's, an expanded Pizza Hut, larger gas stations with gambling available, CBD dispensaries, an enlarged KFC, Burger King, Super Walmart, Taco-Bell, Burger King, and so much more.

"Now that I remember," Kailynn said out loud to the kids, pointing to two older businesses to their right. "The original Long John Silver and Dairy Queen is still here and in business, it seems."

She smiled to herself. *At least not everything has changed.*

"It is the smallest Dairy Queen ever, mom," complained Kayden.

"Huge surprise there, Kayden," responded her brother. "Maybe you could do something UN-Kayden-like and be less negative."

Kayden turned to her mom. "See, he's the one starting things now!"

Her pleas fell on deaf ears. Kailynn was already lost in her own thoughts. She knew their destination was mere minutes away. The reality of now seeing her sister again was looming upon her more heavily.

Kailynn just shook her head, "he has a point kid."

Jackson smiled in victory over the point he had just scored on his sister. Kayden scowled back at him. He knew it would eventually cost him once his mom was out of eyesight and earshot, but it was worth it. Kayden needed someone to tell her the hard facts. Her attitude sucked, and he was getting sick of it.

They neared the McDonald's on the right and Kailynn remembered when it was much smaller. It had been her hangout. Lots of high school kids hung around there on Friday nights when she was younger. Immediately to her left was a Wal-mart Superstore. Other little businesses surrounded it. Last Kailynn remembered, the location was nothing more than a field.

Ah, progress, she thought.

The family drove right out of Harrisburg and into the night. They didn't get very far out when Jackson exclaimed, "Hey, that looks like the junior high school!"

Everyone looked to their right, and sure enough, the sign in the front verified his claim. Jackson had a smile on his face, but his sister simply wore a smirk.

"Well, at least I won't have to see your face every day because the two schools are not connected," Kayden said with disdain.

Jackson continued to smile and simply looked back at his sister and replied, "My luck is getting better already."

Kailynn smiled to herself at the wheel and kept driving onward. It wasn't very far before she saw the exit on the right, Ledford Road.

Now this part definitely hasn't changed much, she

thought to herself.

    She drove a short way and crossed over Tunnel Hill State Trail. The old railroad tracks which used to lead right through Ledford into Harrisburg had been dug up. It seemed the state had poured concrete the whole way, replacing it with a biking or walking trail. Kailynn's memory gravitated to when she was a kid and could hear those trains passing through in the early mornings and in the evenings. For some, it was a nuisance, but for her, it was a comforting sound.

    The car came to a fork where Ledford Road continued to the left and Little Road went to the right. She paused for a moment and took a deep breath. Her kids noticed her hesitation.

    Jackson responded, "You okay, mom?"

    She nodded and quietly said, "Yes."

    Jackson looked over at his sister and their eyes met. Both knew their mom was dealing with some of her own issues, which neither of them had a clue about. Kailynn turned the car right onto Little Road and drove literally to the end. It stopped at a dead end. She turned left onto what was left of the pavement, which adjusted into gravel. Everyone saw the home on their right. It had a few lights on as they pulled into the gravel driveway. Kailynn put the car in park and turned off the SUV engine. She turned around and looked at the kids.

    "I haven't seen your Aunt Hollyn in a long time. I don't know exactly how she will receive me. We left on rough terms and we have some unresolved issues to deal with. Don't worry. None of about you guys. Just, don't be too judgy about her before we get to know her, okay?"

    Kayden rolled her eyes. "Big surprise there,

mom."

"Shut up Kayden," snapped Jackson. This time, he reached over and pinched her hard on the arm.

Kayden about came out of her skin on her brother. She went to punch him, but he grabbed her arm before she could swing.

"Not this time, sis." Kayden was shocked at how strong her brother was when he stopped her. He'd never done that before.

Kailynn ignored her disgruntled daughter and got out of the car. Her preoccupation with this moment made her ignore her disgruntled daughter. She honestly didn't have a clue how this was going to go. Then, a voice called to her.

"Hello, sis."

Kailynn turned to the voice and saw her younger sister standing in the porch's doorway. Kailynn moved around the front of the car to stand in facing her sister. She and Hollyn both stood awkwardly, each taking in the other's appearance.

"Wow, Kailynn, you look... different. It's been so long," Hollyn stiffly stated.

"Yeah, it has. You look the same, though, always so perfect," Kailynn returned graciously.

Hollyn gave a sarcastic smile. "Thank you, I try. So, how have you been? It's been, what, over ten years since we last spoke face to face?"

Kailynn looked down at the ground and strolled towards her baby sister.

"I've been okay, I guess. You know, just trying to make ends meet. How about you?"

Hollyn shifted her posture to a more defensive stance. "I've been outstanding, superb. Just been taking care of dad and dealing with his health issues," Hollyn replied with sass.

"That's great, Hollyn. Congratulations. I bet you were amazing at it," Kailynn spat back in the same sassy manner. All pretenses of niceness were now gone.

"Thanks, Kailynn. I try my best. But I have to say, I'm still pretty upset about what happened with dad's funeral."

Kailynn's face fell.

"I know, Hollyn. I'm sorry." Her demeanor changed to immediate remorse. "I should have been there."

"You should have. I was the only one left in the family TO BE THERE, except for you." Hollyn's voice though upset cracked a little in the exchange.

"I know, and I'm sorry. But it's not like I did it on purpose. I had some really difficult things going on you know that."

Hollyn backed off a bit when Kailynn said that. She knew about her husband and although she didn't approve of him to begin with; him leaving them all was pure shit.

"I realize that, Kailynn, but it still hurts. It hurt me. You and I are all that remains of our family. I was grieving, and I needed my sister, but you weren't there."

"I understand, Hollyn. And I'm sorry. I can't change what happened. But I'm here now. And I want to be a part of this family again. I want to make things right between us."

Hollyn looked at Kailynn for a moment, considering her words.

She stared at the ground for a moment and looked up with her crooked, mischievous smile, "Those are your two rug-rats in the car?" giving a head nod towards the SUV.

"I'll bet they really embraced the idea of coming here to live, didn't they?"

Hollyn didn't wait for a reply. She continued, "Okay, Kailynn. I hear you and I'm glad you're here." Her tone softened. "I've missed you, you know?"

Kailynn returned her smile. "I've missed you too, Hollyn. And I know we have a lot of catching up to do. But for now, can we just start fresh? Can we just be sisters again?"

Hollyn nodded, taking a few steps towards her sister until they were eye to eye and the two women embraced.

"We never stopped Lynni. So, yeah, let's start fresh. I'm glad you're here."

"You know I hate that nickname, Hollyn." Kailynn retorted. There was a pause as each of them looked into the other's face. Slowly, Kailynn answered her baby sister, "Me too, Hollyn."

Both sisters embraced in a truly heartfelt hug. Kailynn couldn't help but tear up and cry. Hollyn pulled back, but didn't let go. She made a quiet shh sound to calm her older sister. They hugged tight again, Kailynn bringing Hollyn in close to her. In Hollyn's ear, she whispered, "I didn't have time to do this with dad before he died. Holding my family again is more painful than I cared to admit to myself. I'm just so sorry HollyBear."

Hollyn smiled at the mention of her big sister's nickname for her. She had always pretended to hate it, but unlike Kailynn, Hollyn liked her childhood name. It brought comfort to her.

"Are we going to go in or stay in the car all night?" interrupted a miffed-off voice from the back passenger side of the SUV.

Both sisters turned to the voice and saw Kayden half-in and half-out of the car, staring at them.

Kailynn looked back at her sister and said, "HollyBear, this is your beautiful, but albeit sarcastic, niece, Kayden."

Hollyn let go of her sister and walked over to her niece. They were both about the same height and looked a lot like each other, age not-withstanding. Hollyn raised an eyebrow towards her niece, whose unsure eyes were taking in her aunt for the first time in person.

"Well, little firecracker," Hollyn said to Kayden, "there's only room for one sarcastic shit in this family, and that title goes to me."

Aunt and niece stared at each other for a short time. Neither showing what they were thinking on their face. Until Kayden's shoulders relaxed a bit and she gave a brief grin.

"Finally," she said to her aunt, "someone who gets me."

Chapter Three: Settling In

The next morning, Kailynn sat down at the kitchen table, clutching a coffee mug with both hands. After getting settled in last night, everyone simply went to the room designated for them and found their beds for the evening. Exhausted from the long drive, packing, and quick preparation for the move; no one really had wanted to stay up and socialize. Each of them had their own thoughts over the last 24 hours and needed some rest. Kailynn had been the first one up the next morning, feeling more comfortable and relaxed than she had in a long time. She was home.

Kayden walked in, still rubbing sleep from her eyes.

"Good morning, Mom," she said, pouring herself a bowl of cereal.

At least she's talking to me, thought Kailynn.

"Morning, sweetie," Kailynn replied. Not wanting to lose a chance at talking alone with her oldest daughter and knowing how hard this was affecting her, Kailynn tried to get her daughter to open up.

"Can we talk about the move for a minute?"

Kayden's spoon clattered against the bowl. Kayden knew the pep talk was about to begin and beat her mom to the punch.

"I don't want to move to some tiny town in the middle of nowhere."

"It's not the middle of nowhere," Kailynn argued. "It's a charming little community, and we'll be closer to your family's history."

"I don't care about our family's history, mom," Kayden grumbled. "I liked it where we were. Everything I needed was within my reach. I just got done earning a starting spot on the varsity, for Christ's sake," she pleaded.

"I know it's hard to leave your comfort zone," Kailynn said. "But we needed to downsize and save money. We couldn't have afforded to stay in a larger city anymore."

Kayden huffed. "I don't want to live in a cramped old house with a yard that seems to be the entrance to 'Deliverance,'" she snorted.

"The old house has a big yard," Kailynn said. "And we can fix it up together. We'll make it cozy and perfect for us."

"I don't want to make it perfect," Kayden replied dejectedly. "I want to stay where we were, where everything was already perfect."

Kailynn sighed. "It wasn't perfect for everyone. I

understand change is hard, but we have to do what's best for our family. It's not just about you, Kayden."

"Well, it's not just about you either," Kayden shot back. "What about Dad? Doesn't he get a say?"

"We don't even know where he is and how can you even bring him up again in such a manner," Kailynn responded. She was becoming more annoyed at her daughter's intentional use of her absentee dad. "He abandoned all of us and you need to make your peace with it, because nothing we say or do will change that. Perhaps I should try to get you in to see a family therapist? Maybe we all should see one together?"

Kayden pushed her cereal bowl away. "I don't know what to think, mom. I just don't want to leave everything I know behind."

"I know it's scary and you feel vulnerable," Kailynn said, taking Kayden's hand. "But we'll be together, and we'll make the best of it. Who knows? Maybe we'll love our new home even more than the other one."

Kayden looked down at their hands, then back up at Kailynn. "Fine, I'll try," she mumbled unconvincingly.

Kailynn squeezed her hand. "That's all I ask."

Jackson meandered into the kitchen. His hair was unkempt. He yawned as he sat down. His sister Kayden who was already in the kitchen, her face twisted in a scowl, looked up at her brother.

"What's for breakfast, mom?" he asked.

Kailynn looked up at her son and smiled. "Good morning to you too, Jackson."

He yawned again.

"Go get yourself a bowl. We just have basic cereal today. Later, we can run into to town and do some grocery shopping kiddo," his mom offered.

Jackson saw his sister, Kayden, already seated at the table. Kayden's face twisted in frustration.

"Good morning, sis! Looks like someone's not having a good day," Jackson said flippantly, as he seated himself next to her at the table.

Kayden rolled her eyes. "Yeah, you could say that. I have to start at a new high school, and I hate it."

Jackson's face took on a feigned look of shock. "What? That's the cool part! I'm starting at the junior high, and I'm super stoked about it. We get to reinvent ourselves. No one at our school knows anything about us, so we can choose what they know or what we want them to know."

"Of course you are," Kayden spat. "You have no idea what it's like to be the new kid. Everyone stares at you, and you have to make new friends."

Now it was Jackson's turn to roll his eyes. "Oh, please. Making new friends is easy. You just have to be yourself and be friendly. Oh, wait, maybe you shouldn't be yourself, pretend to be an orphan. That way, people will feel sorry for you and be more open to talking to you." He laughed at himself.

Kayden immediately got angry. "Oh, it's so easy for you! You're the outgoing one, while I'm the shy one. It's not fair!"

"Shy?" he echoed. "You are many things, but shy is not one of them. More like bitchy."

Kailynn, sensing the tension building between her two kids, quickly tried to diffuse their banter.

"Hey guys, what's going on here?" she interjected.

Kayden whined, "I have to start at a new high

school, and Jackson's being annoying as usual."

Her brother fired back, "Hey, I'm not the annoying one here! She's just mad because she has no one else to take it out on."

Kailynn put her hand on her daughter to calm her down. Their initial conversation had gone as good as Kaitlynn had hoped for. Now, Jackson's mere presence was provoking a new attitude she didn't want to deal with from Kayden.

"Okay, let's calm down. Kayden, starting at a new school can be tough, but it's also an opportunity to make new friends and try new things. Jackson is right about being able to create a new persona, if you will. No one knows us. And Jackson, it's important to be supportive of your sister, even if you don't understand how she feels."

Jackson had a rebuttal for that comment. "No one knows how she feels because all she does is lash out at everyone. I believe it's called a self-defense mechanism," he evaluated. "I read it in an online article."

Kayden sighed. "What does he know about anything? Mom, this is high school. All over again, I have to restart. I'm an outcast. I have to build a reputation and try to fit in somewhere. I do not know about their clicks or who to avoid. It is a swamp, while rocket league boy over here just has to show up and play some video games. Oh, and act like a dork, then boom! He's in."

Kailynn could sympathize. Being a young woman entering a new high school could be very difficult. She knew firsthand how young girls can be so caddy to other interlopers.

"I understand. But you're strong and capable,

and you'll get through this. And Jackson, maybe you can help your sister feel more comfortable by introducing her to some of your friends at the junior high?" Kayden knew that the last comment might diffuse a little of the tension.

"Sure, Mom. I'd be happy to do that," he nodded, "once I make some, of course."

"Ugh... you both are ridiculous!"

Jackson turned to his mom with a grin as he pushed his spoon into the cereal bowl, preparing to eat.

"See? Everything's going to be okay. Let's have some breakfast and start the day off, right?" Jackson declared.

Kayden stood up indignantly with her chair moving back from her with a little more force than she had intended. Suddenly, their Aunt Hollyn came in and broke the tension.

"Harrisburg, Illinois, isn't that bad," Hollyn said in a calming voice. "There's a lot of old tales about superstitions that still swirl around it."

Jackson's ears perked up quickly. "Like what Aunt Hollyn?"

Hollyn's countenance took on a look of someone who was thinking really hard. It was, of course, all for show, but it was apparently the way Aunt Hollyn operated. After a brief pause, acting like she was fully engrossed in activating her memory Rolodex, she answered.

"Well, there's the Big Muddy Monster, the Old Slave House, a time-travel monument in Harrisburg's cemetery..."

"Cool," interrupted Jackson.

"Whatever," responded Kayden to her brother.

Their mother had settled back into her chair,

listening to her sister as a small smile emerged to the corner of her face.

Aunt Hollyn continued unperturbed, "Have you ever heard of the old haunted cemetery near our home?"

Kayden responded surely, "No, I haven't. Is it really haunted?" she inquired.

Jackson surprised everyone with his response, "Yeah, I've heard about it from dad when I was little. He said it's super creepy."

Kailynn's face showed shock at her son's revelation. "When did he tell you that?" she entreated.

Jackson just now seeing his mom's expression gave him a sense he'd done something wrong, so his shoulders slumped a bit. The last thing he wanted was to upset his mom talking about dad.

"He told me one night before bed around Halloween. He thought it would be a cool story."

Both sisters looked at each other at this and Hollyn shook her head as if to say, 'I meant nothing by it.'

Kailynn looked back at her son. Kayden, on the other hand, could tell there was more to their exchanges than just a normal inquiry. Her brother had hit a chord with her mom that had yielded a concern.

"What do you remember about what your dad said?" asked his mom.

Jackson just shrugged his shoulders at the question earnestly. "Honestly, just Aunt Hollyn mentioning the cemetery is all. Honest mom," he pleaded.

Aunt Hollyn interrupted everyone. "That's right Kayden, it's haunted. It's been said that they buried our ancestors in that cemetery, and their spirits still haunt the place to this day." Hollyn's quick interruption broke the inquiry from her sister, changing the atmosphere quickly.

Kayden, understanding that something had passed between her mom and aunt, cautiously replied in a subdued voice, "Wow, that's kind of scary. Why would our ancestors haunt the cemetery?"

"Well, story has it that one of our family members was wrongly accused of setting off an explosion in the local mines here. The explosion killed six people. According to the rumors, mob justice executed him, but they documented it's in the city's history archives: he had died in the explosion as well. Our family passed down a different story. Before he died, he cursed the land and anyone who dared to disturb his last resting place," explained Aunt Hollyn.

"Do you really believe that story, Aunt Hollyn?" questioned Jackson.

As she answered, Kailynn quietly interrupted her by clearing her throat. It was an intentional effort to tell Aunt Hollyn to stop. She looked at her sister. However, the exchange didn't stop her from answering her nephew.

"It's hard to say, but I know that they have reported strange things in the area over the years. Some people claim to have seen ghostly apparitions, while others have heard strange noises coming from the cemetery at night."

It was Kayden's turn to question her aunt. "Have you ever been to the cemetery, Aunt Hollyn?"

She nodded. "I have, but only during the day. It's an old and eerie place. Some Lithuanian society updated it recently, to preserve the historical aspect of the forgotten cemetery. I wouldn't recommend going there at night."

"Why not?" interjected Jackson. His curiosity was getting the better of him.

With trepidation, Aunt Hollyn answered, "Because if the legends are true, it's not safe to be there after dark."

"That's enough about the cemetery guys," Kailynn interrupted. "We have a lot to do today besides talking about some old cemetery."

Kayden, still focused on her Aunt Hollyn, replied, "I agree with you, Aunt Hollyn. Maybe we can visit the cemetery during the day sometime and pay our respects to our family?"

Aunt Hollyn smiled and gave a curt nod.

Jackson gave his nod of support for his sister's suggestion. "Yeah, that sounds like a good idea. I'm still a little scared, though."

Aunt Hollyn put her hand on Jackson's shoulder and squeezed comfortingly.

"It's okay to be scared, Jackson. But sometimes facing our fears can help us understand them better. And who knows, maybe our dead family will protect and watch over us while we're there?"

Kailynn stood up from the table. "Okay, you three, we have a ton of stuff to do. We need to go to your schools and get you enrolled. I have to go to the post office to make sure all our mail is now being sent here to this address, and we also need to go to the grocery store. Let's not forget our stuff will be here tomorrow from the movers. That means we need to help Aunt Hollyn with cleaning and moving the stuff that's in your rooms right now."

"Oh my God, mother!" exclaimed Kayden. "Can't we just take a week off before doing some of this?"

"No," responded her mom with finality. "Let's just get ready and start our day by getting dressed and move on from there."

****

The movers actually showed up early. October in Southern Illinois was cooler than usual. It thrilled Jackson to be moving back into his mom's childhood home. It was a new adventure for him, so his attitude and demeanor were that of excitement. As he unpacked the boxes, memories flooded back. Jackson recalled playing with action figures, collecting cards, and Star Wars items, as well as playing online games. He was excited to be starting junior high school in a new town and hoped to make new friends quickly. As he organized his room, decorating it with Lord of the Rings decor, maybe he would find a new hobby or try joining a sports team here?

Kayden, on the other hand, was not as excited as her brother. She missed her old friends and didn't want to start high school in a new place. But as she helped her mom and aunt carry boxes into the house, she realized she was excited to explore the new town. As she unpacked her room, she made a mental list of all the things she wanted to do in Harrisburg. She started filling her room with pictures of popular music bands and posters of her favorite movies. Memories flooded her of the past when she was younger, her mom and her baking cookies in the kitchen. Every item she unpacked filled her with such memories from the past.

I hate reminiscing; she thought.

Kailynn was busy organizing the kitchen as the moving company delivered the last of their belongings. She was nostalgic about being back in her hometown and surrounded by her sister. Just being in her childhood home made her feel closer to her family, who had passed away in her lifetime. Kailynn and Hollybear were the only ones left now. As she stocked the pantry and refrigerator with food from ALDI's, she couldn't help but feel a sense of sentimentality. She was looking forward to cooking family dinners and spending time with her kids and sister in their new home. As she sat down to rest, she couldn't help but feel grateful for this new chapter in their lives. Although her ex-husband had a major negative impact in that department, all things happen for a reason.

Hollyn was happy to help her sister, niece, and nephew settle into their new home. As they finished unpacking, she suggested they take a day to explore the town of Harrisburg. She drove them around town, pointing out all the local shops and restaurants. They stopped at a family-owned pizza joint called Mackies for lunch. Hollyn took them into town, and they walked around the square and down Poplar Street. Hollyn loved seeing her family happy and excited. She had missed her niece and nephew's early childhood and all she saw now were anxious teenagers.

Oh, well, she thought, *I never had much patience for bratty little kids, anyway.*

She couldn't wait to spend more time with them and make fresh memories of their family. As they were walking, Jackson got excited and ran a few feet ahead of them.

"Whoa!" he exclaimed. Running over to a very lifelike statue, stood Bigfoot. The other three girls walked up with smiles on their faces as they watched the younger teen look on in glee at the enormous statue.

"Mom, it's Bigfoot," Jackson stated.

"Nope," corrected Aunt Hollyn, "it's the Big Muddy Monster."

Jackson turned to his Aunt Hollyn and gave her a scrunched-up face, showing his confusion. Even Kayden's eyebrows raised up at the mention of the Big Muddy Monster, instead of the usual Bigfoot or Sasquatch reference.

"Aunt Hollyn, it looks a lot like how a Bigfoot is described," Kayden responded.

Hollyn smiled at her sister, who winked back at her as both of them who grew up in Southern Illinois knew the legends and sightings along the Muddy River.

She noted that people have routinely seen a large, hairy man along the Muddy River over the decades in Southern Illinois.

Kailynn added, "The Big Muddy River actually starts from the Mississippi River into Southern Illinois. It goes a real long way throughout the towns and eventually ending somewhere by Benton, right Hollybear?"

Hollyn nodded in agreement. "Yeah, they made Rend Lake out of it. It is what feeds the constructed lake. We should go sometime. It has a beach area there we can hang out at."

Kayden perked up over that. Having a place to go to during the summer was on her list of items to research. A beach area, regardless if it is at a Lake was better than nothing and she could get some sun and maybe meet a boy or two there as well. Her brother interrupted her train of thoughts.

"Mom, has anyone seen the Muddy Monster recently?"

Kayden shook her head, "I do not know, honestly buddy. There are lots of things based on the sightings."

"Yeah," interjected Hollyn, "in Murphysboro, they have a brewery called the Big Muddy Brewing Company. The brewery actual has beers based on the legend."

"Let's see," she said, thinking to herself out loud. "There's the Big Muddy Monster, Pumpkin Smasher, Backwoods Monster, S'more Stout... oh, and Winter Ale although which wasn't my fav, but hey, it's a holiday brew."

Kayden smiled inwardly at her aunt. "Experienced a few of their brews, Aunt Hollyn?"

Her mom cleared her throat towards Kayden for her direct comment. If it had any effect on her aunt, she showed no sign of it.

"Quite the contrary," she answered with pride to her niece's question.

"Of course I have Kayden. Do I look like a prude? We live in Southern Illinois where beer, bourbon and whiskey flows," she finished with a look of pride on her face.

"Don't encourage them, Hollyn," snapped Kailynn to her sister.

Hollyn's face turned that of mischievous. "You were no angel as I recall growing up, sis?"

"That will be enough of that Hollybear," the older sister ordered. "We set good examples, not pave the way for bad ones."

Hollyn smiled and just turned around, looking at the statue in feigned interest.

The two teens exchanged looks of amusement over their mom and sister's rehash of the past and gave each other a smile. It wasn't lost on Kailynn, who ignored her two kids and changed the subject.

"Actually, kids, there is a tiny town. Some would

more or less call it a village outside of Harrisburg named Muddy. The Muddy River doesn't run through it, but it has been around for a long time as well.

"The Saline River runs through it. It used to fill the town's old Reservoir, but has since been drained," commented Hollyn.

Kailynn, with a surprised reaction, responded in disbelief, "Are you serious, Hollyn? They got rid of the Reservoir? Dad used to take us all the time there to fish."

Hollyn's face took on one of sympathy for her sister at the mention of a time with their dad. She knew the need for familiarity with people who needed a comforting association with the past. That way, they could visit and remember loving moments in their lives. Kailynn had rather enjoyed the time at the old Reservoir with her dad and Hollyn. They never really fished a bunch themselves, but loved throwing rocks in the water. They chased frogs, avoided the occasional snake, and maybe caught a small turtle. Their dad would fish and watch them play. He allowed them to explore and have the freedom little kids wanted when fresh adventures were at hand.

Hollyn realized the time had gotten late. "Hey guys, let's head home. The two of you have to go to school tomorrow and one of you needs to find a job."

Chapter Four: School

Going to bed was a troublesome matter for Kayden. There were going to be a lot of firsts for her tomorrow. She and her brother were going to use the bus system for Harrisburg's school system. Apparently, they lived far enough outside town to qualify and their mom loved the idea of not having to worry about the pickup and drop-off times. It opened up more options for getting a job by not being restricted to mandatory pickup times. Kayden had heard horror stories about kids on the bus from her last school. Bullying or not having a seat were among them. Of course, it will be her first time attending a new school without knowing a single soul there. Couple that with new teachers, new rules the school employs to its students and, naturally, social life governed by the teens there. No telling how the clicks will be; other than the usual stereotypes which exist everywhere she went. Sleep was not coming easily to her.

As she lay there, a polite knock came at her door.

Great, mom bugging me, she thought.

Kayden didn't answer, hoping her mom would just assume she's sleeping and leave. However, she watched as the doorknob turned and the door swung open. Her Aunt Hollyn strolled in, not only without a care of whether she was waking Kayden up, but with no regard for privacy.

"Hey kid," Hollyn said to Kayden, laying restlessly in her new room.

"You know, I didn't answer your knock for a reason, Aunt Hollyn," Kayden sassed.

Hollyn shut the door behind her and waltzed to Kayden's bedside. She sat down on the side of the bed, having no more care of what Kayden said than the man in the moon.

"I know. I'm the shit in this family, remember? You will have to work hard to fill my shoes if you want the title. Besides, knowing you, probably thought it was your mom, right?" A smile displayed on her face.

Kayden blushed at the comment. Not only did she guess right, but the bluntness of her words kind of stung.

"I came in to just tell you tomorrow will probably suck for you. You'll be stressed, probably get lost at least once. Odds are no one will talk to you and you will end up sitting alone during lunch."

Kayden's eyes almost bulged out of her head at her aunt's callous words.

"Is that supposed to be a pep talk, Aunt Hollyn?" mocked Kayden.

Her aunt smiled at her and winked. "Yep, did it

work?"

Kayden frowned back at her aunt and readjusted to a sitting position. They locked stares at each other, neither backing down.

"You are so weird," Kayden replied.

"Of course! It's what makes me so charming, girl."

"Why are you saying that to me in the first place? You know I'm stressed out about tomorrow already. It's like you're enjoying my pain or something."

"Nah," Hollyn rebuked, "I don't enjoy your pain. You're just a pain, so I thought I'd beat you to the point. You see... I have this image of you waking up in the morning. You'll act like a total shit-wad to everyone because you are 'stressed' about having to go to a new school for the first time. Then you will pick fights intentionally, ruining everyone else's first day as well, and for what? The fact you are insecure over starting over in a new place, as if you are the only one having to suffer the unknown. Then, like a drowning person in shaky water; you want to take everyone else with you."

"What do you know about me?" retaliated Kayden. The bluntness of her aunt's assessment of the situation completely took her off-guard. She needed to regain her composure and control over this conversation better. "I've been here less than five days and you suddenly have me figured out?"

"Yep," she replied casually.

"Who exactly are you to talk to me in that way?" Kayden fired back.

"Well, I'm older than you, more experienced in calling bullshit towards people than you. I'm your aunt, so there's that and I don't like the way you talk to your mom. I hear you two bang away at each other when you are not paying attention and you are very consistent in your behavior."

Kayden opened her mouth to argue, which was her natural tendency with family, but she closed it and squinted with a glare at her aunt.

Hollyn simply smiled back, shrugged her shoulders, and got up to leave the room. She turned back around and her smile had faded. In its place was a serious face this time, which immediately knocked the death stare look off of Kayden's face immediately.

"I say those things to you, little miss diva, because I've dealt with your kind before and can spot you a mile away." She turned to leave by opening the door and paused one more time, then looked back. "I know you, because you are just like me. See ya in the morning."

Kayden was left sitting on her bed, speechless.

What just happened? she thought to herself.

She laid back in her bed, replaying her encounter with her Aunt Hollyn, and fell asleep.

***

Kayden woke up early the next morning feeling very anxious about her first day at her new high school. It was in the middle of her sophomore year, so she knew that she'll be the new kid in the middle of an established social hierarchy. She spent some extra time getting ready, trying to find the perfect outfit to help her blend in and not stand out too much.

After eating breakfast, both of the siblings walked out to the end of their drive. Once there, they started walking to where the street forked with Ledford Road. It was only about five houses down from theirs. They had been told the bus Kayden and Jackson were going to use would stop there to pick up anyone from Little Road, the one they lived off of. It looked like they were the only kids who lived on their road since no one else was there standing outside, waiting for the bus to arrive.

Kayden was getting increasingly nervous and anxious about her first day at her new school, while Jackson seemed excited about his first day.

Typical, she thought.

"Why are you so excited about going to a new school? I bet you're not even worried about making new friends or fitting in."

"Well, I'm a little nervous. But I'm also excited about meeting new people and learning new things."

"Well, I'm not excited at all. I don't want to go to a new school."

"Yeah, I know. You've only mentioned that a million times to everyone," Jackson said in a deadpanned voice.

"What if no one likes me? What if I don't fit in?" she acknowledged to her little brother.

Kayden had just now actually shared her insecurity and fears with her brother. He was more used to her ragging on him and making him feel less than, so her vulnerability caught him off guard.

He responded with genuine concern to Kayden, "Don't worry, Kayden. I'm sure you'll meet some potential new friends. Just be yourself. Don't act all fake. It's how you attract the wrong people."

"Easy for you to say. You're always the popular one. You make friends easily. But what about me? What if I'm not good enough?" Kayden's anxiety over fitting in was on overload.

"I know you never hear me compliment you or anything. It's not really our dynamic, but you're good enough, Kayden. You're smart, sarcastic, and read people pretty well. Just have a little more confidence in yourself. It may not happen today, but people will come to accept you once they are around you long enough."

Kayden took a deep breath. She could hear the bus in the distance. "Maybe you're right, but I don't feel that lucky. Thanks for not making fun of me."

Jackson turned away from her to face the approaching bus and a small smile emerged on his face.

I'll take that as a win, he thought to himself.

As the bus pulled up, they got on and looked around for a seat. They saw an open seat and sat down together. However, no one talked to them, and they sat in silence.

As they traveled back towards Harrisburg, Kayden broke the silence, quietly murmuring, "I thought there would be more people to talk to on the bus. This is so boring."

Jackson just shrugged. "Hey, we're the new kids. Like seeing an alien for the first time. You're curious about them because they look different and are new, but not ready to just go right up and be friendly."

Kayden wondered how her younger brother could be so smart and laid back yet was a total geek. "Yeah, I guess."

As the bus ride continued, Kayden and Jackson said very little else. Each of them was lost in their own thoughts. It didn't take long though, Jackson's stop was first, so once he got off at his stop, Kayden was by herself. At least when she got off the bus, she felt a little more at ease. Jackson's support made her feel a little less alone.

Once she arrived at the school, Kayden felt completely lost. Although she was given a tour of the school when her mom enrolled her, the anxiety she was experiencing made remembering where she was going almost impossible. She couldn't find her first class, and her anxiety skyrocketed. She asked several people for directions, but no one seemed interested in helping her. She finally found her class after the bell rang, but was already tired from the stress of navigating a new place. Even though her teacher wasn't upset at the tardy, knowing she was new, it still was embarrassing to roll in there with the entire class seated and watching her.

Throughout the day, Kayden felt isolated and alone. No one really talked to her, and she was too nervous to start a conversation with anyone else. However, there was one boy in a few of her classes who seemed to be interested in her. He said little, but she could feel his eyes on her whenever she looked in his direction. That added to Kayden's anxiety, making her feel like she was constantly being watched and evaluated.

Kayden's experience at school during lunch period was less than ideal. Being new to the high school, she found it difficult to attempt a conversation with anyone. She sat alone at the lunch table, watching other students socialize and interact. Despite the friendly atmosphere of the school, Kayden couldn't help but feel left out and alone.

As she was sitting alone at the lunch table, she noticed the same boy who had a couple of classes with her. He would glance in her direction now and then, and sometimes smiled at her. He wasn't ugly or anything, but Kayden found this behavior to be confusing, as she wasn't sure what he wanted from her.

As the day went by, Kayden became more curious about the boy who showed an interest in her. She observed him more closely when he was around and realized that he was often alone himself. He never seemed to hang out with a particular group of friends, and Kayden wondered if he was a loner or outcast as she was.

By the end of her last period, Kayden was worn out and ready to go home. However, she had to use the school bus system to get home.

It's just so nerve-wracking, she thought. *No one will sit next to me, and I feel like everyone is staring at me.*

She tried to make herself as small as possible, hoping that the ride would be over soon. As she was looking out the window, lost in thought, she hadn't noticed the bus had pulled into the junior high to pick up the last of the students for the day. Someone plucked down right beside her and took a deep sigh of relief.

Startled, she looked over and saw Jackson was sitting next to her. He didn't look too happy. His look of struggle actually perked her up a bit.

Finally, someone who shares my predicament.

"How was your day?" he inquired with sarcasm.

Kayden looked at her brother, whose expression seemed very lackluster. "Well, got lost. No one spoke to me. I may have a personal stalker, and I'm on this stinky bus," she answered.

"Great," he answered, "mine sucked, too. Apparently, I am too threatening to the Geek Squad on campus with my gaming knowledge and skills."

Kayden hid her smile and echoed, "Geek Squad?"

Jackson nodded his acknowledgment of the name.

"Yep, it's their clicks name around school. They wear it like a badge of honor. I was told through the grapevine by kids who meander around their lockers. In order to penetrate the inner recesses of their organization, I had to prove I was of true gaming quality."

"So, what did you have to do in order to prove your Geek Squad material?" Kayden asked, in part humor, part seriousness.

"I had to challenge one of their ranks to a gaming competition. Turns out they aren't very good losers." Jackson took a big breath and let out an enormous sigh.

"So you won?" his sister prompted.

"Yes, but it didn't go like I had expected," Jackson acknowledged.

Kayden was actually interested in how her brother lost his chance at being inducted into a famous nerd group at school by winning; so she elbowed him to explain more.

"Fine," he responded grudgingly. "They challenged me to a game of Clash Royal on our phones. Turns out it is one of the many games I play, but one of the main games I lock into on my phone. The other ones are on the Occulus and Playstation."

The nerdiness was compounding every second to Kayden, who didn't understand nor care about gaming stuff. Her brother, on the other hand was relentless at it.

"I challenged their leader by accident because I

did not know who was the top dog in their group. He immediately started in with his trash talk and would not engage me, but his buddies reminded him of the code."

"Code," echoed Kayden, "what on earth is 'the code'?"

Jackson wrinkled his nose up, recounting the order of events.

"Their Geek Squad code is anyone who is new to the school can make a challenge to a group member. It was based on the fact a new kid wasn't available at the beginning of the year to 'audition' for a place in their ranks. Therefore, I had clout to challenge."

Jackson kind of took on an air of pride owning up to his newly claimed clout.

He came down off that cloud just as fast as he continued his tale of sorrow.

"So there we are at lunch. We logged in to our accounts, shared our handle and prepared for war. He chose the Lava Hound Balloon Deck. I assumed he chose that once we started because he was pretty good at accurately timing lightning by using his skeleton dragons and lava hounds. I didn't know what to really expect from this group. Since I wanted to impress and compete with them, I chose my best deck; the giant wiz zap. My giant and knight are pretty good defensively and I had no idea what he was going to throw at me."

Kayden interrupted him, "Get to the meat and potatoes knucklehead," she griped.

"I am. Quit interrupting me," he spat back at her. "Where was I?" he paused in thought. "Oh yeah," he remembered. "The wizard can take out tons of enemies, while my minions and archers just keep hitting away at just about anything I figured he could throw at me. It's all about strategy, you know," he pointed out to his sister.

"Jackson," she exclaimed, "for mercy's sake, just get to it. You beat him, then what?"

Her brother scoffed at her impatience, but agreed to her request.

"Fine, yes, I beat him. Humiliated him, actually. He had just gotten that deck, so wasn't very proficient at using it yet, so I won. He was extremely embarrassed and angry; especially after he had talked so much trash and overestimated my skill. Well, I had beaten their leader name Chip Hoyt. According to their code, if the squad is full, then the challenger gets kicked out and you take their place. The squad was full. My win went over like a lead balloon."

"What happened?" replied Kayden.

"Chip called a vote of no confidence to the group, which led into an immediate vote by the rest of the squad. None of them wanted some random new kid to seize leadership of their squad, so they overturned the win by default and I was told to hit the pavement."

"A vote of no confidence?" repeated his sister in confusion.

"Yeah, like in Star Wars when Queen Amidala requested a vote of no-confidence in the Supreme Chancellor. All the senators immediately got to vote to kick out their leader or keep him. I knew once that happened, they rigged the game. At least I'm no Palpatine who had some insidious plan to overthrow their stupid squad," he babbled to himself.

They finally arrived home and both of them were relieved to be back in a familiar environment where they could relax, decompress, and lick their wounds.

At least it was Friday, Kayden thought. Their

mom had been understanding of the stress they'd be under, so she had arranged it for their first day of school to be on a Friday. Regardless of their day, both would have a weekend to breathe and take in all their interactions of their first day at school.

Little did she know, her day was just getting started.

Chapter Five: Friday Night Lights

Aunt Hollyn walked through the front door of the house, setting down her purse and taking off her coat. As she turned to face the living room, she saw her niece Kayden and nephew Jackson, sitting on the couch with hungry looks on their faces.

Kayden was hesitant to talk to her aunt after last night's little interaction in her bedroom.

Funny, some of what she said happened, but nothing like she had predicted, she thought to herself.

She filed that away in her memory for later recall. She was eventually going to talk to her about the whole weird exchange.

"Hi Aunt Hollyn," said Kayden, her eyes narrowed with caution. "We're sort of starving. What's for dinner?"

"Hello, my little firecracker," Hollyn said, returning a mischievous smile. "I'm sorry, but dinner's not quite ready yet. But don't worry, I'll take care of it soon."

The response put Kayden a little more at ease. Kayden and Jackson looked at each other, their stomachs growling.

Jackson felt clarification on the way things would soon unfold as their normal maximums during the school year needed to be cleared up.

"We don't know what to do when we get home from school," said Jackson. "Mom always made us a snack and then dinner later. What's the new protocol?"

Hollyn chuckled. "Well, the new protocol is simple. When you get home from school, have a small snack if you're hungry, and then wait for dinner to be ready."

Kayden and Jackson nodded their understanding, but their minds were still on food. Just then, Hollyn remembered the exciting news she had to share with them.

"Oh, before I forget, your mom got a job offer this morning!" Hollyn blurted.

"What?" both the kids said at the same time.

Hollyn excitedly came into the room, practically bouncing with excitement.

"Kailynn and I had the craziest adventure today. You won't believe it!" she exclaimed.

"Oh, really? What happened?" Kayden asked, intrigued.

Hollyn sat down in the recliner beside the couch and started her story.

"Well, we stopped in at the local ALDI's food store this morning to pick up a few things before we started job hunting. Next thing we knew, we ended up being involved in this wild situation," Aunt Hollyn began.

"What kind of situation?" Jackson prompted, sitting on the armchair of the couch by his sister.

Hollyn smiled in anticipation of telling the story.

"Well, it all started when the key manager of the store just up and quits, right in the middle of his shift. He was arguing with a customer. Apparently, there was a young couple who were having some sort of relationship squabble right there in the store. It was getting heated, so the manager went over to deal with them. Unfortunately, the couple turned their anger at each other on the manager. Both told him to mind his own business. The manager's supervisor came out at about the time his associate lost his temper and started cussing at the couple. Who, to be fair, started the profanity train first. The supervisor scolded the manager right there in front of everyone, further ticking him off. He stormed out of the store, leaving everyone in a bit of a panic," Aunt Hollyn explained.

"Wow, I'll bet that left the supervisor freaked out," Kayden remarked.

"Right?" Hollyn confirmed. "And to make matters worse, there was a tremendous rush of customers this morning, so the store was completely chaotic," Aunt Hollyn continued.

"The grocery store had a rush in the morning? What were they doing, giving away free donuts?" Kayden said sarcastically.

Hollyn paused in her story. "Hey, there's that girl I was talking about last night."

"Busted," joined in Jackson, enjoying his aunt's jibes at Kayden's behavior.

This put Kayden's usual retorts to people on hold. Since last night, Kayden couldn't help but ponder how her aunt of 72 hours could pass such a harsh judgment about her. Now, here she was pointing it out, just as Kayden started in making it a little more close to home in her views about herself.

"Kailynn," Hollyn continued, "bless her heart, was calm as could be. She went over to the couple and apologized for sticking her nose into the couple's argument. She explained their tone and loudness were upsetting other customers; especially the ones who had youngsters in the cart. The other employees there had avoided the whole situation altogether, not wanting to deal with the spectacle. Not your mom, nope. She told that supervisor who was standing with them, her last job was doing her ex-bosses supervising on the floor. The current situation now had gotten her inner bullshit detector moving into overdrive. She knew what needed to be done to keep things running smoothly, so the staff and customers didn't start panicking. The couple started in on her, but she shut that shit-show down fast."

Kayden's eyebrows raised at hearing that. "Really? What did she do?"

Hollyn looked at her niece and answered, "She yelled, 'let's stop this right here. You want to get into a shouting match and scare other people because you cannot keep your relationship straight? No problem,' she reached in her purse," Hollyn explained, actually re-enacting their mom's movements.

"Your mom pulled out her phone and dialed for the police. The moment she held her phone up and asked the couple, 'do I hit send or are we good?' to the two. They both shut up, took their cart to the check-out, and the show was over. Hell, she was practically running the place for a few minutes."

Hollyn paused and laughed out loud over the

whole situation.

"That's amazing. She really said bullshit detector in front of the supervisor?" Jackson asked, caught up with the image of his mom actually cussing in public.

"It gets even crazier," Aunt Hollyn said, grinning and nodding to Jackson.

Kayden's curiosity piqued.

"The supervisor offered her the manager's job."

"That's right," Aunt Hollyn said, leaning in closer conspiratorially. "It turns out that the supervisor was an old high school classmate of your moms. And get this, he used to have the hots for her!"

Kayden and Jackson's eyes widened in shock. "No way! What did mom do?" stammered Kayden, surprised at the turn of events.

"Well, at first it really caught her off-guard. She hadn't recognized him, but then she politely declined the job offer. She didn't want to take a job just because of some old high school crush," Aunt Hollyn said, shaking her head.

The supervisor, named Gavin by the way, wouldn't take no for an answer. He asked her for just a few minutes in the office to interview her officially and if she wasn't interested, he'd leave her alone. A few minutes turned into one hour."

Jackson was the first to respond, "Whoa, what did you do that entire time she was in there?"

Hollyn shrugged her shoulders like it was no big deal. "I finished shopping there and went over to the gas station next door and piddled around a bit, then just sat in the car."

Everyone sat back for a quiet moment, letting it all sink in. Their mom just got hired to be a manager on her first day out and didn't even go looking for it.

"But it was still such a crazy coincidence," Aunt Hollyn said, shaking her head in disbelief. "Who would have thought that Kailynn's old classmate would turn up at ALDIs of all places?"

Kayden smiled at her aunt's enthusiasm. "And offered her a job," she added.

"That's for sure," Aunt Hollyn replied, a glint of excitement still in her eye. "And who knows, maybe one day Kailynn will run into another old classmate who will offer her a job as a CEO or something!" Her joke at her mom's good fortune brought both kids to actually laugh.

She continued, "It was like something out of a movie. And Kailynn accepted the position, of course. She's always had a talent for managing and problem-solving, so it's really a perfect fit for her."

"Well, I'm not surprised," Kayden said. "She loves bossing people around."

"That's for sure," Aunt Hollyn agreed, shocking Kayden. "Anyway, it was quite the adventure today. Who knows what tonight will bring?"

Both teens stopped laughing at catching the word 'tonight.'

"Um, what's tonight, Aunt Hollyn?" Jackson asked meekly.

Hollyn took on a look of utter shock. "Oh, your mom didn't text you?" she said in feigned disbelief. "Well, she got a new job and won't get off until later, until her new supervisor is done getting her ready to start on Monday. We are going to the football game tonight. The Dogs are 7-1 right now and play the Red Devils."

Jackson looked a bit confused. "The Dogs?"

"Yeah, your school's mascot, Bulldogs," she

answered, "They take on rival Murphysboro. Should be a hell of a game. Kick-off is at 7:00 pm. Better get ready, it's already close to 5:00 and I need to get my butt in gear making dinner if we don't wanna be late."

Neither of the teens wanted to go to the football game after the day they had in school, but no one wanted to argue with Aunt Hollyn. Their mom was hard enough to deal with, but their aunt was too unpredictable. Pausing for a moment, looking at each other; they made a B-Line to their rooms. Both of them needed to plan how they were going to survive tonight's unexpected journey into the depths of their non-existent social lives.

****

Aunt Hollyn, Kayden, and Jackson stood in line at the high school football ticket booth, waiting patiently for their turn to pay and enter the stadium. The line was barely moving, and they could hear the buzz of the excited crowd in the distance. Aunt Hollyn was trying to lighten the mood by making small talk, but Kayden and Jackson remained silent.

Kayden was feeling very self-conscious after her first day at a new school. She had moved to Harrisburg just a week ago, and she was struggling to make friends. She had hoped to spend the evening at home, but Aunt Hollyn had other plans to get her exposure to the community by bringing her to the game. As they stood in line, Kayden kept her head down, avoiding eye contact with anyone. She felt like everyone was staring at her, judging her, and she couldn't shake the feeling of being out of place.

Jackson was also not feeling too enthusiastic

about the game, either. He had had a tough day in junior high, and he was feeling defeated. His lunch battle for entry into the geek squad hadn't gone well at all. He didn't want to be there, but he didn't want to disappoint Aunt Hollyn or abandon Kayden. He kept his hands in his pockets, staring at the ground, lost in his own thoughts.

Finally, they reached the ticket booth, and Aunt Hollyn paid for their tickets. As they made their way into the football bleachers, Kayden and Jackson followed Aunt Hollyn, both feeling a little unsure of themselves. The bleachers were packed with excited fans, and the energy was palpable. Aunt Hollyn led them to an open spot somewhere in the middle upper area of the crowd, and they sat down, still feeling a little uncomfortable.

As the game began, Kayden and Jackson relaxed a little. They watched as the Harrisburg Bulldogs took the field, and the crowd erupted into cheers. Aunt Hollyn would steal a few glances at the two teens checking on their demeanor. She knew they were having a little trouble acclimating to the new little town. Hollyn was quite aware of how small towns can be hard to break into fitting in with generational biases passed down from families rooted in its rich history. Harrisburg was no different, and she knew this firsthand. The name Toth was as old as the town itself. It also had a stigma to it and here she was the last of the generational name. Well, almost. Kailynn had taken her maiden name back and consequently, the kids had wanted the same thing.

Man, their dad had done a number on his wife and kids, she thought.

Aunt Hollyn tried to interact more with them. "

Hey guys, how are you liking the football game so far?"

Kayden frowned a bit. "It's okay, Aunt Hollyn. I had a really tough day at school today.

"Same here, Aunt Hollyn. It's been a rough first day," agreed Jackson.

Aunt Hollyn asked, "What happened?"

Kayden was hesitant to respond honestly based on her conversation last night with her aunt, but decided there was no reason to lie.

"No one talked to me at school. I felt so alone."

Jackson chimed in, "And I tried to join the geek squad, but they didn't let me in, even though I beat their group leader in a challenge game. I'm really bummed about it, even though I should have known better." Jackson looked out over the crowd in the bleachers, hoping not to see any of the geek squad members.

Aunt Hollyn didn't really know what the hell a geek squad was, but it sounded like a ridiculous group to be associated with. What did she know? Things in the teen world were so different from when she went to school.

"I'm sorry to hear that. But don't worry, there are plenty of other clubs and groups you can join," she said, trying to be supportive.

Kayden said, "I wouldn't even know how to find them. I got lost trying to get to my class today."

"Yeah, well, at least you didn't outright get rejected and somewhat bullied. You just shrunk yourself so no one would see you. I take a chance and now I'm enemy number one to the squad," Jackson retorted.

"Well, we could start by asking your teachers or the school counselor for suggestions. They should be able to help you find groups and clubs that interest you," replied Hollyn. She was trying to come up with some solutions, but she knew although her suggestion was how adults dealt with stuff, it was lame as far as teens went.

"No offense, Aunt Hollyn, but I'm not going to a teacher or counselor for help," Jackson replied.

Kayden nodded her head in agreement with her brother and added, "Yeah, it's hard to make friends when no one talks to you."

Aunt Hollyn looked quickly at Kayden and said, "Keep in mind that is a two-way streak, Kayden." She was getting frustrated with all the complaining and no effort at finding solutions. "I understand, but don't worry. It takes time to make friends, especially in a new school. I know this sound cliché, but just try being yourself and strike up conversations with people in your classes or in the hallways in-between bells."

"Expert advice," she replied sarcastically. "I'm going to the concession stand before half-time. I want to beat the traffic."

"Me too. Good thinking. Can I come too?" Jackson asked.

Aunt Hollyn smirked, "You're welcome, guys," she replied in her own sarcastic manner. "Just remember, you're not alone in this. We'll all work together to help you two acclimate to your new school and town." She turned back towards the game and her two companions got up and headed to the concession stand.

***

Their plan had backfired on them because

apparently, it seemed like everyone else had the same idea of beating the rush before halftime. Kayden and Jackson stood in a very long line, waiting for their chance to buy snacks.

"I hope they have either hot dogs or polish sausages here," commented Jackson to no one in particular, "otherwise I'll just go for the popcorn in a bag."

Kayden didn't really reply, just sort of nodded. She was lost in her thoughts. Her eyes quietly darted around the line and all over the area, taking in the teens running around and making mental notes. Kayden stood in line, fidgeting with her phone. She was feeling shy and reserved, preferring to keep to herself rather than engage with the other students at her high school. But as she stood there waiting for her turn to order, she felt a tap on her shoulder that made her jump.

Turning around, she saw the boy from her school standing behind her, grinning mischievously. She had noticed him today in class and in the hallways, always making eye contact with her, but they had never spoken before.

"Hey there, Kayden! What's your favorite thing to get from the concession stand?" he asked, a playful glint in his eye.

How did he know my name? she thought to herself. Her brother beat her to the punch.

"Wow, how did you know Kayden's name? I'm sure she didn't bother to give it today at school," Jackson said smugly.

Kayden felt her cheeks heat up as she stuttered out a response, surprised by his sudden attention and her brother's embarrassing statement.

"Shut up, Jackson," she quickly responded to her idiotic brother.

"Whoa, didn't mean to start a fight, just needed a quick conversation starter," the boy returned politely.

"Don't worry," Jackson responded. "She's like that to me all the time. It's kind of our thing."

The boy smiled earnestly back at Kayden. He nodded his head like he understood completely.

"Little brothers right?" he said to her. "I have one too. They can be challenging."

Kayden smirked a little back at the boy. "Challenging is putting it lightly," she retorted.

He smiled again. "I apologize. I heard your name read out loud when Mrs. Turner was taking roll today in class. I didn't mean to seem like a creeper or anything. You just didn't seem approachable today."

Hearing this, Kayden crossed her arms and kind of shrank back into herself. The boy noticed this immediately and reacted quickly to dispel her discomfort.

"It's totally cool, you know? New kid on the block is one of the worst situations for anyone moving to a new school. I'm more of a wallflower if truth be told, but I'm sure my friends would disagree."

"Wallflower? I'm confused then about your ability to come up and start a conversation then. Wallflowers sit back and watch everything."

Now it was the boy's turn to shrink back. Kayden saw it in his posture and expression. She softened immediately, allowing a smidge of her walls to come down.

After all, he attempted to communicate and he wasn't exactly vile.

"I don't know any wallflowers, so I just have the

character Charlie as a reference from that novel, *Perks of Being a Wallflower*."

The boy nodded. "I get it. Good book, the movie had a pretty decent acting group in it as well. I'd say opinions vary on what a true wallflower is, but no worries."

They stood there a second, not talking. Jackson pretended not to be interested in their conversation when she finally broke her silence, "so what's your name, anyway?"

The boy's face took on a look of self-inflicted stupidity at not introducing himself.

"My bad," he held his hand out politely, "my name is Drake."

She reached out hesitantly and took his hand, shaking it lightly. They broke the ice. As they continued chatting in line, Kayden noticed Drake was more open and outgoing than she was. However, there was still something mysterious about him she couldn't quite put her finger on.

"Hey you never answered me. What's your favorite concession stand food?"

Kayden shrugged, "Uh, I don't know. I guess I usually just get popcorn or a hot dog."

"Oh cool, I'm more of a nachos guy myself."

As they reached the front of the line and placed their orders, Drake surprised Kayden by paying for her and Jackson's snacks. He insisted it was just a friendly gesture. As they walked away from the concession stand, Kayden felt grateful for the unexpected conversation. She needed the chance to connect with someone at school.

Jackson invited Drake to sit with them after he bought their snacks. Kayden couldn't object, even though she was still hesitant. Drake accepted his invitation and a very surprised aunt Hollyn moved over to make room for him.

Over the course of the football game, Kayden and Drake continued to chat and get to know each other better. Kayden slowly came out of her shell, thanks to Drake's easygoing nature and genuine interest in learning about her.

Drake then asked a very scary question. "Have you been to any parties lately?"

This caught her by complete surprise and her family as well, who indirectly had been listening in on their interaction.

"No, I haven't really gone to any big parties before," she said honestly.

"Well, there's one tomorrow night at my friend's house and it wouldn't really be classified as 'big'. You should come! It's going to be a lot of fun. It's more of a fire-pit gathering outside. You know, typical teens outside in 60 degree weather standing around a couple fire-pits solving all the world's problems."

"I don't know. I'm not really sure if I want to go to a party," Kayden replied timidly at the fact she was being thrust into the social stream at warp speed.

Drake smiled knowingly. "Come on, it'll be a good time! You can meet some new people and have fun with us. Plus, you already know me, so it won't be too intimidating."

"I'll think about it. I'm not fantastic with crowds and outside music," she lied.

He shrugged and said, "I guess if you take no chances, you never have to worry about disappointment or embarrassment, right? Nor do you ever meet anyone, either."

She could tell he was being sarcastic, of course. "Look, Kayden, here's my number. You can text me if you are interested. I'll leave it to you to decide and reach out. If you are interested, we'll make plans. I promise I'll keep you safe and if at any time you need to bounce, we're out and I'll bring you home. Think on it."

He stood and said his goodbyes. Kayden found herself looking forward to the next time they would see each other.

"Nice guy," Hollyn said absently as the final horn blew to signal the end of the football game.

"Yeah, way too nice to be talking to Kayden," Jackson said in jest.

Jackson's words went unheard as Kayden was too lost in her own thoughts again. Hollyn and the kids made their way to the car and remembered they hadn't seen their mom all day.

*****

Kayden and Jackson walked out of the high school football field with Aunt Hollyn, feeling a mix of excitement and disappointment. Their team had lost (it was customary to feel down when your home team lost), but they still had a great time watching them with their aunt.

As they piled into the car for the drive home, Aunt Hollyn turned on some music.

Just like in the movie *Stepmom*, they all sang along to an old classic from the 90's. Vanilla Ice was bringing the funk with *Ice, Ice Baby*. All three were doing their best to sing the rap lyrics along with the beat of the track. It made for a silly moment and both the kids actually forgot about their social lives.

When they arrived home, they found their mom, who had just started a new job that morning, asleep on the couch. Jackson gently shook her awake, and she rubbed her bleary eyes and asked how their first day of school had gone. Kayden and Jackson both sighed and shared their not-so-good experiences. Their mom listened sympathetically, nodding along as they spoke.

Aunt Hollyn, sensing the exhaustion in the air, quietly slipped off to bed. The three of them continued to chat for a bit, but the day had taken its toll on them all. As they finished their conversation, they called it a night and headed off to bed.

As Jackson climbed into his bed, he felt grateful to have such a caring mom and supportive aunt. He knew that even on tough days (like today) he had a strong family dynamic to rely on. And with that thought, he drifted off to sleep, dreaming of how he would redeem himself to the Geek Squad next week.

Kayden was settling down and kept looking at the new contact on her phone. Drake. Who would have thought that hours after finishing a lousy day at school, she would have made a new friend of sorts and already got invited to a party? It was scary, but felt nice to be noticed and asked to join something.

Should I text tonight and say I'd go? Kayden felt the conflict, but a voice startled her as it came from her doorway.

"You should text him, you know?" came her aunt, who had snuck up to her open door and was watching her.

"That's creepy, you know, Aunt Hollyn," said Kayden, miffed.

"What is?" she returned innocently. "Oh, yeah,

the sneaking part. Well, what good is being all respectful to you, like your mom? I'd never find out all the good stuff and see you at your moments of doubt," she quipped.

"Do you just act mean to me on purpose to get a rise out of me or are you genuinely disturbed?" Kayden returned.

Aunt Hollyn showed a big smile at that remark.

"It's all part of my charm and the method behind my madness," she shot back, but in a gentle, relaxing way.

Kayden frowned, but acknowledged her aunt's efforts at getting her to relax. She was still upset over last night's visit and told her aunt about it.

"You know, what you said last night was really mean and it has bothered me a lot today. What's worse, most of it was true or happened just the way you predicted. It made me very self-conscious."

Aunt Hollyn's smile dissipated and a serious expression took its place. She walked into Kayden's room and sat down on the side of the bed next to her niece. She extended a hand and put it on top of her niece's hand, that was lying on the bed beside her comfortingly.

"I know it upset you, but it needed to be said for a couple of different reasons, kiddo. One, you carry that attitude around and swing it like a hammer too much. It is a tool you need in life, but you can't use it all the time in every situation. Second, all you could think about was your social anxiety that night and never would have gotten to sleep, so I gave you another avenue to think about, me!"

She stressed the word 'me' with a kind of proud declaration.

"Last, I wanted you to be aware of how you operate, so when you actually went to school, you might not do some things I predicted you would. The other stuff, well, anyone would have probably done. For example, getting lost because it was your first day there. Your nerves alone would have caused that."

Kayden shrugged in her understanding of what her aunt was telling her.

"Besides," she continued, "you got asked to a party, met a boy, and have the coolest aunt on earth to thank for it."

Smiling, Kayden shook her head and laid down, calling it a night. She turned her back to her aunt and made ready to sleep. Hollyn got the picture and got up and headed for the door. She almost made it out when Kayden stopped her.

"Aunt Hollyn," she said with her back to the doorway, "thanks."

Hollyn gave a wry little smile and closed the door, when her niece followed quickly without looking, "and stop smiling."

Hollyn really smiled then and closed the door.

Chapter Six: The Party

    Everyone woke up late on Saturday. A late October day with all the makings of how a potential Halloween movie might look. The colors of the sky, temperature, and fallen leaves marked the beginning of the end of fall and the start of winter. Just not yet.
    Kailynn had gotten up first among the inhabitants of the house and took a shower. After the long, but very fruitful day yesterday, she needed to recharge her batteries. As she was walking back to her room, she heard a fast knocking noise. It wasn't overpowering and loud, just annoying. It was coming from Kayden's room. Without thinking, she opened the door quietly and peeked in. Kayden sat on her bed, nervously tapping her foot against the floor.
    Kayden hadn't noticed her mom yet and was

thinking about texting Drake, the boy who had invited her to a party after the football game the following night. Her heart raced with excitement, but she couldn't help feeling a little anxious.

Her mom, who had poked her head in the doorway, startled her daughter, who was just staring at her phone.

"Expecting a text or call?" Kailynn asked innocently.

Kayden jumped in fright. "Mother, you scared me. Why didn't you knock?"

Kailynn saw the opening to communicate with her daughter.

"Hey, I'm sorry, kid. I just heard this knocking or tapping sound coming from your room and just wanted to make sure you were okay. I figured you were sleeping in, so I didn't want to wake you."

Kayden softened, knowing she was the one making the noise and knew if she had been asleep, she would have more than likely snapped at her mom for waking her up.

"It's okay, mom. I guess I'm sort of stuck on deciding about something."

Looking at her mom, Kailynn nodded, but then fell forward from the door into the room. More like stumbled, as her aunt emerged behind her mom, clearly having bumped her from behind.

"Sorry," Hollyn said unapologetically.

"I'm sure you are Hollyn," retorted Kailynn dryly. "Always butting in the conversation, aren't you?"

"Naturally!" Hollyn replied jovially. "You can't be the head white girl in charge if you don't."

Kayden smiled at the sisters' playful banter. Seeing that both of them were in the room gave her the courage to open up. After initially hesitating, she talked to her mom and Aunt Hollyn about her dilemma. Kayden poured out the events of the previous evening and what she was struggling to decide. They were both very supportive and understanding. They also cautioned her to be careful, but encouraged her to put herself out there. Kayden appreciated their advice and took it to heart, but she couldn't shake the butterflies in her stomach.

They all three went down to the kitchen for breakfast. Jackson was already there with a glass of milk and a doughnut. He looked up from his phone while he was eating and gave a head nod to everyone. Apparently, her mom had purchased a box of doughnuts for everyone last night and had brought it home as a surprise. Jackson discovered them and began his assault.

"Looks like Jackson found the doughnuts," Kailynn remarked to the other girls. "He has a nose like a hound dog."

"And an appetite to go with it," Hollyn added.

Everyone sat down and ate the yeast rings of sugar, enjoying the quiet of the morning. Hollyn made coffee for her and Kailynn. Kayden took some as well, but watered it down with milk and sugar. No one had much to say, still reeling over the whirlwind Friday, so they just ate and kept each of their thoughts to themselves. Kayden brought her phone to the table, which was a no no, but she looked at her mom and she in return gave a smile and look that said, 'go ahead.' Kayden texted Drake and gave a quick message, 'I'll go tonight.'

As the day went on, Kayden couldn't stop thinking about the party. What was she going to wear?

She opened her AccuWeather app to check the temperature and it said it would be around 60 degrees, so she knew her basic coat and long-sleeve shirt would do the job. She kept checking her phone to see if Drake had replied to her text. When he finally did, they started a back-and-forth conversation about the party and what time he was coming by, along with the address of where they were going. Kayden was nervous, but also excited to see Drake in person and hang out with him at the party, but scared about meeting his circle of friends.

As the day progressed, the night of the party finally arrived, and Kayden spent hours getting ready. Drake had told her he'd be by around 8:00 o'clock that evening. It was 7:48 and she was feeling a wreck. She put on her favorite outfit, did her hair and makeup, and was nervously waiting for her ride to arrive while sitting in her room. Aunt Hollyn and Kailynn had left Kayden alone for the day and were doing stuff around the house and yard. Jackson had been helping with the yard for a bit and then went exploring outside of it. He had re-emerged later with a weird look on his face, but had gone to his room immediately, having not talked to anyone. No one had noticed because they were all aware of Kayden's friend coming to pick her up and no one wanted to miss that event.

Like clockwork, Drake pulled up in a black 2003 Chevy S-10 pickup truck. Kayden could see it from her bedroom window. It looked like it was in pretty good shape, considering how old it was in years.

So, he's a truck guy. Could be worse, she thought to herself.

Her aunt quickly broke her internal reflection by yelling up from the bottom of the stairs. She had company.

Ugh, Aunt Hollyn is having fun with this, Kayden said to herself internally.

Kayden came down awkwardly. She had on blue jeans from American Eagle, a shirt from the Shein website (all teens flock to it) and a coat, faux fur from Northface. She had pulled out all the stops with some of her best clothes. She wanted to impress and at least fit in with fashion. It wasn't important, but first impressions here were important. She also wanted to make sure Drake saw as well and feel him out. When she made it downstairs, Drake was waiting for her at the door. He looked ruggedly handsome and confident, and Kayden couldn't help but feel a little red in the face.

"Wow," Drake immediately commented upon seeing her descend the staircase, "you look very nice."

Kayden's face continued to blush even more and squeaked out, a barely audible, "Thanks."

Aunt Hollyn came up and put her arm around Drake and pulled him back and forth like a Yo-Yo. "Yep, ya got your hands full tonight, fella. Kayden here is a chip off the old block. Well, my block." She let him go, then came around to stand beside Kayden. "Kayden needs to be home no later than midnight."

"Whoa, we didn't agree with that," Kailynn interrupted. "Her time was 11:00 pm."

"C'mon Kailynn, it's freakin' Saturday and the address they are going to isn't even ten miles away. If Kayden gets upset or needs rescuing, Aunt Hollyn is there in five minutes or less. Give or take how 'Silver Streak' revs up," Kayden's aunt quipped regarding her car.

Kayden looked at both of them, and a large

grimace appeared on her face. Her mom sensed they were breaking their promise not to embarrass her. Kailynn knew she was dangerously close. Not wanting to push her daughter's trust away, especially after her confiding in advice this morning, she caved quickly.

Kayden's grimace quickly disappeared and she nodded. She turned to Drake.

"I have to be back by midnight, cool?

"Cool," he responded, unperturbed. "Better go. We want a good spot by one of the fire pits. There's only so many make-shift seats there."

"Make-shift?" Kayden asked.

"Yeah," said Drake. "My buddy's family carves seats from logs and puts them around the pits. Their prime real estate."

Both of them left Kayden's house and got into Drake's truck. He opened the door for her and then went around and got into the driver's side. The truck was a standard, which Kayden did not know how to drive. Plus, she wouldn't turn 16 until June of next year, anyway. Drake backed it out of the drive after shifting around on the stick and pulled out towards the night and the party.

***

The party was a whirlwind of activity, with music blaring, a few people dancing; the drinks seemed to flow freely. As they arrived, they mingled with some of the other guests, enjoying the festive atmosphere. It was an average high school get together, but outside. Kayden had been to a couple of parties from her old hometown, but they usually were indoors. Here, they were all outside with four fire pits rolling. There was a bit of a fall breeze, which carried the scent of the falling leaves from the trees with it. The scene looked pretty down to earth and relaxing. Drake pulled Kayden over to a fire pit, which had eight kids hanging around it. It was one of the smaller groups, but they had saved both Kayden and Drake a seat at the table, sort of speaking.

As Kayden sat down at Drake's urging, he signaled to a guy across from him who was sitting on top of a red cooler. The kid, looking to be around sixteen or seventeen, lifted and grabbed two canned beers from the cooler. He tossed both of them to Drake. Drake caught them and sat down.

"I don't know if you drink or not, but I took the liberty of just having a few on hand if you were interested. Do not feel pressured. Oh, and don't worry about me and driving while intoxicated, either. I have a designated driver for the evening and I never drink enough to get drunk." He handed her a silver can.

"Why is that?" Kayden asked, accepting the beer from Drake.

"Because he can't function very well if he does," quipped a girl who sat to the right of Kayden.

"Okay, introductions are all around," informed Drake. "The vivacious lady to your right is Sadie. The girl to her right is Brooklyn. However, don't let Brooklyn fool you. She's best buds over there with Ayelyn, the blonde. The guy sitting next to her is her boyfriend, Owen. He's one of my close buddies."

"Miss," Owen said, tapping his cap to Kayden. Kayden smiled and said hello back to both of them. Ayelyn grabbed Owen's hand and made sure he knew whose girl was his. This simply made Owen smile and laugh a little. Ayelyn elbowed him in the side.

"Watch it, Owen," joked Brooklyn from across the fire. "Ayelyn's elbows are bony and they hurt."

"Shut up Brooklyn, they're not bony."

"Sitting directly across from you," continued Drake, "on the red cooler is Shay. Now he's probably the most laid back dude you'll ever meet. Always chill."

"That's because you've never seen him when we're alone," challenged the dirty blonde beside him.

"Which brings me to his opposite, the most unchilled girl you'll ever meet, Olivia. She's our town athlete. Runs cross, track and is hard core on the basketball floor."

"Damn straight, Drake. However, it's nothing compared to how I protect my man," she said, looking directly at Kayden in defiance.

"Relax baby girl," replied Shay, "we're drinking and watching the flames of relaxation. No one is interested in trying to hook your Shaydy."

Everyone at the circle smirked or covered their soft laugh at Shay's reference to the nickname Olivia had obviously designated to him.

Olivia looked around at everyone. "Something funny?"

Everyone in the group quickly replied no, with some even holding up their hands in submission.

Drake rolled his eyes at this and finished his introductions. The other two sitting on either side of the happy couple I just introduced are Braelyn, a true blonde and Gage. He's just passing the time before he jumps ship, right, Gage?"

"Screw you Drake. Just because I'm dropping out of school when I hit 17 years old doesn't mean you have to keep introducing me as 'that guy' to everyone."

"Gage, you've been saying that shit since junior high," interrupted Owen.

"So?"

"So you are full of crap, man. We all know you like the attention it gets you from the teachers; trying to save your soul and all. Gives you an out too if you screw up in class since you are dropping, right?"

Gage stood up in anger real quick at Owen's question and comments.

"You obviously want me to take those shit-kickers you have on and whale them upside your head, don't you hillbilly?"

"Bring it burn out," Owen challenged back.

"Gage," Braelyn quietly, but firmly, called, "enough, please. Drake meant nothing to it. It's a party and we are all just poking fun at each other. Otherwise, try going to some of the other fire pits and hang out with those guys. We are chill here, got it?" she ordered.

Oddly enough, Gage's body language shifted to a more relaxed posture and he nodded towards Drake, who raised his beer in return.

Kayden looked at her can of beer before she opened it. "What's Keystone Light?" she asked Drake.

Owen answered before Drake could even open his mouth. "Only Southern Illinois' finest spirit," smiling in a self-congratulatory manner.

"You've never had a Stone before?" Shay asked earnestly.

Shaking her head, Kayden popped the can.

"Go on," Gage ordered in an amused manner, "it won't bite you. Actually has a pleasant finish to it and it isn't overly strong in alcohol content. Somewhere in the 4 percent area."

Kayden mimicked Drake and raised her beer to Gage and then took a sip. Gage smiled at this and looked at Drake. "I like her."

Suddenly, a very flamboyant personality who seemed to materialize out of nowhere disrupted the moment. The young male teen vaulted over Brooklyn's head, almost giving her a concussion with his crotch. He gave a loud, "Whoa no!" upon sticking a very shaky landing, almost falling into the fire pit. He was skinny, wore a flannel shirt open to a white tank top, presenting zero muscles. On his face, he wore a pair of sunglasses with yellow lenses. Drake immediately went into action, catching the kid before his momentum carried him into the fire pit.

Brooklyn yelled, "Dammit Shades, your skinny crotch almost got you castrated. You are lucky I didn't get up and slam those ridiculous sunglasses into the fire!"

Shades smiled and whirled on Brooklyn, "You'd only be so lucky to get Shades' crotch on you, Brooky," the boy teased.

Drake got between them before Brooklyn could stand up and respond.

"Whoa guys," he said to both of them and then turned to the young teen, "Kayden, this here is the life of the party, our host and my best friend, Shades."

Shades turned to Kayden and immediately went down on one knee, grabbed her free hand and brought to his lips. "My Lady," he said in a chivalrous tone. "Young Drake has been all awash about how this new girl with dark hair and green eyes has come into our midst. Yet, here she is in all her splendid glory, blessing us with her mere presence. I am humbled," he finished, lowering his head down.

"Um, nice to meet you, Shades?" she choked.

Shades looked up and smiled a crooked grin. "I like her D. She is already using my pseudonym!"

"His real name is Jeremiah Van Ormer," whispered Drake to Kayden conspiratorially.

Shades stood and turned abruptly to Brooklyn. He walked over to her and put his right hand into his back pocket. He pulled out a pair of sunglasses and held them in front of him.

"My apologies, Brooky. I come bearing gifts. Here are the Dezi angular cat eye sunglasses I've teased you about. Got an extra pair just sitting there and I know the cat eye look is your thing. Accept this as a peace offering." Shades handed them to a shocked Brooklyn like he was bequeathing her a sword hilt first. She took them almost apologetically.

"You didn't have to do that, Jeremiah," she answered.

"Oh, but I did! Think of it as my apology for breaking the strap on your purse."

"Jeremiah, it was more than a purse. It was a Michael Kors Dover Half Moon Leather Shoulder Bag and for the record, my dad fixed it."

"Be that as it may," continued Shades unfazed, "they are yours. Enjoy!"

Shades turned to Drake and held out his hand.

Drake looked at Shay. "Beer him, Shay."

"Coming right up, compadre!"

****

Kayden and Drake spent most of the night together, talking and laughing and a few times dancing with the group. They didn't really mingle with the other kids at the party, but some came and went, saying hi to some of the group or thanking Shades for a place to party for the night. The vibe of the group, mostly, was pretty laid back. Ayelyn was fine as long as nobody was acting like they were hitting on Owen. Brooklyn struck Kayden as the fashion guru of the group. Braelyn and Sadie seemed to be close to each other also, even though Braelyn had some kind of connection to the loner, Gage. Gage kept mostly to himself and his demeanor always seemed defensive. It reminded Kayden of an abused dog whose master was always beating it, so it was always in defense mode and distrusting of others.

Now Olivia, she was altogether about one thing: Shay. Shay, however, was about everyone and hardly paid attention to Olivia's constant fawning over him. Shades was the life and clown of the party. He was a free spirit, who had no issues expressing his nerdiness, yet intelligence. As the night went on, they grew more comfortable with each other, and Kayden felt like she was really getting to know them and Drake. Maybe this could be a group she could hang out with and fit into?

Before she knew it, the party was winding down, as some teens there had left, but it was only about 10:30. Not too late, but not her curfew time either. Things took a sudden turn for Kayden when a group of people approached her, asking her about her last name, Toth. At first, Kayden was happy to talk about the little of her family history she knew, but she soon realized the tone of the conversation was turning negative.

The goth girl in black leggings and bride of

Frankenstein's monster hair spoke up. She inquired if her family had been involved in a terrible accident in the coal mines a long time ago.

Without having time to answer, another girl next to her asked, "Do you know the history behind your family name in this town?"

An overweight boy who looked on the older end of high school looked at Kayden directly. He said, "your family descendants were involved in a scandal that rocked this town decades ago. It's a pretty horrific tale."

The news of the accident in the coal mines shocked Kayden. "I don't know what you're talking about," she replied.

Drake, who had been standing next to Shades talking, moved to intercept the group who were gathering around Kayden. He put himself between them and her. Shades followed and stood beside him.

The goth girl interrupted Drake, pressing her advantage. "It's a long story, but the short version is that your great-grandfather or something was involved in some shady business dealings with the local politicians. There were rumors of bribery and corruption, and it caused a tremendous uproar in the community."

Another goth kid chimed in a disgusted tone. "He and the other members of your family involved in the scandal were all buried in the Hungarian cemetery on the outskirts of town."

A short quiet fell upon everyone at the mention of the cemetery.

Kayden stood up behind her two protectors and responded, "I've never heard of this or that place before."

Drake noticed Kayden's discomfort and tried to intervene. "Hey, guys, let's not jump to conclusions here. It's just an old story. No one knows what happened other than there was a terrible accident."

Owen stood up and moved over beside Kayden after hearing this. The three formed a protective ring around her.

Kayden's heart sank as she heard the terrible rumors. She couldn't believe that her family could be involved in something so tragic. But the worst part was the way the people at the party were treating her. Some of them began giving her dirty looks and whispered behind her back.

Owen broke his silence and aggressively said, "Listen, hauss, you can take your tone and attitude and back off. We were enjoying our evening until you shit-disturbers showed up. No one here cares about your Gothic need to stir up the past because of your dark desire to play with Ouija boards."

This got some of the other teenagers riled up. They began bad-mouthing Owen and Drake for sticking up for a total stranger who was a Toth. The damage had been done. Kayden felt isolated and alone, like she didn't belong at the party anymore. She touched Drake on the shoulder.

Quietly, she said, "Maybe you should just take me home, Drake."

Shades, overhearing Kayden's request, interceded on behalf of his best friend.

"Awe Kayden, don't let those losers bother you. I let everyone hang out here, even if I don't hang out with everyone. Can't let the trolls or woke kids have something bad to hit me with on social media, ya know? However, I won't allow them to stay here any longer. Just hold tight."

With that, Shades sprung into action, kicking the teens out. Some of the goth kids were cursing at Shades, but made their way to their cars. A few guys, though, who had been hanging out with the overweight kid named Rolland Dickerson, were trying to cause problems. She learned his name fast, as her new friends used it repeatedly to tell him to leave. They seemed to have drunk too much and were itching for a fight. Braelyn came up behind Kayden and put an arm around her comfortingly. It completely surprised Kayden who was feeling like an outcast at this point.

"Listen to Shades, Caviar. Rolland is a dick and bully to everyone, even to his cronies over there by him. He is all mouth and every school has its share of unlikable people," Braelyn informed her.

"Why did you call me Caviar?" Kayden asked, perplexed.

"Raven-haired is such an overused term to describe hair color and we all need nicknames. Caviar suits you best," Braelyn responded light-heartedly.

"I agree," Ayelyn cooed, coming up to Kayden's right. "It is already growing on me. Just keep your eggs away from Owen," she warned in a joking voice.

"Eggs?" Kayden echoed again.

"What are you a parrot?" came Sadie's voice from her seat at the fire. Sadie was a very skinny, short blonde who seemed to have drank a little too much.

One drink could probably get her drunk, thought Kayden.

"You know, eggs... fish eggs... Caviar?" Olivia butted in on the conversation.

"Oh, yeah," Kayden quickly responded, suddenly understanding the reference.

"Good one," Brooklyn said to Ayelyn.

"Thanks, girl," Ayelyn smiled, "you girls keep settin up dem' softballs for me to hit and I'll knock'em out."

Kayden couldn't shake the feeling of unease. She still wanted to leave, to get away from the judgmental stares and hurtful comments. But she decided she couldn't leave until she had learned the truth about her family's history or at least the rumors which surrounded it.

Some scuffling sounds came away from the girls and they immediately turned to see what was happening. Owen and Rolland were pushing back and forth on each other. Rolland was a big boy who threw his weight around, but Owen was a typical country boy. He was strong and unafraid. Drake was in-between Shades and the other two boys who were fat boy's cronies. Drake was trying to keep Shades from getting pummeled as both the cronies were grabbing his shirt from both sides and pulling back and forth. Shades feverishly tried to disengage from them. Drake was getting into the middle and was pushing both sides away from his body, but was being bounced around more than being able to push.

"OMG," cried Ayelyn. "Owen is taking on Dickerson." Ayelyn grabbed Kayden's arm and squeezed it hard to show her worry.

Braelyn looked on and saw Shades pull away from the cronies to fall hard on the ground, sunglasses flying off his head. She growled, "Are you going to sit there or are you going to do something?"

Kayden did not know who she was talking to until she heard his voice.

"Dammit, Braelyn."

Next thing Kayden saw was Gage fly by her and the other girls, running right at Drake. Drake was next to get slammed to the ground by the two bullies just as Gage arrived. Gage threw a hay-maker at the one on the left, clocking him solidly in the face, dropping him to the ground. The other kid backed off, but Gage moved toward him, lifting his foot up hard to kick the kid right in the groin. The crony grabbed his junk from the impact with both hands and fell backwards, like in a movie. Gage, fully energized now, turned to Owen and moved towards him and Rolland.

Rolland saw Gage coming and immediately turned and semi-ran away from Owen to avoid Gage. His pants were sagging in the back to where his butt-crack was hanging out. Gage continued to follow, catching up to the large, lumbering teen. Gage pushed him from behind with his foot, using his momentum running to send Rolland flying head first to the ground. His sheer volume of weight sent ripples all over his body of fat.

"Get out of here fat-ass," sneered Gage.

The heavy-set teen had trouble picking himself up, but used the car he had fallen down close to, to help him stand up.

"You'll regret that Gage," Rolland spat. He had a bloody lip and bruised cheek from where he fell from Gage's push.

"Next time you should think before acting like an asshole," retorted Gage. He turned around and started walking back to his group of friends, unconcerned.

The group of friends reformed their circle around the fire pit. While the commotion was going on, Shay had added logs to the fire to prepare for the returning combatants. When they all sat down, each had their own quiet conversation. Ayelyn was looking over at Owen to check for injuries. Braelyn pulled Gage aside and was having a word as well. Gage didn't seem overly upset, but responded to whatever it was she was telling. Kayden and Drake were both talking to Shades whose glasses had broken in the struggle. He seemed none the worse for wear and was excited his party had a fight story to talk about at school. To Shades, his street cred was on the up-tick. Once they were all done calming down, everyone popped another can of beer and just sat looking at the fire. It was now 11:00 pm.

Kayden alone with her emotions on what had happened with the kids coming over and telling her about the Toth name couldn't hold her thoughts any longer. She would talk to her mom and aunt about it tomorrow, but wanted a better gauge of her classmates' thoughts sitting around her.

She said out loud to no one in particular in an innocent, but confused tone, "This is all so wild. I did not know about any of this. Do you think it's true about ghosts?"

Braelyn, staring at the fire, replied softly, "Who knows? But it's definitely a creepy place to visit. We should all go there one night and check it out."

Brooklyn looked at her with a gleam in her eye and a wry grin. "It's said that the spirits of the people buried there are still restless and seek justice for the wrongs committed against them."

Kayden shook her head at the madness of it all. "What exactly is the issue here with the people who died?"

Shades stood up and gave a grand bow to everyone, as he was renowned for his storytelling ability.

"Allow me," he quipped to everyone in the group. He turned to Kayden and began.

"Toth had always known that being a coal miner was a dangerous job. After all, it was the late 1920's. Every day, he descended deep into the mines, knowing that he might not make it back up again. But he had a family to support, and so he continued to work hard, day after day."

The emotions displayed by Shades were infectious by the light of the fire. As the shadows of the light played on the orator, Shades continued dramatically.

"One day in the 1930's, Toth and seven other miners were working deep in the mines when disaster struck. In the early morning hours, eight miners burned to death in a gas explosion in the Saline County Coal Corporation mine at Ledford, five miles south of here. Rescue workers found the bodies charred almost beyond recognition. The rescue team's efforts could not save them. They pronounced the eight miners dead as they were recovering the bodies at the bottom of the main shaft."

Shades paused, motioning to the memory of the minors by raising his can of beer. The others sitting around mimicked him to keep the drama unfolding. After a small drink, Shades continued to build the rising action of his story.

"The explosion was because of the ignition of a pocket of gas, presumably from an open, lit lantern used during this era. It could also have been the older helmets they used before electricity. The helmet held a candle or something in it they lit with a match. At least three hundred miners who worked in other sections of the shaft area ascended to the ground level in safety after the explosion. Rescue workers, for a time, held the slender hope that the eight victims, who were missing, had retreated somewhere safe in the mine. Unfortunately, they simply could not leave the mine. The community of Ledford was heartbroken by the loss of these brave men, but as the years passed, their memory faded. The cemetery, their last resting place, became forgotten and unkempt. The graves became overgrown with weeds and the headstones weathered and wore out. The graves had become sunken in and looters had defiled their resting place."

Shades looked at Kayden and Drake as he spoke. "The old cemetery had become a place of criminal activity. People used it as a location to conduct their shady dealings of drugs, violent acts, and rumor even had it as a devil worshiping site. As time went on, strange things happened in the cemetery. People reported hearing eerie noises and seeing ghostly apparitions. Some even claimed that they had seen the ghosts of the eight coal miners, still trapped in the mine and searching for a way out, but burned horribly."

Kayden interrupted Shades. "What do you mean by searching?"

Shades ignored her question and continued ramping up the crescendo. "At first, people dismissed these reports as nothing more than superstition. But as the paranormal activity continued to escalate, it became clear there was something going on in that forgotten cemetery."

The group was leaning in towards their narrator, listening in on his every word.

"Visitors to the cemetery reported feeling a sense of unease and foreboding, as if they were being watched by something unseen. The atmosphere was heavy with the weight of the past, and many people avoided the cemetery altogether. But one day, a group of paranormal investigators investigated the strange occurrences at the cemetery. Armed with cameras and recording equipment, they ventured into the unkempt graveyard, determined to uncover the truth."

Shades then turned and sat down, becoming quiet. The others awaiting the climax wore looks of confusion. When Shades said nothing else, Drake motioned to Shades, "Well?" he asked.

"Well, what?" Shades responded.

"What happened to the investigators?" Drake inquired a little frustrated with his friend.

Shades shrugged, "I don't know. They published nothing, nor reported their findings. In fact, no one really knows what came of it. Maybe something happened that scared them away or perhaps they never came out? Your guess is as good as mine."

The groups looked at each other. Gage was the first to respond.

"I'm with Braelyn. Perhaps we should just check it out tonight."

Drake immediately spoke up to the group. "I don't know. It's a little past eleven and I promised Kayden's family she would be back at midnight."

Owen asked, "how far away is her house?"

Drake responded, "actually, she lives within walking distance to the cemetery."

The group responded together, "no way... whoa... really?"

Brooklyn stood up. "That settles it. We leave now and go there. It will take us less than ten minutes to get there from here. We can hang out for twenty or thirty minutes and Drake will have plenty of time to get Kayden home. Who is with me?"

They all stood up except Kayden.

Drake took her hand. "We absolutely don't have to go if you are uncomfortable with this," he informed her seriously.

The story horrified Kayden, but she felt a sense of relief. She understood why people were acting so strangely towards her. It wasn't about her personally, but about her family's history. However, with her being a Toth it was going to create scandal. She decided they should go. She would be with a group who seemed to care about each other and moved to protect her tonight even though they barely knew her.

"Okay," she said standing, "let's make our way to the Hungarian Cemetery. We'll see what all this fuss is about."

Everyone packed their stuff up and headed for their cars. Drake, Kayden and Shades all got into his truck and the others followed. The night was about to ignite.

Chapter Seven: The Cemetery

Shades, Drake, and Kayden, along with their friends, began their journey towards the Hungarian Cemetery. The clock read 11:15 pm. and the darkness enveloped them like a thick fog. Drake had said they were only ten minutes away, which he told her on the way to the cemetery. It was literally less than a minute's drive to her house from there. This gave some relief to Kayden because of her curfew, but Drake was more worried about getting her home on time than she was. He didn't want to disappoint her aunt and mom.

As they drove, the headlights illuminated the road ahead, casting eerie shadows across the desolate night's landscape. The trees rustled ominously in the wind, adding to the unsettling atmosphere. The fall evening had dropped to a colder feeling given the breeze and the fact they were no longer huddled around the fire pit.

Finally, in what seemed only seconds given their anticipation of the event, they arrived at the cemetery. As they approached the entrance to the cemetery, Drake's headlights shone on the newly placed marker. On the slab, it said, "St Casimir Lithuanian Cemetery" as they slowly drove in.

This made Kayden wrinkle her nose, because everyone was calling this the Hungarian Cemetery.

Lithuanian is not the same as Hungarian. In fact, her name was of Hungarian descent, so why even call it Lithuanian? she pondered.

The cemetery was small, enclosed by trees growing outside the entire place. It seemed to be designed in a circle. Based on the lights of the truck, the road just drove around and came back to where the driver initially came in. There was nothing to stop anyone from coming into the cemetery. The gravestones were old and weathered, some of them tilting at odd angles. The ground was uneven but it was better kept than what Shades had described. There were no weeds and vines creeping over the graves. The place, although it looked old, seemed to be taken care of.

The group got out of their cars and met in front of Drake's truck. They stood there looking out at the old cemetery. The moon light was eerie because of the random cloud cover. The silence was deafening, broken only by the occasional rustling of leaves and the distant howl of a coyote.

Even with the recent renovation, the cemetery still had a spooky vibe. The gravestones seemed to loom over the group, and the wind whistled through the branches of the trees, creating an unsettling cacophony. The air was thick with the smell of damp earth, and a misty fog began settling over the graves.

Drake checked his phone. It was now 11:35 pm. The teens were visibly nervous and anxious, their faces lit by the flickering glow of the phones in their hands. They had heard stories of the cemetery being haunted by ghosts and paranormal entities, and the creepy environment only added to their fears.

As they stepped out from the truck, their footsteps echoed through the silent cemetery from walking on the gravel path. The gravestones cast spectral shadows, and the misty fog seemed to swirl around their feet. Despite their apprehension, they pressed on, determined to explore the spooky graveyard and uncover its secrets.

The cemetery had an unmistakable air of mystery and foreboding. It was as if the spirits of the deceased still lingered, trapped between this world and the next. The teens looked around nervously, unsure of what they might encounter in the dark and creepy environment of the Hungarian Cemetery.

Drake pointed toward the small path which formed to the right of the cemetery. It was a tiny worn out trail, through the grass and weeds. It went through what looked like a tree line.

"If you take the pathway right there," he said with confidence, "it will end up in Kayden's backyard."

Kayden's eyebrows went up in surprise. She hadn't known how close her family lived in proximity to this cemetery. The others kind of nodded or gave a little noise, showing their understanding of Drake's comment.

They felt a sense of unease looking back at the

issue at hand. They were determined to explore this historic place as they reached the starting point of the cemetery.

Brooklyn looked around at the group members and asked quietly, "Well, now that we're here, what should we do?"

Gage made a noise which undermined the scariness of the location. "Who cares? The place seems deserted and there are no idiots here but us."

As the group of eleven walked deeper into the cemetery, Owen gave orders for everyone to split up. Half of them would take one side of the cemetery and the other half the other.

Shades, Drake, Kayden, Braelyn and Gage were part of the latter group, and as they walked away to the right, the others took the left side. As they slowly made their trepidation along the tombstones, Kayden's group couldn't shake off the feeling that they were being watched.

With Shade's group taking the right side, they wandered through the sporadic rows of headstones; they felt a sense of somberness wash over them. The old, weather-worn grave markers stood like sentinels, watching over the last resting places of those who had passed on.

"The place is definitely creepy," Kayden whispered.

"It is a cemetery and it's nighttime," replied Shades, who kept his newly replaced yellow sunglasses tightly on his head. His bravado though had become very somber.

Kayden, without thinking, had linked her arm around Drakes and pulled him closer to her. Drake reassured them calmly, "Don't worry, guys. It's just a typical October night."

"Other than it's the Halloween season you mean? What exactly are we looking for as we're walking?" Braelyn inquired, looking back and forth from the gravel path they were traveling.

"Ghosts or strange things," Shades said in dramatic fashion. "The ancestors of yore are here remember?"

Kayden thought about the events of the last hour. The kids had said her relatives were supposedly responsible for some event which happened in the mines. She thought about her last name and just said the thought.

"We're looking for a grave marker with the last name Toth on it."

The others stopped walking for a second and checked out the tombstones; they were passing up; now that they had a solid idea of what to look for.

The air was heavy with the smell of old stone and musty decay. Suddenly, they heard a faint whisper, and they froze in place.

"Do you hear that?" asked Drake to the group.

"Yeah," responded Gage who now was on alert.

"Maybe it's just the others trying to play an early Halloween joke on us?" Shades replied, trying to make sense of the whispers.

"They are too far away from us and even if it was them, there's no way they could have snuck up on us right here. Too much open room among grave markers," Braelyn returned logically.

They listened closely, and the whispers grew louder, until they could make out words.

"Whoa," cried Shades, "those were actual words I'm hearing."

"I can't really put what is being said together," Gage said to nobody in-particular.

"Maybe we should go back?" Braelyn suggested in a terrified voice.

"I want to see," responded an emboldened Kayden. "This is supposed to have one of my family members buried here. I want to see their resting place."

"Okay," Drake returned assuringly to her. "Just in case, let's tighten our group. We want nothing we can't see jumping out at us individually."

They all complied immediately. Not even Gage was showing unnecessary bravado. Just like out of a horror film the entire area went quiet, with only the faint sound of rustling leaves and swinging branches moved by the wind. The clouds were moving ominously in front of the moon, casting even more shadows in the areas of the grave markers. Everyone stopped moving and strained their ears to figure out what was making the whispering words in the air.

Suddenly, they heard a rustling sound from behind a nearby gravestone. They turned around to investigate, but saw nothing. Just as they were about to dismiss it as their imagination, they heard it again, louder this time. They started moving again, but this time towards the sound.

The group cautiously made their way over to the source of the noise, their heartbeats quickening with each step. As they reached the gravestone, they saw a figure materialize, standing in front of it. It was a ghostly apparition of a middle-aged man dressed in some kind of dirty overalls, with brown boots holding something in front of him. On his head was a cap which looked to have possibly had a candle holder built in it. Soot covered the figure's face. A handkerchief was tied around his neck. Another small whistle swung in front of his chest. A thick coat covered his shoulders and body. He just stood there looking sideways at a grave.

The group froze in terror as the ghostly man slowly turned his head towards them. His eyes glowed a luminescent white on the darkened, sooty face underneath the cap.

"Oh my God," breathed Kayden. "The man's eyes are glowing," she quietly stated.

The rest of the group didn't respond to Kayden about the tombstone. They were more worried about its visitor.

"That isn't normal," stammered Shades, pointing to the thing's eyes.

Gage replied, "No, it isn't," clearly shaken by the sight before them.

"Who are you?" challenged Drake in an unsteady voice.

"Um, maybe you shouldn't be so brazen, Drake," a terrified Braelyn muttered.

"Yeah, man. He doesn't seem well, look at the dirty face and the glowing eyes. I'd say we're freaking seeing a ghost right now," Shades quickly added.

The figure limped towards the group. It muttered the words 'help.' It reached out towards the group.

"That's enough for me," Gage said with finality. "Let's get the hell out of here, Drake."

Drake looked at Kayden who couldn't take her eyes off the eerie figure.

"C'mon Drake, we need to get out of here now," echoed Shades. "Halloween fun be damned dude."

Drake nodded in agreement and turned away from the approaching figure when Braelyn let out a terrifying shriek. The entire group turned. Forgetting about the supernatural man approaching and looked at the terror-stricken Braelyn. Their eyes moved in the direction she was staring. What they saw all around them from the other tombstone markers were dark figures emerging. They looked mangled and deformed. They started walking towards the group.

    Gage looked all around him and nodded to himself. "There are seven of them out there, Drake."

    "That makes eight total then, if we count creepy who is getting uncomfortably closer to us," Drake answered, looking back over his shoulder.

    "Didn't you say there were eight coal miners in that accident Shades?" Kayden quickly inquired.

    "Yeah, but who's counting?" he replied without taking his eyes off of the scene unfolding before him.

    Kayden used her phone and turned on the flashlight mode. She shined it at the closest disfigured entity moving towards them. What the group saw was a figure who looked burned from some type of accidental fire. The clothes or whatever it had been wearing, seemed cauterized to its blackened skin. The clothes were also melted to protruding charred bones as it slowly hobbled towards them. The scorched creature turned translucent when the light hit it. It stopped and wailed from the light touching it. The others did the same.

    The young teens tensed at the loud whining of the surrounding entities. As they stopped, a small flame ignited at the top of each of their heads. Kayden's phone light shut off. She panicked and checked her phone. Something completely drained the cell phone of power.

    "My phone's battery just went dead," she

informed the group nervously.

"I'll use mine," Braelyn offered. As she pressed the button to open her phone screen, she noticed hers too had no battery power. "Guys, my phone is dead, too."

The rest of them checked their phones only to find they were dead.

"What do we do?" cried Braelyn.

"Whatever it is, it better be fast. They are only a couple cars' length away, man," Gage stated in sheer panic.

Drake looked at the little candle flames above their heads. It was mesmerizing. As he looked, he felt a real calm come over him. He wasn't afraid or anxious. In fact, he felt relaxed. He didn't want to run or get away. Just serene. The candles had a real tranquil effect on him. Kayden looked up at Drake and noticed he looked as if in a trance. Braelyn and Shades were acting the same way. Only she and Gage were still in panic mode.

"Gage, the others are in some kind of trance."

Gage turned to look at Braelyn. Braelyn had a lost, vacant stare, while gazing at the oncoming things, so Gage yelled at her, but she didn't hear it. Gage started shaking her hard by the shoulders, yelling for her to wake up.

Kayden was having the same issue with Drake. All the while these things were lumbering awkwardly toward them like the Thriller Video by Michael Jackson. It was the part when he and his girlfriend walked by the cemetery. Kayden couldn't help but remember that scene as it flashed before her in real life. She became so frustrated with the whole thing. First, her dad leaves them. Next, her mom moves them to a new town and school. Now, just when she thought she found a group to fit in with, they get killed or worse by freaking bogeymen? Bogeymen which apparently her family had some dark secret about? Her instincts took over. With the specters of the dead almost upon them, she hauled off and slapped Drake as hard as she could, knocking him down. The slap jolted him out of his hypnotic state and he was back to himself. He shook his head to get the cobwebs out. Kayden yelled his name and reached down to pull him up as Drake worked to make sense of things.

As Kayden helped Drake up, the first ghostly figure with the glowing eyes had reached them. The three who were still coherent heard distinctly from what looked to be an old miner who still was very much dirty, wearing clothes of another time. He muttered, "help me."

Just when it seemed like the ghostly man was about to touch them, he suddenly vanished, leaving the Drake and Kayden standing there, dazed and trembling. They couldn't believe what they had just witnessed.

The other wretched looking things were still very much there and almost upon them. They did not seem as harmless and were reaching out for their victims while shrieking in pain. Drake had enough.

"They are blocking our way back to the cars. Gage, throw Braelyn over your shoulder. I'll put shades on mine. Kayden, see the path I showed you earlier over there?" Drake instructed, pointing at the place with his stretched out finger.

Kayden nodded, seeing the way just a few feet from them.

"We take that path and head to your house,

now," Drake ordered with the air of authority.

No one argued. Gage picked up Braelyn like a sack of potatoes and lifted her easily onto his shoulder. Drake did the same with his lanky, best friend. As he hoisted him on his right shoulder, the sunglasses fell off his face. Kayden bent over to pick them up, but Drake grabbed her with his free hand. "No time, lead. We will be right behind you. Go!!"

The zombie apocalypse was upon them.

Kayden immediately turned and started running through the quickly closing opening of the macabre scene before them. Gage went next, with Drake following behind. None of them looked back. They punched through quickly and an extra burst of adrenaline seized them all. Kayden followed the path straight into a roughage of trees and overgrown grass. They bobbed and weaved through the entanglement of foliage until all at once they came into a clearing.

Kayden stopped and looked around. In front of her was their home. Aunt Hollyn's car was still in the driveway, parked. She fell to her knees. Exhaustion consumed her. All the emotional strain had played itself out, and she allowed her tense body to relax. The result was extreme fatigue. The others crashed through as well and did the same thing. The two boys slung down their now heavy burden to the grass and sat back, trying to catch their breath.

Shades stirred almost immediately and in a groggy voice asked, "What happened? Why am I laying on the ground in the dark?"

No one answered, still in shock over the last few minutes of excitement.

"Awe, dammit Gage, you got grass stains on my shirt," grumbled Braelyn.

"Are you serious right now?" yelled Gage back at Braelyn in disbelief.

"Yes, I'm serious. Do you have any idea how hard grass is to get out of clothing? Mom paid good money for this shirt and now it's ruined. What am I supposed to tell her?" snapped Braelyn back.

"How about thank you, Gage, for saving me from those creatures?"

"What creatures?" she replied defensively.

"What creatures?" echoed Kayden. "The charred remains of whatever it was in the cemetery lumbering towards us?"

"You guys are full of shit," stated Shades. "I guess this is another one of your pranks to get me scared, around Halloween time, huh buddy?" he said to Drake.

"You really don't remember what just happened?" Drake asked earnestly.

"Hey, where's my glasses dude? That's two pair in one night," whined the skinny teen.

"Wait," ordered Kayden. "Neither of you two remember anything that just happened?"

"Sure, I remember what happened," responded Braelyn. "We were searching for ghosts in the cemetery when apparently Gage and Drake threw us on the ground here."

Gage looked at Kayden and Drake in disbelief. Neither of the two recalled what happened. Drake internally thought about the series of events. He too had been lulled by those candle flames on top of the specter's heads, when...

"The candle lights," he said out loud, shutting everyone up. "When those candles lit up on those things' heads, all the power went out of the phones. All

I could see or concentrate on were those tiny flames. Everyone and everything disappeared and they simply mesmerized me."

"That makes sense," Kayden agreed. "Only after I slapped the crap out of you did you come to your senses."

"Exactly," he pondered, "When I came out of it, everything came rushing back to me like a tidal wave; which, by the way, flat out hurt," he exclaimed, reaching for his face.

Kayden made eye contact and could see he wasn't upset, just rattled.

Laughter broke out from the least expected person there, Gage. He pointed to Drake's face. "Man, you have a red hand print the size of California on your face."

Shades joined Gage in laughter, seeing the huge whelp sticking out on Drake's face.

Kayden breathed a sigh of relief. "Well, we survived the infamous Hungarian Cemetery," she said to no one in particular.

A large flashlight coming from the house suddenly illuminated them.

"Stay right there," shouted a female voice coming around the garage. It was Aunt Hollyn and Kayden's mom.

"Great," muttered Kayden. "Who is going to explain this to Aunt Hollyn?"

Drake looked down at his watch. It was 12:15 pm. They missed Kayden's curfew.

Nice, he thought, *so much for first impressions on a first date.*

"How long have you horny teens been hiding back here behind the garage?" Hollyn accused menacingly.

"It's not like that Aunt Hollyn," Kayden replied, trying to diffuse the situation.

"Really?" Hollyn retorted. "Two girls and three guys who went to a party. They sneak back to one of their houses and are hiding behind the garage on the cold ass ground in a circle. Two questions, one; where's the bottle at and two; where did you stash the truck?"

"Why would we have a bottle?" Braelyn asked in earnest to Hollyn.

Kayden's mom spoke up first. "Spin the bottle game? Don't act like you don't know about it."

The teens all looked at each other in confusion. Shades replied, "Is that like some drinking game or something?"

Both sisters looked at each other perplexed. Hollyn fixed her stare on Shades. "You really don't know what spin the bottle is? The kissing game?"

The teens laughed out loud despite themselves. Both women felt foolish at this and Hollyn yelled, "what the hell's so funny?"

Gage answered. "It's called spin the phone game. The app has a spinner on it and we pass around the phone. The person holding the phone taps the screen and the phone spinner spins. When it lands, that's who you kiss."

"Yeah, among other things," added Braelyn.

"Other things?" Kailynn asked.

"Mom," Kayden said embarrassingly, "the app adds challenges to the spin, if you want. You can determine how many people are playing and their seat in the circle. God, you guys are so old," she finished, completely annoyed.

An uncomfortable silence passed between

everyone. Finally, Aunt Hollyn cleared her throat.

"Either way, it's past your curfew," pointing to Kayden. She turned to Drake. "You did not get her here on time young man." She paused, looking at the handprint on Drake's face with her flashlight. "No means no stud," Hollyn said with viperous intent. "I think it's time for you and the other three there to head on their way back to wherever you stashed your truck."

All five of the teens made a shocked sound with their breaths. It didn't go unnoticed by the two adults.

"Where is your truck?" Kailynn asked.

"That's a long story, mom," returned Kayden timidly.

"How bout you get started with it now then," remarked Hollyn.

"Well, it's back at the Hungarian Cemetery," Kayden admitted truthfully.

Now it was the adults' turn to experience a bit of shock.

"Why did you leave it there and why did you even go there?" Hollyn dared to ask.

"We were just going to explore Aunt Hollyn. Just to show all the rumors about it being haunted were lies," Kayden explained.

"And?" Kayden's mom asked curiously.

"Well," Drake answered for all of them. "The stories are true."

Chapter Eight: Ghostly Encounter

Jackson had been numb from the moment he had returned to the house after his little adventure. He hadn't really told anyone about what he had discovered on the other side of the tree foliage in the backyard.

"Hog Rider!" yelled the digital character from the game Jackson was playing online.

Jackson had needed something to distract him. This was the game he had defeated playing the leader of the Geek Squad. Jackson opened it on his tablet and just played whatever deck he randomly chose off the game. He was currently playing the Gob-Hog Cycle deck for this round. He liked the game because it was fully strategy based. He had been building his battle deck for over a year. He entered the arena where he battled against other deck holders. He originally had started his own clan with his old schoolmates. They had broken ranks and formed their own clans eventually because they couldn't play to Jackson's level. Feeling inadequate, jealous, and disrespected in the gaming world, his buddies all went their separate ways. Every once in a while, they would see each other online and play, but it never returned to their former gaming relationship.

He had got himself into the League and actually had a few shots at playing in a few global tournaments. Those players could flat bring the challenges. Brilliant minds played these kinds of games, but Jackson couldn't count himself among them. He was 14, after all. He did really well against those his age, but competing against adults was a different story.

"Hog Rider!" the game went off again. Jackson was using the Gob-Hog Cycle deck characters against a new foe who was using the Ice Bow Deck. Jackson was having trouble against their Tombstone card. This deck was primarily a solid choice when playing the defensive game against an opponent. Jackson was familiar with the move his opponent was attempting to use. They were using Phoenix and Ice Wizard cards. He already was destroying the Phoenix with his own powerful Wizard. He simultaneously used his Hog Rider and Battle Ram with the Canon to lay out his opponents' defensive barrier.

Tombstone, thought Jackson, *stupid tombstone is the last thing I want to think about.*

His thoughts were wandering back to the series of events he had experienced in the late afternoon today. He had gone exploring and felt a tug of sorts to expand past the tree line in the backyard. Upon clearing it, he discovered a cemetery. Thinking it pretty

The Hungarian Cemetery Secrets Within Backup

cool to be living so close to a cemetery given his world of gaming; he visited it. The place was pretty cool overall. The cemetery was small by cemetery standards and many of the tombstones were old. They dated back around the 1920s before the Great Depression era. He had been learning about that era in school. Apparently, people liked to drink illegally, dance, and party. That decade gave rise to the original American gangster.

As he had been walking, he had come upon someone standing over a grave marker. Out of respect for what appeared to be a man, he walked by him a couple of yards away. As he was passing by him and looked away, he heard a quiet voice on the cool day breeze. Jackson couldn't make it out fully and assumed it was coming from the guy. He stopped and turn to see the man looking towards him. Jackson was actually seeing this guy for the first time. He looked awfully dirty and his headgear was way outdated. It actually had a candle built into it.

To Jackson this guy looked like an old remnant from the past he had seen from his social studies class. Not being the rude teen, he responded to the quiet voice.

"Excuse me sir, but were you talking to me?" Jackson questioned timidly.

The form of the human awkwardly stepped toward Jackson, startling the young teen. His movement seemed unnatural and it sent the hackles on the back of Jackson's neck standing on end. The man reached towards Jackson a few feet away. Jackson started slowly backpedaling away from the approaching figure.

"Help me," the quiet but clearly stated words came from the man.

"Hel-l-l-p you with w-w-what?" Jackson asked, frightfully.

"Help me save them," answered the approaching man. As he got closer, Jackson saw his eyes. They weren't normal. They actually had a soft glow to them. Actually, they had no eyeballs. He tripped over another marker he had absently backed into, trying to keep the distance between himself and the ghostly figure.

"Save them," repeated the scary figure.

Jackson righted himself quickly and all thoughts of escape clamped down on his spinning head. He turned and ran away. He ran out and around the figure towards the way he had come. He ran as fast as he could toward the tree line. Once there, he broke through the trees to the other side and found himself in their yard again, safe.

Jackson came out of his thoughts as the countdown sound of the sudden death feature of the game filtered into his head. He had been playing on auto-control without even knowing what he was doing, lost in his memories of the scary events. The game ended with Jackson winning the sudden death.

He took a deep breath to release the pent up breath he had been holding, remembering the scary thing in the cemetery. As he was getting ready to turn off the game, he saw a new friend request. He looked at the name, **BgMone$y_gsquad** link.

He looked at the ending in the name. Could this be a member of the geek squad from school? Jackson got nervous. Should he accept? The overwhelming sense of curiosity was too much for him and he clicked on the link. He started a new game and was now friends with a new unknown. He immediately checked with Facebook to see who this random request had come from. The profile belonged to a Boyd Baker.

That's the infamous Double-B. He's the head leader's number one guy, Jackson realized. *Why did he want to be friends with me?*

Jackson's sister, mom, and Aunt Hollyn barged into the house, interrupting his thoughts with their argument. It wasn't the usual arguments he was used to hearing; the voices had concern in them. He checked his phone: 12:35.

Wow, Kayden came home late, he concluded.

Not waiting for a chance to miss the action, he crept out of his room, leaving the game and focusing on the conversation down below.

The conversation was all over the place as Jackson descended the stairs. No one seemed to notice him. To his surprise, his family wasn't the only ones downstairs. There were three boys and one girl. As he listened, he got the strange feeling he wasn't the only one to see something weird today.

"All I'm saying is what we saw wasn't normal," Kayden clarified to her mom.

"You shouldn't have been wandering around there at all," her mom argued.

"Now Lynni, let's not get too carried away here. We used to do worse things when we were her age. Going to a cemetery, even if it's at night, isn't the worse thing she could do. Besides, she technically was in our backyard," defended Hollyn.

"Hollyn!" Kailynn turned to her sister in disbelief. "You were just now outside about to bring the wrath of God down on everyone and now you're dialing back your position?"

"Well, to be fair who would have even thought they would have seen something like that there?" she innocently responded.

"Miss Toth," Drake interrupted, "I take full responsibility for this. I drove her there, even though she was a little apprehensive about the group's suggestions for going." Drake was standing next to Kayden, in a sort of protective stance, which wasn't lost on Kailynn. She could see a young man who would have protected her little girl if anything bad would have happened, but her daughter was still as guilty as the rest of them were.

"I appreciate you taking ownership of the situation, Drake. Kayden is bullheaded enough to make her own decisions. I know you weren't taking her kicking and screaming there," Kailynn replied.

"Man, if she hadn't been there though, there's no telling what would have happened to the rest of us," Shades added from the corner of the room. He was standing by Gage and Braelyn.

"OMG!" exclaimed Kayden. "What about the others?"

"Others?" Hollyn repeated questioningly.

"Damn," Gage said reflectively, "there are a few more of us who went the other way in the cemetery. We took off when we were dealing with those ghost things. Drake, we have to go back there man," he stated seriously to his friend.

Hollyn attempted to interject, but her nephew interrupted her.

"Mom, I saw it too," exclaimed Jackson.

Kailynn and Hollyn both turned immediately to Jackson, who no one had apparently noticed standing on the stairs. Everyone stopped talking to look at Jackson as well. Kayden walked over and pushed herself between her mom and aunt to stand in front of

Jackson.

"What do you mean you saw it too?" questioned Kayden, in a disbelieving voice.

Jackson quickly went into his account of events which happened earlier that evening to everyone. When he finished his retelling of the story, everyone stayed silent for a short time, thinking to themselves.

Drake walked up behind everyone and moved to the front door. He paused and looked at the rest of the people in the room.

"Look, it's obvious what is happening in the cemetery isn't a figment of our imaginations. Jackson's story matches ours in terms of the creepy ghost figure in the cemetery. No one will believe us, though. No one will believe our story about ghosts. We need to go back and check on the others and get our cars."

Gage moved to follow Drake with Braelyn hot on his heels.

"Wait," Hollyn said, stopping them. "I'll take my car and Kailynn, you take yours as well. Gage, Brooklyn and Shades go with me. Kayden and Drake, go with Kailynn."

"What about me?" asked Jackson, feeling left out.

"I want you here, Jackson," Aunt Hollyn replied. "If we are not back in thirty minutes, I want you to call the police. Got it?"

He didn't like the idea of being left behind alone in the house, but logically his aunt was right. They needed someone available to get help if things got out of control.

The two groups left and got in the cars. The ride would take less than two minutes.

* * *

***

As Hollyn pulled up behind the cars sitting in the cemetery. Gage noticed none of the cars had moved. His and Drake's were parked beside each other, while Shay and Owen's cars were there, too.

"Well, looks like they haven't taken their cars either," Gage mused as they parked and turned the car off.

Braelyn was already showing concern, since no one's car had left. Even though she and Shades didn't remember too much of the event, the fact four other people could with confidence vouch that it happened. She was worried about her missing friends.

"What will we do?" she asked, getting out of the cars.

Hollyn had brought her hand-held spotlight and turned to the kids.

Kayden's aunt looked around and then asked Gage and Braelyn if the place they went was over there, pointing to the left of the cemetery where a dirt path led.

Both of the teens looked at her strangely and shook their heads. Gage questioned, "Why would we go that way into the trees?

Hollyn looked quizzically back at the kids, "Well, because that is where the Hungarian Cemetery is or what's left of it anyway."

The kids all looked at each other perplexed. Shades asked, "I thought this was the Hungarian Cemetery," pointing towards the one they had originally entered. "Why would it be that way?"

Hollyn responded. "The gated one is the local cemetery which is still active and taken care of in

Ledford. The original Hungarian Cemetery is that way," she said pointing towards the darkened path. "It has been in complete disrepair for a while and many of the headstones have been damaged, while other grave sites have sunken into the ground."

"We didn't know that," Shades replied.

"Normally I'd just say to get in your cars and get out of here, but I don't know exactly who we are looking for. How many others are there again?"

Shades spoke up quickly. "We're missing Ayelyn, Sadie, Olivia, Shay, Owen and Brooklyn.

"I do not suggest we split up," came a voice from behind them.

Drake approached in front of Kayden and her mom. He definitely was itching to get looking for the others.

"I say we take the direction they walked and see if there are any clues to their whereabouts?"

Everyone agreed mostly, so Drake and Hollyn led the group. Kayden and her mom were in the back and the others stayed in the middle. They hadn't gone far when Gage yelled out Owen's name. Braelyn called out for Brooklyn as well. They all waited in tense anticipation for a reply. Nothing echoed back at them.

Hollyn whispered to Drake as they continued walking. "Where about were you when the incident happened?"

Drake knew exactly what she was speaking of. He shook his head.

"We haven't walked far enough around the cemetery to see it. We took the other way around. We didn't go super far around and we didn't see them at all."

Gage, being close enough to them heard their

exchange and butted in with his own thoughts.

"Perhaps," he said quietly, "they ran off too. If they did, they would have gone somewhere in the opposite direction we did."

Hollyn stopped walking and turned to everyone.

"Gage had a pretty good thought. We are going the way they went. If they got spooked, they probably would have run over that way," she said, pointing in the dark's direction.

Kayden quickly responded, "Aunt Hollyn, what if they didn't? What if they continued walking to where we saw those things? I do not know what would have happened if they saw the ghosts and did not run, but that should be the place we should go back to."

Shades immediately responded. "Look, I don't exactly remember what happened there, but I have a terrible feeling about going back there."

"What if the group is there right now and needs our help?" questioned Braelyn.

"Not all of us have to visit there again," responded Kailynn from the back of the group. "Hollyn, Drake, Kayden and I will go there and you other three go back to the cars and wait for us. The group might actually come back for their cars and see ours. We don't want them taking off searching for us. We'll be walking in circles. We will go to the place you guys had your encounter and then simply come back to the cars."

Shades nodded his head, "yeah, now you're talking."

Gage wasn't so sure. He didn't enjoy leaving his friends by sitting in their cars and protested. Braelyn grabbed his arm and whispered in his ear, "if you go, then it will just be me and Shades. Who will protect me then? Please come with us?"

Gage's shoulders slumped a little in acknowledgment and grudgingly started back in the lead of his new little group.

Hollyn's group formed up and she fired up her spotlight and they started walking around to where this all started. They slowly made their way towards the place where events of the past few hours had occurred. Kayden squeezed her aunt's arm, when they came upon the original site.

"This is the place Aunt Hollyn," she whispered. She pointed at the tombstone marker which had the name 'Simatis' on it. Hollyn raised an eyebrow at seeing the marker. Without hesitation, she started walking at a faster pace toward the grave. The others almost tripped over each other, not being ready for the change in walking speed.

"This is the exact tombstone the thing was standing in front of?" questioned Hollyn to the two teens. Both of them nodded their heads in acknowledgment.

Kailynn stepped up behind the teens and moved to stand next to her sister. The two siblings stared at an unfamiliar sight. The marker was old and withered. The name Aras Simatis was eerily glowing in the light of Hollyn's spotlight.

"Well?" Kayden asked nervously. "Why are you two just standing there staring at the tombstone like that?"

Kailynn looked at her daughter. "We know who rests here sweetheart," she informed Kayden. "It belongs to our great-grandfather Joseph Toth's mining friend. He died in a coal mine accident back in the 1930s."

"That explains why the figure we saw looked oddly dressed and had what looked like an old coal mine outfit on," followed Drake. "It also explains a little about the weird hats those other charred looking things had on as well."

"Hats?" asked Hollyn curious and confused.

"Yeah," responded Drake. "The hats were like a hard hat, but held a lit candle on it and not an actual light."

Hollyn nodded her head in understanding. "Right, it was old-school lighting. The coal mine tunnels didn't have electricity or batteries. Those weren't exactly available during the roaring 1920s and even into the 1930s everywhere," she informed the group.

"But why would anyone look like that now?" Kailynn asked not really understanding.

"Um... because they're like ghosts, mom," answered Kayden sarcastically.

Kailynn's body posture stiffened at her daughter sassing her. "You don't have to be so sarcastic Kayden," she responded.

Hollyn stepped in quickly, before things could escalate. "What happened after you saw the figure standing where we are now?"

Drake motioned behind them. "We were standing right over there," pointing to the spot.

"Then what?" Kailynn asked, looking at the spot Drake was pointing at.

"That's when the other figures emerged behind us over there," Kayden answered, pointing.

Hollyn turned her spotlight to each area the teens had pointed towards. As the spotlight moved slowly, she spotted a shoe and stopped on it.

"Do you remember seeing a random shoe sitting on the ground?" Hollyn asked the kids. Both looked at each other, trying to remember, but shook their heads no. Kailynn walked over to the shoe sitting on the ground. The others followed her.

Upon getting to the shoe, Kayden bent down and picked it up.

"It looks like Sadie's shoe," said Drake, recognizing the footwear.

Everyone started looking around the tombstones for some kind of clue to their friend's whereabouts. Hollyn's light moved over the tombstones slowly, scanning the area. Grass, tree limbs, leaves, and bushes were blowing in the wind here and there, which gave the illusion of movement around them. As her light left an area, Kayden saw something.

"Aunt Hollyn, point the light over there again," she ordered, pointing to a spot on the ground behind one tombstone. The light settled on the object she had caught from the edge of the spotlight.

"Oh my God," Kailynn said in blind shock.

Sticking out of the ground was an arm from the elbow up. The hand had formed into a claw-like position. It looked like the arm had fought to dig its way out of the ground only to be stopped short. Drake ran over to the arm, followed by Hollyn. Kailynn and Kayden stayed back and watched in staunch horror.

There was a ring on the hand. It was a silver ring with an emerald in the middle.

"Holy shit," he cried. "That is Sadie's ring."

"That's because the hand may very well belong to Sadie who is underneath the ground," Hollyn responded hollowly.

Drake looked at the area around the arm.

"Hollyn, I don't see any disturbed or torn up ground around the arm," Drake said as he looked around the area.

Hollyn saw what he was talking about and backed away, grabbing Drake's shoulder and pulling him with her. They backed into Kayden and Kailynn. Both had heard Drake's and Hollyn's comments.

"What does that mean?" Kayden said almost imperceptibly to Drake.

He answered in a very low and quiet voice. "They did not bury her. The ground was undisturbed. It's like they stuffed her under the ground without the ground breaking open to put her in it." He was looking all around him now.

"Okay guys, we've seen enough. We need to get the hell out of here and back to the cars," Hollyn ordered.

No one argued and they quickened their pace by speed walking with Hollyn who led the way. It didn't take long to see the cars.

As they rushed up, they could see Gage, Braelyn and Shades sitting in Gage's car. The three saw the panic of their pace, which made the three get out of the car, looking behind them as they approached.

Gage asked, "Did you find anyone or anything?"

Hollyn answered with an order to the teens. "Listen, Gage and Drake get into your cars and follow me and Kailynn back to my house now."

"Why?" asked Braelyn in a demanding voice.

"There's no time to sit here and talk about things. We'll talk once we get home in a safer environment," Kailynn chimed in with her sister's request.

"Is there a need for a safer environment?"

Shades questioned in a more nervous tone.

"Jeremiah, get in my truck now!" ordered Drake. "Gage, don't think. Just do it, man. I'll explain when we get back..."

A loud shrilling shriek emerged from the cemetery. No one waited to find out what that was. Everyone hustled to their cars and got in. Kailynn backed her car up, with Hollyn following closely in her car and started away from the cemetery, but slowed. They checked in their rear-view to make sure the other teen's cars were following. Everyone had their cars on the move and they made their way back to Hollyn's home.

***

In a matter of minutes, the group of vehicles made it back to Hollyn's house. Once in the house, Hollyn got on the phone with Kailynn on her heels, and started calling the police in the other room away from the kids.

Drake paced the living room back and forth, with Gage leaning against the wall. Braelyn was crying while Gage embraced her into his chest. Shades sat on the couch with his eyes locked on the floor, in disbelief at what was told to him.

Her little brother showed visible signs of being shaken up. The revelation of the events in their attempt to find their friends had unhinged him. Kayden had her arm around him to give him some comfort.

"Drake," said Kayden. His pacing stopped as he looked at her. "Use your phone to text some of the others who are missing. Maybe they're actually safe somewhere and we just haven't tried that avenue of communicating with them?"

Drake started at the idea. He hadn't checked his phone since it had run out of juice over their first encounter.

He had stuck it on a charging chord to his car and had left it there. It hadn't really been able to charge. He dashed outside to his truck. He got his phone and the charging cord. Getting back into the house, he looked at the other three of his friends.

"Have any of you been able to use your phones after our first encounter at the cemetery?" he questioned.

"No man," said Gage. "When have I had the time?"

"D," answered Shades, "none of our phones have recharged. All our chords are at home or in the cars. We went back to the cemetery with just flashlights, dude."

Drake nodded his understanding and asked Kayden for a block to plug in his chord. Once he plugged it in, the charger immediately started charging the phone. Since it had drained all the power, Drake had to wait a few minutes for the phone to store enough juice to fire it up. Once it turned on, the dings started hitting his phone from his text messenger.

"Dude, your phone is blowing up. Who is texting you so much?" inquired his best friend.

Drake's face lit up. "It's the guys. I'm getting tons of texts from Shay and Owen," he explained.

"What do they say?" Gage asked, walking over to Drake.

The phone rang just then. The name on the caller ID was Owen.

"It's Owen," confirmed Drake. He immediately

answered it. "Hello?"

"Drake? Where the hell have you been, man?" A concerned, but irritated voice came from the other line.

"Owen," Drake acknowledged, "man, it's been a horrible night. We have had no cell phones available. They all got the power zapped out of them or something when we were in the cemetery."

Drake immediately broke the story to Owen about what had happened to them. He told him about seeing ghosts, running away, and stumbling into Kayden's backyard. He relayed their events about going back out to the cemetery to look for them and then coming back quickly into Kayden's house. He left out the part about Sadie for now.

Owen didn't answer for a minute, sitting in a partial stunned state, trying to comprehend everything Drake was telling him.

"Owen, you there, man?" Drake asked, looking at everyone in the room.

After another few seconds, he answered. "Yeah, Drake. Look man, we couldn't find you guys after a short while. We thought we heard you guys making a commotion on the other side of the cemetery. When we got there, you guys were nowhere to be seen. Some of the girls got a little worried about you being missing. We fanned out over the cemetery looking for you. We went into groups of two. We should never have split up."

Drake took notice of that last statement. "Why, what happened?"

Owen paused a second and blew out a large breath he was holding in. The sound emanated loudly from the phone speaker. The other teens were sitting by the phone in Drake's hand. He had held it out and on speaker so they all could hear.

"Well, there was a weird vibe going on among the grave markers. I can't really explain it. It was just off. As we separated, there was a really loud shriek. It sounded like one of those screech owls. Scared the shit out of me and Ayelyn. Brooklyn screamed. Next thing I knew she was running straight towards us. On the other side, Shay and Olivia were there. We were missing Sadie. Brooklyn swore she lit out away from her towards the other side of the cemetery where Kayden lived. Shay suggested we go to the cars and drive over there to look for her."

Everyone in the room exchanged looks.

"We never got to the cars, man."

"Why not?" asked Kayden interjecting.

"Oh, hi Kayden," Owen said. He immediately continued. "When we got close to the cars, there were these black figures moving around them. At first, we didn't see them because they were literally black. They had these lights or something on them, maybe candles? Anyway, we heard Sadie scream way off in the distance somewhere. It spooked us and we took off away from the cars, cemetery, and to our shame, Sadie."

Owen's voice was cracking and everyone knew he was almost in tears.

"Owen, it's okay, man. We saw the same thing and they almost got us if it hadn't been for Kayden and Gage. You did the right thing and skinned out of there."

"Yeah, but Drake, we left Sadie."

The room was silent.

Gage spoke. "Owen, all our phones are still down. Text the others and let them know what happened to us. Let them know we went back to the cemetery looking for you guys. We didn't just abandon you."

Owen was quiet for a moment. "Gage, I'm sorry about what I said to you earlier at the get together."

Gage closed his eyes and sighed. "It's cool Owen. Just blowing off steam. Let them know and we'll see them on Monday at school and talk."

"What about when you went back? Did you find Sadie? She's not picking up on her phone either."

The entire room was quiet. What could they say? Did they even know what happened? Just then, a knocking came from the door. Hollyn and Kailynn appeared from the kitchen to answer. By the flashing lights outside, the teens knew who was there.

Drake came out of his stupor and took control of the conversation.

"Owen, the police are here. I'm pretty sure we all are in trouble with our parents. We've had no phone access to even call them." Drake looked at his phone and it said 1:30 AM. The time had passed by fast and he was sure there were going to be some angry parents. Worse, if that hand was Sadie's, then the whole town was going to be buzzing. "We have to go. Text the others like Gage said and we'll talk on Monday when we're together."

"Alright man. I hope the police finds her. Brooklyn is beside herself. Bye."

Owen hung up. Everyone could hear the exchanges going on at the door. After a moment, two officers walked in with solemn expressions on their faces. The taller of the two stepped forward towards the kids and eyeballed all of them.

"Seems you guys had a night of excitement? We'd like to get this all squared away quickly, so we'll start with you," said the officer, pointing to Drake.

Joshua Banks

Drake stood up from sitting on the sofa holding his phone and addressed the officer.
"Sir, what do you need from me?"

Chapter Nine: Echoes of the Past

The night's events had played out for the teens, but for Sheriff Warren "Whip" Anderson, the night had just gotten longer. Whip, as he was known around the area had been at the job for over 20 years. He had started out as a young local police officer fresh out of the police academy. He went back to serve his home town as an officer of the law. On his way to the scene in Ledford, he passed the local junior high school. His thoughts shifted back to how he even thought of becoming a police officer while he was driving.

***

Warren had a penchant for being someone who stuck up to bullies in school. He hadn't been afraid to mouth off to his teachers as well. Youth had given him a bit of an attitude coupled with a notion for fighting. Makes sense as he used that aggression to wrestle. He liked to 'whip' their ass. A statement which earned him the name 'Whip.'

Out of school, he didn't exactly know where to apply his brand of fun in the working world. The military had been one option, but Whip didn't like being told where he had to go and when.

He took work in Carbondale, which was about 45 to 50 minutes away from Harrisburg (depending on how fast he drove). He had landed a job as a bouncer for a local dive bar, which catered to college kids.

He was only 18 at the time and under age. The owner needed help and since technically he would put Whip outside to ID and keep the masses at bay; he wasn't inside where the booze was being dished out. Besides, the age to enter was 18, but the age to drink was 21. Everyone knew many of the 18-year-olds had fake IDs or someone who would score them drinks. It simply was the college standard and Whip had been told this in no uncertain terms. His job was to keep the peace when those who drank too much and got a little outside the norm were to be escorted out or barred from coming in.

Whip had no problem complying with this. He knew most of the time he'd have the upper hand in a dust-up. The patrons were sloppy and inebriated. He was sober and in good shape. He knew pressure holds and how quickly to take down anyone who was getting too physically aggressive with other patrons. It was a free ride to be physical to shit bags and allowed him to make money while figuring out his future career.

As it happened one night, there was a particular

scuffle between some SIU college jocks and him. A few of the Saluki football players were nice and juiced up. They had come there with a good buzz and looking to start a fight. It just so happened a patrol officer had positioned his squad car next to the lot to just monitor the evening. Usually around 11:00 pm. to midnight before the place closed, those looking for trouble always seemed to emerge. Whip had been doing his usual, when four of the Saluki's showed up at the door.

    Whip could tell right away these guys were itching to cause trouble. He asked for their ID. The first two slung them out in an asshole manner to Whip. They seemed insulted to be asked to show their licenses. Once Whip let them pass, the other two said they were with the two he identified as 21. He knew these guys weren't 21.

    "No problem, guys. I just have to mark your hands that you are under age," responded Whip.

    One of them answered, "We don't need that shit on our hands. There's only about an hour left for this place to be open."

    He pushed past Whip, trying to strong arm him out of the way.

    Whip immediately arm barred the jerk, spun him around and pushed him out of the doorway back into his friend.

    "Whoa there stud," Whip said, "you made two mistakes. One, you refused our house rules dealing with minors. Two, you put your hands on me, which is a no - no. Now, you two take yourselves out of here. You are not getting in tonight," he commanded.

    Both of the players looked at each other and laughed.

    "Is there an issue here?" came a voice from

behind Whip.

Whip turned to see the first two of the group who he passed to go in come back out to assess why their other two friends had not entered yet.

"I'm sorry, sir," Whip said, "but they won't be permitted inside as they laid their hands on me and declined to get their hands stamped to prove their age is not 21."

"Surely you can make an exception for a fellow Saluki football player?" the larger, dark-haired player said.

"No sir, I cannot. It is the law."

"Screw the law," came the kid who had tried to strong-arm his way in. "Just get out of the way or you are going to find yourself on the pavement boy!"

Whip taking a quick assessment of the situation knew they flanked him. He noted who was his best option at taking out before the others had their opportunity to take him down.

"Listen, I'm going to ask nice one more time," said the player behind him.

Whip turned, moving his body where each set of players was on his left and right. He figured to keep these guys as far away from the door as possible until back up came.

"No," was the only response given by Whip.

"Then you are going to get your ass kicked... whoa," roared the younger player to his right, taking a step to be right next to Whip, but he never got to finish his sentence. Whip went into motion, pushing the kid's pointing finger and arm away from him and grabbed the kid with a quick choke hold. He used his momentum to pull his verbal abuser away from all three of them, positioning their friend between him and them. The kid flailed helplessly at Whip who was overpowering him easily.

The leader of the group moved his blonde buddy who had entered the club originally to his right and moved the younger friend who wore a Saluki jersey to his left.

"Let him go now or we will put you in the hospital!" roared the dark-haired leader.

Whip had his adrenaline in full effect and everything slowed down. He used his hip and weight to flip his captive and throw him against a parked car's front bumper. The kid went down, trying to catch his breath and holding his face from where he had connected with the car. Whip immediately went after the leader in front of him, driving at him like a wrestler taking his legs out from under him. He didn't pull back, like on a soft mat, though. He continued driving with his weight on his adversary. The leader smacked his head on the concrete hard with both his and Whip's momentum coming down on the player. The impact took the fight out of him.

Probably has a nice concussion from that, thought Whip.

Whip continued his momentum to shuffle off the prone body of their leader. Coming up, he got a hard fist into his stomach from the blonde player. It took the wind out of him for a second. The jersey kid popped him in the face on the other side. Blondy used the distraction to get behind Whip and grab him at his waist. He had hoped to slam Whip down, but Whip knew how to break this amateur's grip. Positioning his feet out, stabilizing his frame, he used hard driving thumbs to the locked wrists and broke it easily. He grabbed the hand and quickly rotated around Blondy and grabbed his waist. Using the momentum, he slung his ass to the ground hard. The guy hit his shoulder hard. Whip could tell he was not used to being thrown. Whip knew that landing he just gave the kid possibly tore or dislocated his shoulder from the impact. Whip stood up shakily. He was winded, but ready for the last one. The jersey kid backed away at seeing the odds. He took in the scene, looking at his buddies on the ground and pointed at Whip.

"You are lucky," he said while retreating and leaving the entire scene.

"Not bad," came a voice from behind.

Whip turned to see a police officer walking up. Whip was a bit confused.

"O-Officer," he fumbled. "You were watching this the whole time?" he asked a little miffed.

"Yeah, wanted to see how you handled yourself. Pretty good in a scrap."

"Why didn't YOU help stop them?" Whip asked angrily.

"Well, these here boys are part of the Saluki football team. The college is an excellent source of revenue for the town, so we go a little easier on them here and there. Of course, we report them to their coach and let him deal with the issues more directly. Here," he said, reaching for his pocket and pulling out a card. He handed it to Whip.

"It says policy academy," Whip said, reading the card.

"That's right. You have the stuff, kid. Ever think about being a cop? You would do well as one I think. You can use me as a reference."

***

The Hungarian Cemetery Secrets Within Backup

* * *

The memory of that encounter reminded Whip of why he had started in this profession. The memory, though, came and went as he pulled up to the crime scene. The cemetery had been closed off by police tape.

The ambulance and four of his officers were there on the scene. Whip was deep asleep when his phone went off around 1:30-ish this morning. McCormick had been on the other line explaining a murder had more than likely happened sometime that evening at the old Hungarian Cemetery. He got dressed and headed out.

Whip walked up to the crime scene. Officer McCormick was there with the other two officers and two paramedics. His officers had set a parameter around the lone arm sticking out of the ground. The paramedics were looking stumped and all three officers were arguing with each other as Whip came up.

"At ease, gentlemen," he said, interrupting their heated exchange. "What is the issue here?"

"Sheriff," answered a skinny officer. His name was Mitchell. "We're having an issue figuring out how this happened?"

Whip walked between them. They parted and he squatted down at the scene. The body had somehow made it under the ground of undisturbed soil and grass. It was baffling. It looked like whoever was under the ground had tried to push from being under the ground up to escape their trappings. Yet, only the hand and upper arm had made it.

"I'm confused," Whip said.

"I'd be worried if you weren't," responded McCormick. "We asked the paramedics if they had ever seen anything like this. They were stumped, too. How does a whole body get stuffed underground without digging up the dirt first?" he asked.

"Where's the coroner?" asked Whip.

"He's on his way," replied Kramer, the other officer at the scene. He was short and stocky.

"We need to call the forensic duo," Whip said to no one in particular.

"Already called, sir," answered McCormick.

Everyone stared at the scene before them.

"Do we know the identity of the victim?" Whip inquired.

The other officers shook their heads no. The body hadn't even been exhumed from the spot to look at it. If there had been another cause of death besides asphyxiation from being buried in the ground, they sure couldn't see it.

"The victim may be a female by the name of Sadie," replied the fourth officer who had been over by another tombstone. He had been squatting down in what seemed to be an investigative stance in that area.

"Ramsey," replied Whip. "What do you have?"

Ramsey sundered over to the other officers and the sheriff. "I came from the Toth house. Hollyn Toth made the call and I followed up. Upon getting there, I interviewed the family along with a group of kids. There are some other kids mentioned who were involved as well, but I haven't followed up on them yet."

The sheriff stiffened at the name Toth. It was not a very popular name among locals based on their continual generational biases passed down in this small town. He had known Hollyn Toth's father before he passed. They had a mutual understanding and respect for each other. He and Ramsey respected the fiery

Hollyn, too. They had been working together as partners before Whip had elevated himself to the sheriff with the voters.

"What did they say happened here?" Whip asked perplexed at the situation.

"Alright Whip. You need to prepare yourself for this."

The officer scratched his head a bit and took out his pad where he had taken everyone's statements off the cuff and thumbed through a few pages.

"Well?" Whip questioned impatiently.

"According to the kids, they came out here a little before midnight to goof around over the rumors of the place being haunted. They broke into two groups walking into the cemetery. One group encountered some kind of..." the officer fumbled on the next part.

"Of?" echoed the sheriff.

"A ghost maybe?" Ramsey answered.

"A ghost? Are you freaking serious Ramsey?" asked Whip irritated at the initial explanation and relieved it wasn't something worse. He knew the Toth family had dealt with a lot of shit over the time he had been in this town.

"Yes sir. They saw a ghost over there," Ramsey said, pointing to Aras Simatis grave site.

"Simatis," repeated the sheriff. "The witnesses' names also were Toth, correct?" the sheriff inquired just to make sure he heard it right, thinking it was far too connecting to be a coincidence.

"Not all of them were Toth Sheriff, however I see the connection you are alluding to," returned the deputy. Ramsey also had a more private, yet complicated connection to the Toth family, specifically Hollyn.

Ramsey adjusted his stance and pointed at the spot the supposed ghost came from.

"The ghost started coming towards them and as they backed away, a group of blackened forms were surrounding them from behind. They got spooked and ran off. The second group must have heard them and began searching for them. They too saw something and got spooked. They ran the other way to get to their cars, but apparently these blackened forms were there too. Scared, they took off in the opposite direction away from the cemetery. Unfortunately, one of them got separated."

"Miss Sadie I would guess?" responded the sheriff.

"You got it Sheriff. Her name is Sadie Stone."

Whip, who had let his gaze move around the cemetery area, immediately turned his sight back on Ramsey. "Sadie Stone? Chris Stone's daughter?" inquired Whip.

"The same Sheriff."

"Dammit," shouted Whip to no one. "I went to school with her, old man. Chris won't take this news well at all. He especially will not like the fact the 'Toth' name is involved."

Whip took his hat off and used his hand to move his hair back over his head in frustration.

"Ramsey," Whip said with sincere concern. "When you were taking statements and questioning the Toths, did you get the sense that what they were saying was on the up-and-up?"

Ramsey took a step closer to the Sheriff, since he knew exactly what the Sheriff was getting at. "Look Warren, they all were shaken up. Hollyn called it in and asked specifically for me to come to the house. She was frightened, but very well aware of what this story sounded like. She is very concerned for her sister and the two kids."

Whip raised an eyebrow in shock. "Kailynn is back in town? How long ago had this happened?'

His deputy shrugged. "I didn't ask, but it's very apparent it couldn't have been too long ago."

"Damn," the Sheriff murmured, "another unfortunate coincidence."

"Well," stammered McCormick, "we haven't exactly identified the victim yet. It may not be her," McCormick finished, trying to offer some hope.

"Trouble seems to always find that family," cracked Kramer to no one in particular.

"The Toths are good people, Kramer. They keep paying for the sins of the past, which none are alive to even warrant it," said Ramsey defensively.

"Just cause you have a little sweet tooth for the Hollyn girl," shot Kramer.

"That's quite enough from you, Kramer," snapped Whip.

Whip needed to think. He did not know how the body got to where it was now, but that is what a forensic team is for. He needed coffee to clear his head. He knew he wouldn't be going back to sleep for a long time, given these circumstances. Why would something like this occur? It made no sense from a police officer's point of view. There was no motive.

Looks like I'm going to have to look into everyone involved and find the motive, he thought.

"Kramer, make yourself useful and snag me and the boys some coffee from Huck's gas station. Ramsey," he called to his deputy. "Give me that list of names involved. It's time to go to work."

Chapter Ten: Bad News Travels Fast

Sunday was a whirlwind for the Toth family. Whip had paid them a visit in the late afternoon to follow up on some questions he now based on his forensic team's findings. Ramsey had come back with him and they assured the family that they were not suspected in the case. The body had no fingerprints, forced physical trauma, or evidence to point to them. They sent a lot of the surrounding samples of DNA from the body, clothes and ground to the lab. They hoped to see if traces of anything could shed some light on the grizzly cause of death. It was obvious poor Sadie had died of asphyxiation under the ground, but no one could figure out for the life of them how she had gotten there.

It really shook Jackson and Kayden up over the

situation. They were already trying hard to fit in at school and now an enormous scandal tied to their family was already rocking the Saline County area. Drake and the other teens had their parents come and pick them up from Hollyn's house at Ramsey's request when he had taken their statements. Ramsey and Whip told Kailynn and Hollyn they were going to each of the teen's families who were involved in going out to the cemetery that evening.

Whip had learned about a fight that had happened at the party between the boys, which then begged the question, what had started the fight? Once they learned it was over the Toth story from the past, those kids had become potential targets to interview as well. Things were heating up and both sisters were very concerned for the kids. They suggested perhaps that they call in sick on Monday to let the gossip run its course for the day, but Whip disagreed. He thought not going might sway the community that the Toth family had something to hide and make new rumors. Both of the sisters agreed. Ramsey said he and McCormick would come to the school at different times to just check on the school environment. He wanted to get a pulse for how the students were handling the news about Sadie.

Drake had texted Kayden back and forth that evening about what was going on with the other kids. Brooklyn wasn't taking the news about Sadie well at all. Gage had gotten permission to hang at her house to help with her shock and anxiety. Owen and Ayelyn were handling things okay. Shades was running damage control to the school masses who demanded the inside scoop on all the rumors that were spreading on social media. Drake said Shade's street cred was on the rise after last night's events. Shay and the rest of the group were on lock down by the parents, so he wouldn't know much until they got to school tomorrow.

Kayden had really gained respect and appreciation for Drake. He was a stand-up guy and seemed to be genuine in his efforts. Kayden would need his support tomorrow when she hit school. He offered to drive her to school, so she didn't have to face criticism on the bus. He also didn't want her entering the school by herself. He and Shades would be there in the morning to get her.

Jackson now had a new potential ally in his crusade to be acknowledged by the Geek Squad. Apparently, one member slyly became friends with him on his gaming site. Jackson, being skeptical of the intentions of the effort was prepared for some kind of backstabbing effort. Any chance to demean Jackson's obvious gaming skills was in the Geek's Squad's best interest. At least, in their leader's best interest. Hollyn volunteered to take Jackson to school as well.

Hollyn and Kailynn had been juiced up on caffeine and sugar all day. Their buzz in the evening had a gigantic crash. They each fell asleep early. Being completely exhausted in all ways possible, they had retired to their bedrooms and fell asleep almost upon contact with the bed.

****

Kayden awoke to her cell phone alarm clock going off. She peeled away the covers and meandered to the bathroom to get ready for another dreaded day at school. Jackson was already up and moving. He had made his way to the kitchen for his patented bowl of cereal. Aunt Hollyn and Kailynn were already up as well. Both looked like they had pulled an all-niter at a bar. Each of them sat across from the other sipping the mornings newly brewed coffee.

"Good morning," Jackson said cheerily to his aunt and mom.

"Hey kiddo," Kailynn returned.

"Rat," Hollyn responded despondently.

The young teen got his bowl, milk, and cereal. He sat down and ate. The two women's eerie silence made Jackson a little uneasy, to be honest.

He scooted his chair out and picked his bowl up.

"Where are you going?" asked his mom.

Jackson shrugged his shoulders and looked at each face, staring at him. "I felt like watching some TV in the living room while I ate."

Hollyn sat up a little in her chair and cleared her throat. "We eat in the kitchen. Neither of us feels like cleaning up kids' eating messes today," she said, pointing to her sister and her.

"Yeah, well, the climate in this room is off and I'm not starting my day off with negativity."

"Who is being negative?" asked Hollyn. "We haven't even said a word."

Jackson squared his shoulders to his aunt. "You don't have to say anything. You and mom's demeanor is more than enough. My cereal is getting soggy." With that, he turned and went into the living room.

"He's right you know," agreed Kailynn. "We are right now."

"Only because you won't tell the kids about our family," countered Hollyn. "They need to know about their heritage and what is going on."

"They are kids and we have never even talked

about our family, ever."

Hollyn took a sip of her coffee. "We can thank Pavilonis for that Kailynn."

Kailynn stiffened at Hollyn, throwing out her ex-husband's name. Pavilonis was his last name and the only one Hollyn ever referred to. His first name was James. Hollyn had never approved of him and to make matters worse, held him responsible for her leaving.

"You don't have to bring his name up Hollybear," Kailynn responded with a little edge in her voice.

"And you don't have to pretend he was something he isn't, Lynni."

That was all it took. Both sisters took in to arguing.

Kayden meanwhile had just descended the stairs to hear them squabbling in the kitchen. She had heard them talking about telling the kids something, but what, she did not know. Neither of them saw her enter the room because they were so focused on arguing.

Kayden interrupted them by asking, "What do you think you should tell us Aunt Hollyn?"

The arguing ceased immediately. Hollyn being surprised, looked at her sister and then curtly said, "Good morning Kayden. Now isn't the best time." Hollyn stood up and walked past Kayden in a rush. "I need to get ready to take Jackson to school." She headed up the stairs.

Kailynn watched her sister go and motioned to the seat next to her. Kayden sat down. "I'll get you a bowl of cereal Kayden. Want juice or anything to drink with it?"

Kayden shook her head no, so her mom proceeded to getting Kayden her breakfast. While she was moving around the room putting it together, she talked to her daughter.

"Excuse us for being typical sisters. We disagree on a lot of things, but it isn't through meanness. We just have opposite thought processes in how we run our ship, so to speak."

"I gathered as much," responded Kayden. "Look mom, I know things have been tense lately and last weekend's adventure seems to be the icing on the cake. Please don't be mad at me for going to the cemetery."

Kailynn stopped what she was doing and turned towards her daughter.

"It isn't the fact you went there, Kayden, which I'm upset with. I am more upset with myself, if I may be frank."

Her response caught Kayden by surprise. "YOU? Why would you be upset with yourself? You did nothing wrong."

Kailynn finished getting the cereal together and put it in front of her daughter to eat. She then sat down and addressed her issue.

"I have never talked about Harrisburg or our family history to you or Jackson. I left you completely unprepared for what the town's view of our family might be. It goes way back, but I had hoped all that crap had subsided and those people had left this place. Unfortunately, we now know differently. Aunt Hollyn wants us to tell you guys about it. I'm not so sure," she said conflicted.

Kayden stopped crunching on the cereal and answered her mom with a mouthful of food.

"I agree with Aunt Hollyn."

"I do too," said another voice standing in the entryway. Jackson had snuck up on them again during their conversation and felt like giving his vote.

Both of the girls turned to see Jackson standing there, looking concerned. He walked up and sat down at the table as well.

"Honestly, mom, keeping this stuff from us will hurt us more than help," Jackson reasoned.

"Yeah mom. I hate to agree with him, but he's right."

Kailynn looked at the expecting faces of her kids and sighed. She smiled at them.

They have grown up so fast. Where did the time go? she thought to herself.

"Fine," she conceded. "Tonight, when you two get home, your Aunt Hollyn and I will discuss things about our family. I warn you, it is a topic we try to avoid talking about."

Kailynn's expression was one of seriousness. It wasn't lost on the kids. They were all shaken out of their bubble by the knocking on the front door. Drake had shown up to take Kayden to school.

"Looks like your boyfriend is here," said Jackson playfully.

"Shut up dork," retorted Kayden. "Tonight mom. I gotta go."

Kayden got up and went to the front door. Drake was standing there looking expectant when she opened it. He had a weird look on his face, which gave Kayden pause. Drake noticed her reaction and realized he must look stupid.

"I'm sorry," he blurted. "I hadn't seen you since the police, so I didn't know how you would react to seeing me again."

Kayden blushed a little and smiled coyly. "Don't worry, Drake, you and the others are the only ones right now who have actually treated me nice since I got here."

Her comment gave the 16-year-old teen renewed confidence. Drake stepped out of her way and motioned to his truck. "Your chariot awaits," he quipped.

Smiling, she grabbed her stuff and headed to the truck. She could see Shades duded up in some Halloween attire. His sunglass frame was in the shape of skeleton bones. He had a quirky expression when Kayden got to his door.

"My Lady, permit me the courtesy of giving you my seat," he said in his usual manner. Getting out, he opened the door for Kayden and she moved to the middle. Both boys got in and Drake pulled out of the driveway. They headed to school.

Kailynn who had quietly been watching the exchange rolled her eyes and looked at Jackson.

"Your sister is more interested in Drake than she lets on," she commented.

"What makes you say that?" asked Jackson.

"Because she doesn't talk shit to him," responded Hollyn as she bounded down the flight of stairs. "Also, she allows him to take a protective stance around her when confronted with unpleasantness."

Kailynn raised an eyebrow at that comment. She nodded her agreement and went to putting the dirty dishes in the sink.

"C'mon kid," Hollyn said to Jackson. "We need to get you to school. You feeling up for it?"

Jackson smiled at his aunt. "Round two," he said with confidence.

"That's the fighting spirit," Hollyn replied, slapping him on the shoulder.

Jackson took off out the front door and Hollyn stopped short of it, looking back at her sister.

"You okay Lynni?" she asked with sincere worry.

"It's technically my first day of work at the store, so we'll pick up tonight where we left off at the table. We'll talk to the kids about our family. Just use kid gloves, please?" she requested of her sister.

"When have you ever known me to do that?" she fired back sarcastically and shut the door behind her.

****

Drake's truck pulled into the back of the school parking lot. They weren't too early, but had agreed to meet around 7:15 AM to have a little time to talk before the first bell hit. They pulled up alongside Brooklyn's car. Gage was inside along with Braelyn. A couple of empty car spaces down were Owen and Ayelyn. Shay and Olivia hadn't gotten there yet. Everyone got out of their cars and headed over to Drake's truck. Shades pulled down the tailgate and sat on it. He patted with his hand a spot next to him to Kayden, who smiled and sat next to him. Drake came up on the other side of her and just leaned on the gate.

The rest of the teens gathered around the three. Gage gave Drake, Owen, and Shades a hand slap, acknowledging them. He fell back between Brooklyn and Braelyn. Owen was holding Ayelyn's hand as everyone stood there solemn and remorseful.

Brooklyn started to tear up. "We shouldn't have gone there. It's all my fault."

Drake spoke up immediately. "Hey, we can't look back in hindsight and beat ourselves up. Besides, how is it your fault Brooky?"

Gage put his arm around her. "I was the one who suggested going in the first place."

Kayden unexpectedly spoke up. "Not one of us here in our wildest imaginations could have ever known or suspected something like this would have occurred. I've never seen a ghost before. Has anyone here actually interacted in something like this?"

Kayden's question was rhetorical because everyone knew the answer, but it needed to be stated. No one, of course, raised their hands.

"I appreciate your words Kayden, but you weren't the one who left her and ran away. I was the one who did. Now she's dead. What can I even say to her parents? We hung out a lot." With that, she started crying. Gage held onto her, trying to comfort.

Shades popped off the tailgate of the truck and looked at Owen. He took his glasses off.

"Did the police actually identify the body as Sadie officially?" he asked gently.

Owen grabbed Ayelyn's hand tighter and his body stiffened up. "The sheriff stopped by my house Sunday afternoon. He said the coroner had identified the body and her parents were called to the morgue to make it official. I overheard my dad talking to mom about it when he thought I wasn't in the room. He said Mr. Stone was furious and upset."

"Who wouldn't be?" responded Drake. "I cannot imagine being told about how my daughter died."

"Well, that isn't where it ends." Everyone looked at him, except Ayelyn who probably had already talked to Owen about it. "Mr. Stone blames Kayden's family for Sadie's death."

"My family?" Kayden responded in disbelief. "Why would he do that?"

Owen shifted uncomfortably his weight from one foot to the other and answered. "I heard my dad say something about the Toth family. Since you were there and that's your last name, it obviously had to be your fault somehow."

"That is ridiculous," said Shades. "She was with all of us the entire time. She even saved Drake and me."

Gage growled softly. He looked towards Drake and shook his head back and forth. "Damn town and the grudges they pass down." Gage had felt something of the same to an extent when he had moved to Harrisburg in middle school. His last name was Ratcliff. Some parents associated the name with trouble-makers. He hadn't even grown up here, but the stigma caused many potential friendships to dry up quick. If Drake and Shades hadn't befriended him, then he probably would be a solo act.

"I take issue with that on a personal level," Gage retorted to Owen.

Owen let go of Ayelyn's hand and held both of them up like he was being arrested. "Hey dude, I'm just repeating what my dad told mom. They aren't my words."

"Okay," Gage he said. "Let's dig a little deeper. Exactly what is your family's opinion on Kayden or the whole situation?"

Owen's eyes lowered to the ground. His lack of response said it all.

"See?" pointing his finger at Owen. "Your family is just as bad. Going along with these backwood's bumpkins!"

"Screw you, Gage," Owen yelled.

"Can't handle the truth?" Gage returned. "Exactly how it works. You'd never know because you haven't ever had to deal with the public's bullshit opinion about your last name. Who you are means nothing. It's all about where you came from."

Drake stepped away from the truck and got in between both of them.

"Stop it, Gage," he ordered. "You know that is not how Owen works. He cannot help how his dad or mom react. Those are their issues, not his." Drake looked at Owen.

"He's upset and this hits close to home."

Owen looked at Gage and nodded his understanding. Ayelyn nestled her head on his shoulder and reacquired his hand again in hers. Kayden had been watching the exchange between the two and was understanding Gage a little better. It still didn't change the topic.

Kayden felt hopeless. It was an issue she couldn't change.

"What am I supposed to do?" she asked the group. "It's not like I can change my last name and I really do not understand all the resentment towards my family."

Drake looked back at her and moved to sit beside her again. Shades had already sat back down next to her.

"Honestly, Kayden, I cannot remember the last time things around here had been so shaken up. It's not anyone's fault, but it is apparent your family's arrival is turning some eyebrows up."

Brooklyn had pulled herself together again. She wiped her nose on Gage's sleeve.

"Gross Brooklyn," he exclaimed. This got a chuckle out of everyone, lightening the mood instantly.

"We all know what happened, but no one is going to take our word for it," Brooklyn stated in a sad voice.

"Yeah, what do we say?" Ayelyn asked, looking up at Owen.

"I've actually been interacting with different factions of the student body," answered Shades. "You know how rumors get going? Lots of them were floating around on social media. I headed off a bunch of them, but the main one which continues to filter everywhere is about Toth being some kind of witch or supernatural summoner."

Everyone looked at Kayden.

"A witch?" she returned. "Seriously? I don't even dress in black," she stated.

"No Caviar, you actually have pretty good taste in outfits," agreed Brooklyn.

"What else are they saying?" asked Drake. Shades looked at his best friend.

"Nothing that I haven't discussed with you already good buddy. There were stories like we sacrificed animals to bring back the dead. The girls plotted Sadie's murder because they were jealous. Gage killed her because he found out she was pregnant..."

"What in the hell?" Gage bellowed. "Tell me what dick said that?"

"Someone added it anonymously," Shades said with a shrug.

"Shit-ass town," he growled again, looking at Owen.

Owen just rolled his eyes.

Drake looked down at his feet. They needed to stop this rumor train, but he knew from experience it had to play itself out initially. The masses would be onto some other juicy gossip soon enough. Just not soon enough for him and his friends.

"It also didn't help that Gage put fat-boy on his ass at the party. Someone had taken a couple of cell phone pics of the whole thing and snap-chatted it," informed Shades. "It was a great shot though Gage," Shades joked. "It had his butt-crack way out there for the entire world to see."

"Dammit," Gage said, releasing his arm away from Brooklyn. He looked over at Braelyn. "You see? Exactly why I don't get involved in shit like that. That stupid picture is going to cause me more grief." Gage had a blood vessel emerge on his temple from the anger which was building up inside along with the anxiety of learning this additional issue.

Braelyn went over to him and hugged him, pulling his ear to her lips and started whispering to him. Kayden could see again that whatever she was saying to him calmed him down.

"What did we miss amigos?" came a chipper voice from outside the group. Cars had been slowly pulling into the parking lot as time closed and class approached. Everyone saw Shay approach, with Olivia walking beside him. Shay was holding her bag along with his backpack.

"Everything," replied Shades.

"Don't get worked up, Jeremiah," replied the fiery Olivia.

"I told you not to call me that," Shades retorted.

Drake saw the puzzled look Kayden had at the exchange and leaned towards her and said, "Jeremiah VanOrmer prefers people to use his nickname Shades."

"And he hates it when they don't," replied Shades to Kayden, looking directly at Drake.

"Hey, she needed to know your actual feelings on the name dude. It's standard protocol among friends."

Kayden looked around at everyone and realized she only knew their first names. With everything that had happened to the group, she hadn't any time to really know more about them than what had transpired on Saturday.

"Actually, I don't know any of your last names," she said embarrassed.

Shay laughed at this. "Of course you don't, we didn't offer them kid. Let's change that. My name is Shay Randolph. She's Olivia Bell," pointing to his girlfriend. Motioning over to the other love birds, he said, "Owen Nelson and Ayelyn Shoemaker."

To her left came another reply. "I'm Gage Ratcliff. This is Brooklyn Church," turning his thumb to the girl on his right, "and she's Braelyn Patton."

Drake offered his hand to Kayden who took it. "I'm Drake Steele."

"Suites you," she said shyly.

Just then, the first bell rang. Free time was over and the time for class was at hand. Everyone looked at each other with trepidation about interacting with the masses in the hallways.

"Oh, let's go," commanded Olivia. She began walking and Shay followed.

Drake took a quick look at the others and nodded, as if internally deciding something. "No one walks by themselves this week. We stay in groups."

"Shades, you go with me," Braelyn ordered. Jeremiah nodded and hopped off the tailgate and they started walking together.

"Smart choice," said Drake to Kayden. "Both of them are pretty good at deflective banter. They'll field a lot of the shit we're going to hear today. Just everyone stay cool and don't say anymore than you have to."

Everyone else knew their partner. Gage and Brooklyn would stick together while Drake escorted Kayden. Owen and Ayelyn were already glued to each other's hip and wouldn't separate. They all made their way to class and the day began.

Chapter Eleven: The Past Revealed

By 3:05 pm that day, Kayden's newly formed group of friends were exhausted and ready to leave. The whole day, students hammered them over the death of Sadie. The emotional spectrum was off the charts. Brooklyn didn't even make it to third period. Rumors were running rampant and at one point, a senior boy by the name of Kris Olson started shaming her for leaving Sadie in the cemetery by herself. It happened during passing period in the halls. Gage who had a small engine and repair class had made his way upstairs to meet Brooklyn by the Chemistry teacher's room. Upon getting to the top, he saw Brooklyn walking away from the stairs and going the opposite direction. He also saw two boys pursuing her closely. Their intent looked unsavory.

The Hungarian Cemetery Secrets Within Backup

He ran quickly and caught up to her. She immediately curled up into his chest, sobbing. He didn't have to ask what was going on. Kris immediately rode in hard on Gage by making fun of him for being a friend to someone who abandons their friends in a time of need. Gage didn't even hesitate. He let go of Brooklyn and tackled Kris to the ground. Kris was twice Gage's size, but the larger teen did not know how tenacious and unafraid his attacker could be. Gage started pounding his fists anywhere they would land on his verbal abuser. Gage was yelling the whole time about no one in school has a real clue about what they were going through. It was all the kid could do to cover up against Gage's rage.

None other than Officer Byron Ramsey pulled Gage off Olson. The deputy, true to his word, had come by in the morning to check on the school climate. He heard the commotion upstairs gathering audible momentum. Enough time on the force had given him experience to know something was going down outside the norm. Once he pulled Gage off and held him against the wall, Brooklyn came up beside the deputy and helped calm Gage down. Ramsey recognized Gage and Brooklyn. He pulled Gage away from the Olson kid and escorted him downstairs to the principal's office. Brooklyn had followed and told the principal what had happened. Normally, an act of violence against another student was not tolerated. However, since Kris bullied Brooklyn, Gage received only a three-day suspension. Kris got five days of in-school suspension for his role in the event.

Officer Ramsey called Brooklyn's parents to come and get her based on her emotional state. He recommended to the principal and her parents that

Brooklyn get counseling and take a few more days off. Just a safety precaution to protect the poor teen's mental health. Ramsey then drove Gage home from school with his parent's permission. The Deputy felt an escort for the young lad (who he didn't blame at all for the incident) was in his best interest as well. After that had occurred, then no one would directly poke the bear. McCormick ended up coming by the school during the last two periods of the day. The police presence was a welcomed safety net for Kayden and the rest of the group. Although no one directly came up to them after Gage's brief scuffle, there were whispers, stares and finger pointing.

    Unfortunately for Kayden, the presence by the police added more fuel to the rumors about the teens involvement in Sadie's death. When they all got to their cars after school, Shades informed the group what was buzzing around school. He told them the word on the street was the police were investigating their group because they were in on their friend's death. It had become a nightmare for Kayden. If Drake hadn't been there to walk her to every class, things could have gotten worse. None of the teens really had anything to say after school. It was all so overwhelming. Drake dropped off Kayden after he walked her to the door.

    Kayden had beaten everyone home, so she went to her room and started crying.

    ****

    Kayden awoke to her brother lightly shaking her shoulder. She had fallen asleep and did not know what time it was upon waking.

"Hey sis," her brother calmly said. "Mom wanted me to wake you up for dinner."

Kayden rubbed the dry crusted tears from her face. Jackson looked at her with concern on his face.

"Looks like your day didn't go very well, huh?" he asked her.

"No," she replied, covering her face with her hands. "It was rather shitty if the truth be told. How about yours?"

Jackson wrinkled his nose a little at the question. "It was weird for me."

Kayden removed her hands from her face and looked at him questioningly. Jackson moved to sit on the end of the bed by Kayden's feet. She moved them out of the way and sat up, looking at him expectantly.

"Well, the kids there were all excited having heard the town gossip over the weekend. Sadie apparently has a younger sister who is a 7th grader. She wasn't at school today for obvious reasons," he said matter-of-factly. "The other girls were saying terrible stuff about our family and your new friends. To be fair, no one said anything directly to me, but there were tons of whispers behind my back. Sucked," he finished.

Kayden let out an enormous sigh. "That's the weird part? You knew that was probably going to happen," returned Kayden sarcastically.

Jackson didn't react to the insult. He went on to the next part of his story.

"A kid befriended me today, but in secret. He asked me to friend him on our online game. Turns out he is in that group the Geek Squad, at school. He was the number two guy in their group. His name is Boyd Baker."

Kayden raised an eyebrow up for that bit of information. She thought he had made enemies of the entire group after that botched challenge at lunch Jackson had told her about.

"Boyd said he thought I should be the group's new leader, since I beat their guy fair and square. Unfortunately, Chip had been their group leader for over a year and wasn't about to give up his position. There's five guys in the group and three of them do whatever Chip wants. Boyd was always getting picked on by Chip. He felt it was mainly fear over anybody being a better gamer than him."

"That makes sense," Kayden said, stretching and getting ready to get out of bed to eat supper.

"Boyd wants to hang out sometime this week after school and just game it up. He was interested in seeing my abilities, but doesn't want anyone at school to know it just yet."

Kayden smiled. "Not ready to shake things up among his friends, huh?" she surmised.

"Yeah," replied Jackson. He followed her downstairs to the kitchen where her mom and Aunt Hollyn had already sat down to eat, but were waiting for them.

Aunt Hollyn took a drink from her glass of red wine, Kayden noticed. She seemed preoccupied. Kailynn smiled at her two teens and stood up to give them both a hug. Each of them accepted it with no fuss. A rarity, but the situation had put everyone in a vulnerable state. Family bonding was at an all-time high. Kailynn sat back down and waved at the food.

"C'mon guys, tonight is Kentucky Fried Chicken," she said over elaborately, showing the spread. "Compliments of Aunt Hollyn."

Both kids smiled at their aunt. She looked at

them and put on a fake face for them. Jackson and Kayden could see through it.

"Looks like Kayden and I weren't the only ones who had a tough day," Jackson observed to no one in particular, as he reached for the mashed potatoes.

Hollyn blinked and replied, "Pardon?"

Jackson sat the potatoes down. "We know something is bothering you Aunt Hollyn. We can see it on your face." He looked at his mom. "Both of us had a trying day too," he said, motioning to his sister.

Kailynn put down the chicken leg she was about to bite into. "I thought as much. I'm so sorry you two must deal with this and not even a week into school."

"They aren't the only ones, Lynni," interrupted Hollyn.

"What does she mean?" asked Kayden, picking up on her aunt's tone.

Hollyn without missing a beat said, "Your mom got an earful from one Chris Stone today at work."

Both of the kids looked at their mom together, recognizing the name of Sadie's dad.

"What happened, mom?" Kayden inquired.

Kailynn looked at her sister with displeasure, but Hollyn wasn't one to really keep secrets. She preferred getting things out there and done with.

"Don't look at me that way Lynni. These two need to know and understand, less they themselves have a run in with some of the unhappy folk around her," she spat with disdain.

Kailynn looked back at her kids with concern. "Guys, Sadie's dad came to the store. He heard I had been hired and paid me a visit. As you can imagine, he was very upset over his daughter's passing."

"His daughter's murder," retorted Kayden. "We

all know how shady this situation makes us look. Who would believe us?"

Jackson sunk into his meal quietly, not getting involved in the uncomfortable conversation.

"Yes, I agree Kayden. We know it was no accident, but how it happened versus what others think is the way it has always been."

Both kids looked at their mom. Hollyn lifted her eyes to her sister and took another drink of wine.

"Always been?" echoed Jackson.

Kailynn paused.

"Go ahead Lynni, you opened the door. Explain things to them," instructed Hollyn.

"Our family first migrated to America in the mid 1850's. Our original family member was Ferdinand. He was of direct German descent; Lithuanian, to be more specific."

"Like what people around here call the cemetery behind our home," rationalized Jackson.

"That's right," nodded Hollyn. "Our descendants started in Indiana, but with the rise of the railroad, our family migrated here to Ledford. It's where our great grandfather was working when a mining accident occurred."

"Aren't we more Slavic, mom?" Jackson interrupted again. "I've been looking our family heritage up online. It says we're sort of on the German border by Poland and Ukraine."

Kailynn gave her son a look of admiration. Jackson always wanted to understand the background of what he was trying to learn.

A good foundational trait, she thought.

"Well, there's debate among past family members, but what we know is Ferdinand was related to an up and coming Russian Orthodox Priest by the name of Alexis Toth. Bishop Nicholas Toth had ordained him. They were Lithuanian."

Kayden blurted, "Wow! We actually have a priest in our family line?" Kayden never thought her family had any religious affiliation besides being Catholic.

Kailynn continued, "When Father Toth came to America, they placed him in Minnesota. At some point, he petitioned for Ferdinand to come and visit on a matter of great importance."

Jackson perked up at the new mystery unfolding. "Great importance? You mean like church importance or family?" he asked his mom.

Hollyn intervened and answered the question. "It seemed everyone did not exactly want him in Minnesota," she said. "The church had sent him there, but not every leader in the church appreciated or recognized his rank in the church. It is a well-documented story that Toth who was an Eastern Rite Catholic rubbed another man of the cloth's beliefs wrong. It was said, a Bishop Ireland, who was of the Roman Catholic Church didn't approve of this Eastern Rite priest. Ireland was "Americanizing" the west and this priest worked against his efforts," Hollyn reported.

"The actual issue we need to talk about though is how our family comes into play," Kailynn barged in on her sister. "We can always do a history lesson later," she informed them.

Hollyn stuck her tongue out at Kailynn. Kailynn continued, "Father Toth called upon Ferdinand for 'unofficial' business. It seemed the Catholic Church had motives other than Father Toth's instructions. He was to help establish and build a Russian Greek Latin Orthodox Catholic Church. Eventually, it would just become the Orthodox Church built on former Roman Catholic ties."

Kayden was getting sick of the history lesson. She had been casually eating the Kentucky Fried Chicken, but was getting full. All this talk about the past was starting to bore her.

"Can we get to the point, mom?" Kayden belly ached.

"You need to learn some patience, Kayden," her mom responded. "I was just getting to it."

Kailynn took a bite of her chicken and washed it down with a gulp of wine. Everyone else sat waiting. Once she was clear of food, she continued.

"Turns out the Toth family had been distant crusaders for the Catholic Church dating way back."

"I'll say," exclaimed Jackson, looking at his phone. "Listen to this, we derived our name from the German word 'toto' which means 'death' or 'tote' meaning 'god-father." Either is cool."

"Great," followed Kayden in sarcasm. "We mean death, which we all got to see this weekend. Or, we are known as the god-father. Lots of mafia ties to that name," she spat sarcastically. "As if I couldn't feel worse."

"Give it a rest, Kayden," retorted Hollyn. "We have an important role historically. Unfortunately, no one outside of certain circles knows this."

"And why not?" questioned Jackson. "Are we cursed or something and what is our role?"

Kailynn interjected. "Wait. First, we're getting off topic. Second, our name doesn't mean exactly what you are connecting it to. When Ferdinand met with Alexis, the priest gave him a secret task. Our family ties link us to a lot of the unexplained phenomena you hear about in the news. The things you might hear about in the occult."

Everyone at the table became somber at the mention of this. No one said anything.

Kailynn sensing she had their full attention proceeded again.

"Alexis was here to build the Orthodox Church, genuine enough. There was also another reason they sent him. According to Ferdinand, our family was tasked with the job of finding and stopping some of the supernatural events which seem to occur all over. The Toth family were asked to serve the Midwest area. Alexis had dubbed Ferdinand's lineage to protect the Southern Illinois region. It is why our great-grandparents moved here. They tasked Alexis with the Minnesota area."

Hearing this declaration from their mom seemed ludicrous to the two teens. Jackson didn't know if his mom was pulling his leg. Kayden felt this conversation was moving towards calling the guys who put people in straight-jackets. Hollyn could see the doubt in the teens faces and interceded before Kailynn could delve deeper.

"What I think your mom is trying to tell you," she chimed in, "is that our family lineage started all the way back to Europe. Our family has been involved in events which are not recorded necessarily in the news. Your mom and I found out when we were a lot younger than you guys and it has plagued our current family you see here at this table."

Hollyn looked at her sister and to the kids. Normally, their parents would have indoctrinated the two teens into this little secret a long time ago. Kailynn had forsaken the family by cutting ties and moving away. It was another link in the chain of events leading them back to where they started.

"Your mom and I were all that was left of the direct line of Toths. Only now, you two spit-fires came into the picture and are the future. Yet untrained."

Kailynn saw where Hollyn was going with this and argued quickly with her sister.

"Hollybear, they are only teenagers. You aren't even giving them a choice in the matter."

"What choice do they have?" fired back Hollyn. "You cannot escape our family's legacy. Look where you are now? Right back here and no sooner than a week later, your kids stir up a hornet's nest," she challenged.

"Wait," yelled Kayden. Everyone stopped talking and turned to her. "What exactly are you saying? By my take, it sounds like we're some kind of ghost, witch, or spirit hunters who go around stopping unexplainable crap."

Kaitlynn looked her daughter hard in the face with a no-nonsense expression. "In a word, yes."

"Whoa," cried Jackson. "We're like the Ghost-Busters, Supernatural, or Lockwood & Co?"

"Who is Lockwood?" inquired Kayden.

With a huge smile on his face, he answered, "Only the coolest ghost hunting group on Netflix right now. They are these British kids. The story is set in a dystopian future. This young mysterious guy named Lockwood leads these guys..."

"Okay, shut up," interrupted Kayden. "I'm sorry I asked."

Hollyn sat back in her seat a little miffed at the teens' reaction. Kailynn just gave her sister the look of 'be patient'.

"Mom, do you guys wear like outfits or anything?" asked Jackson, getting his imagination ramped up.

"Just stop," commanded Kayden. "I am not sure where any of this is going, so can someone just stop with all the dramatic background crap and give it to me straight?"

Kailynn's patience was also waning. She had just as a trying day as any of them and was low on patience as well. "You want the short of it Kayden? Here it is."

Jackson sat back. He saw it was serious mom now and knew where this was going. No one could bring out frustration in his mom better than Kayden. Kayden also saw this, but felt similarly angry over everything and was ready to ratchet this conversation to a level 10 if needed.

"Your grandfather taught Hollyn and me about our family legacy. He officially indoctrinated us into it when we were in high school. He started training us around 10 years old. I was part of his group who engaged in behind-the-scenes cleaning."

"Cleaning is getting rid of the problem," chimed in Hollyn.

"Right," she said, looking at her sister. "I wasn't too keen on the whole thing because it was dangerous and I hated how the town felt about our family. No one knew what we did, but when the shit happened, they always found one of us to be at the center. Obviously, because we were called to deal with it. Therefore, our family name has been surrounded by lots of scandal. We have a few friends and distant relations who we can trust and talk to…"

"But they are becoming more scarce," interrupted Hollyn again.

The two sister's eyes met each other at Hollyn's

last statement. An unspoken understanding took place.

Hollyn took over from there. "Kayden. Your mother met your father, James, in college. They had a few run-ins together and it didn't set well with him. Eventually, James gave your mom an ultimatum to either leave with him or he'd leave. You know the result. James had harsh words with your grandfather over the issue, but your mom followed James, anyway. The truth about our family has been hidden away from you."

The kids could tell this was a touchy subject between their mom and Aunt Hollyn. Her last words had a tinge of bitterness to them.

"I wanted the kids to have a different life than we did," spat Kailynn to her sister.

"Well, what kind of life do you know they want if you don't allow them to choose for themselves?" fired back Hollyn.

"I was not about to have them indoctrinated while they were small children. Children who had no business being subjected to such things," retaliated Kailynn. Kailynn clinched her fists and clenched her jaw in anger at her sister.

"It's who we are Lynni. You cannot fight against who our family is. You left us when we needed your help. There were four of us left after you turned tail and ran off with Pavilonis."

Kailynn stood up, knocking her chair back. She glowered at Hollyn. "I always told you I hated doing that shit. The only reason I did was to protect you."

"Bullshit," yelled Hollyn, standing up equally to her sister. Her chair flew back. "You used me as an excuse. You left our family out to dry. Dad could have used your help, but because you left we didn't have a seer anymore. Because of that, you are the reason he ended up getting hurt and eventually passed."

There it was. The kids finally understood where the animosity and pain came from between the two sisters. Hollyn blamed her sister's leaving for their dad's eventual death.

"I killed dad. Is that what you really think?" accused Kailynn. "You think because I left, dad got hurt?"

Hollyn's bottom lip quivered and tears were forming in her eyes. "You left us Kailynn. We needed you. Instead, you abandoned us."

Hollyn fell to the floor in a seated position. Her whole body was limp. This topic had been eating away at her for years. Now, like ripping a scab from a wound, it bled out again. Kailynn walked around the table and kneeled down by her sister. She put her arms around her and whispered quietly into her ear.

"Hollybear...you know better than that. I loved both you and dad, but I hated doing what we did. It was scary and dangerous. Most of our family succumbed to the dangers. I didn't want that kind of life."

Hollyn didn't move but responded. "You just took off without a word."

Kailynn kissed her sister on the cheek. Tears were now flowing from her as well. "I cannot apologize enough about that. I was young. I didn't know how to break the news to you. I thought you would never allow me to leave and I didn't want to be talked out of it."

Looking at her sister, Hollyn felt completely deflated. Her usual chipper, cocky demeanor was gone. "What about dad?"

Kailynn sat down beside Hollyn. "I told dad what I wanted. He accepted my choice of leaving the family to make a new life."

This was news to Hollyn. Her talks and memories told her the opposite.

"He always hated you for leaving and constantly talked about how your shiftless husband stole you from him," she responded.

Her older sister smiled at the thought. "I'm sure he did. He accepted me leaving for a better life. He did not accept me leaving with James. Dad didn't like him."

Finally, she accepted the fact verbally, something that Hollyn never thought her sister would do. A fact Hollyn knew, but never thought her sister would verbally accept. Hollyn smiled for the first time since they started in on this dark topic.

"What are you grinning at?" she asked a little confused.

"You," responded Hollyn. "Dad hated James, which pushed your rebellious ass towards him even harder," Hollyn accused.

Kailynn almost immediately objected, but caught herself. If she truly looked inside herself, what Hollyn had just said was true. All she could do was nod and say, "probably."

Hollyn reached out and hugged her sister. This was the closure she needed. All this time the pain and stress of the past had plagued her and the issue festered beneath her skin like a slow spreading disease. Now, her sister's honesty had released that malignant void in her life. She let out a deep sigh.

The two kids watched on as their mom and aunt made amends with each other. A sibling fight which had spanned almost two decades had finally ended.

Both of the sisters realized they still had an audience looking on and composed themselves again.

"I'm sorry you had to see that," Kailynn said to her kids in a more subdued voice.

Jackson answered, "I'm not. It's about time all the cards were on the table. What exactly do we do now?"

Hollyn looked at Kailynn. Again, something passed between them unseen. Hollyn looked at the two teens and answered.

"Even if you do not wish to be a part of this legacy, you will have to be trained, anyway. The simple fact is we're drawn to these things whether we want to be. You will need the basic knowledge to defend yourselves. And you..." Hollyn said, pointing to their mom, "you are very rusty. You will need to practice also if you are to get back into the game."

"Great," cried Kayden. "I'm supposed to be freakin Nancy Drew combined with the Ghost-Whisperer."

"Could be worse," responded Jackson. "You could be that red-headed girl on Stranger Things who gets messed up in season three."

Kayden punched Jackson in the arm hard. "Ouch!" he cried.

"You watch too much Netflix," she said.

"Great!" Hollyn said to everyone. "I will start the preparations and we will begin training tomorrow after school. Lynni, I will take them to Muddy and start their practice. You and I can practice on things when you get home from work and situated. Deal?"

Kailynn looked at her eager younger sister. There was a familiar feeling to this part of the gig. She at least had enjoyed working with her sister during some of their past ghostly huntings. She nodded her agreement.

"What's Muddy?" Jackson asked in curiosity.

"Our central base of operations," Hollyn answered.

"Awesome!" the young teen exclaimed.

Kayden just shrugged her shoulders and complained to no one in particular. "Just wonderful. We're now headed to the Batcave."

Chapter Twelve: The Toth's Legacy

    The next morning started out just like Monday. Drake and Shades picked up Kayden for school, while Hollyn took Jackson. Kayden was extremely quiet on the drive there, which worried Drake a bit. He wondered if he had done something wrong to upset Kayden. Shades, oblivious to the social signs of a female in the car banged on and on over the drama ensuing over the death of Sadie.

    Apparently, the police had issued out a statement to the local news and town. Sadie had died of asphyxiation from being trapped under the dirt in the cemetery. They had no leads or persons of interest. The forensic results had yielded no fingerprints, DNA or clues into the mysterious death. The police were currently researching events where someone could make the ground look untouched, but have a hole dug underneath. Unfortunately for them, no cases, at least on file, were available to present a better understanding. In a nutshell, it simply looked like it sucked her into the ground and upon covering her returned to its normal state. The only reason anyone knew of her plight was because of her protruding arm.

The day progressed a lot like yesterday in the halls as well. Drake walked with Kayden to all her classes. Brooklyn had taken a leave of absence for the rest of the week. They suspended Gage from school. The others took their lumps of accusations here or there. Shades and Braelyn continued to run counter-interference with the rumor mill. This made the initial shock from yesterday weaken.

Jackson, on the other hand was having a whole other experience. Once it got around, he was involved with the high school kids over the cemetery issue; his street credit had gone up. Boyd Baker had wasted no time using Jackson's newfound popularity to create even more drama. He officially left the Geek Squad and told everyone he was joining Jackson. They hadn't come up with a name for their group yet, but were mulling it over. Boyd's decision rocked the Geek Squad. Now the Geek Squad numbered at four with Chip still in charge. This created a new rumor mill about some of the other member's jumping ship. Jackson, of course, had no actual hand in any of this. The talk took on a life of its own. Boyd talked about their joining up as friends on Clash Royale and the other gamers started geeking out over it. Many of them went online to check out Jackson's status there.

By the end of the day, Jackson was the talk of the junior high. Who was this kid from out of town?

How had he infiltrated the top gaming group on campus? He must be cool to hang out with high school kids on the weekend, right? This definitely wasn't the hype and social attention he needed right now.

    Aunt Hollyn was waiting for him at the end of school outside in the front. Jackson almost ran to her car to get away from all the attention. Boyd had asked when they could hang out. Jackson, not knowing what his aunt had in store for him gave him an unsure answer because of the series of events which recently happened. Baker loved the answer, because it showed even more the intensity of Jackson's outside affairs. Affairs which no one but the Toth family knew about. Boyd had decided Jackson was the coolest thing to come to Harrisburg since he could remember. He was determined to be involved in it and genuinely wanted to learn more about Jackson.

    Over at the high school, Kayden waited for Drake outside her classroom. She had slowly gotten her school stuff together and was intentionally last to leave the room. When she got to the door, she stood off to the side of the entrance to the classroom, scanning for Drake. A voice met her off to her right.

    "Looking for your boyfriend Toth?"

    Kayden turned to see the goth girl she had the run-in with at the party. She was by herself, dressed in black. Her eyes were outlined in a dark black cascade of overly pronounced eye-liner. She wasn't very tall and had part of the side of her hair shaved close to her head. The other half was still long and braided. In the shaved part was an infinity symbol.

    "What do you want?" Kayden responded curtly. She continued to scan for Drake among the students, running around like ants in the hallway.

"With you? Nothing," the Goth girl responded. "However, since you came to town, bad luck seems to have followed you. I don't find it coincidental. Do you?" she purred in a sarcastic tone.

Kayden turned to address this interloper. "What's your name?" Kayden asked.

"Why?" returned the girl in black.

"Because I would at least like to address the person who is indirectly blaming me for something without actually saying it."

The girl stood there, staring at Kayden. Kayden could tell she was internally struggling with how she should answer. Slightly grinning, she answered. "My name is Felecia Wolfe. You would figure it out, eventually. Small town and all."

"Well, Felecia, as small towns go, you of all people should understand what a rumor is, right?" Kayden asked in an equally sarcastic voice.

"Oh, I do Miss Toth," Felecia answered in a low voice. "I can also smell bullshit a mile away. Perhaps you should go back out to that cemetery of yours and bury yourself."

The comment completely surprised Kayden with its directness and negative tone. However, a familiar voice arose from behind Felecia.

"Miss Wolfe, always a pleasure, but a little dark even for you don't you think?" Shades had emerged on the scene and heard the last comment from Felecia to his friend.

"Shades, naturally poor timing," Felecia returned.

"Or perfect timing," he quipped. "Why are you so hard on Kayden, Wolfe? She has done nothing to you or anyone else here in Harrisburg. Seems you decided the moment you saw her to start conflict." Shades lifted his glasses up and propped them on top of his head for effect.

"Not that it's any concern of yours, VanOrmer, but Toth here has a history with our town." Felecia had turned around and faced Kayden again after addressing Shades. She put the emphasis on 'town' to make sure Kayden knew she was an outsider.

"Now that's just rude, Felecia. True. Toth is a known name in these parts of Southern Illinois, but it is debatable to how you are depicting it wouldn't you say?" The question hung in the air.

"I'd say trouble and two-faced would sum it up in 'my' depiction," Felecia acknowledged.

Shades put his glasses back down and replied, "Or it depicts wrongfully accused and under-appreciated."

Just then, Drake showed up and saw the threesome gathering. He could tell from the expressions, the conversation was not pleasant.

"Is there a problem?" he asked. His gaze specifically locked in on Wolfe.

She returned his stare and walked up to him. Reaching for his face, she seductively caressed his cheek with the back of her fingers. "No Steele, no problem at all. I was just conversing about the weird coincidences that keep happening since Kayden started school. However, with you protecting her and all, I'm sure there's no reason for anyone to be suspicious, right?"

"Suspicious Wolfe?" repeated Drake questioningly. "Suspicious as in the unfortunate situation about Sadie, you mean?"

She smiled seductively and started walking away

with her hand rubbing ever so slightly down Drake's arm. "You said it, not me." With that, she walked away without turning back to look at any of them.

They all looked on. It left an unpleasant taste in Kayden's mouth, but she didn't know if it was from what Felecia had said or jealousy over touching Drake.

"She was an abused child," joked Shades. "C'mon, let's get out of here. The bell rang. There's no need to torture ourselves."

"Agreed," nodded Drake.

All three of them shuffled out of the school building to the parking lot. Drake started small talk to keep them engaged with each other. A useful tool when everyone around liked to stare and whisper.

"I guess Felecia was doing her normal?" he asked Shades.

"Yep," he answered. "She can't go a day without torturing some poor soul. Guess it makes up for her lack of friends."

"Oh, she has friends, Jeremiah. They are just not the fun sort to be around."

Kayden took mild interest in their banter, but changed the subject.

"Anyone heard from Owen or Shay today?"

Drake made a throat clearing noise to hide his initial response.

Shades keeping it light responded. "Both of the couples were a little frustrated today. It seems Owen got into a verbal exchange with Rolland in the hall. Ayelyn got between them and pushed Owen away, but it's not a good thing. Tension is building up on those two since last Saturday. Just a matter of time."

Kayden was becoming so frustrated over the whole situation. These guys were in this situation with her, whether they wanted to be. It didn't help that most of the bullies hammering down on them were upper class-men at the high school.

"I just hate that for Owen. Having a senior bullying him like that," Kayden fumed.

"Don't worry about Owen, Kayden," replied Drake. "He can take care of himself. Besides, their issue stems back to junior high when fat boy was in 8th grade and Owen 6th."

Shades followed Drake's comment, "Dickerson has always been a verbal bully and picks on younger kids. Since he's fat, he falls along that line of thinking he's a victim of anyone who might be thinner than him. Therefore, his verbal attacks are perceived by him as standing up for himself. Even though no one has really 'attacked' him."

Kayden squeezed her eyes shut tight and stopped walking. Both the boys flew past her and stopped looking back at her. Kayden growled and opened her eyes and looked at them.

"So what you are saying is because he's overweight, he thinks by bullying other people he is really sticking up for himself?" Kayden asked.

Drake and Shades simultaneously both said "Yep," at the same time.

Kayden then began walking again and they all fell in line with her. "That's idiotic guys."

Drake just shrugged. "Hey, we didn't say it was okay, just explaining the dude's mental state."

Shades smiled at that statement. "Mental state," he repeated. "Good one Steele. He's more like Fat Bastard from the Austin Powers movie *Goldmember*."

They both laughed.

"Excuse me," came a voice from behind them.

All three turned to see Deputy Ramsey walking up behind them. All of them immediately became worried and defensive at the same time. The police hadn't come close to solving the murder and they all knew who the town suspected as the murders.

Shades quietly hissed behind teeth to Drake, "Dude, should we ask for an attorney before saying anything?"

Drake shrugged in confusion over the entire situation.

"Miss Toth," Ramsey said, addressing Kayden politely, "I was hoping you might be open to talking with me?"

Kayden felt surprised, but not entirely shocked. After all, this was becoming a par for the course lately.

"I was just heading home, officer," she replied curtly. "I'm sure if you needed to talk to me it would be better if my mom or Aunt Hollyn were around for it."

"I understand completely Miss Toth. It is for that reason I'm actually here."

This caught all of them by surprise.

"What exactly do you mean officer?" Kayden responded, bewildered and a little nervous.

"You can call me Ramsey, miss or Deputy Ramsey," he informed her. "No need for all that 'officer' banter. You guys are not in trouble and I'm not fishing for information about the crime," he explained to them. He looked at Kayden with soft, non-menacing eyes and explained further. "I'm actually pretty good friends with Hollyn. She told me I could talk to you today after school. I thought, I mean, if you were open to it; I could give you a ride home?"

This request shocked everyone. Kayden didn't know how to answer, but Drake did.

"That's very nice Deputy Ramsey, but she has a ride." Drake's tone took on an element of jealousy and a protector.

Ramsey smiled genuinely at his response and held both hands up in defeat. "Whoa now, this isn't some creepy deputy hitting on a high school girl, Drake," he said. "I actually am friends with Hollybear."

The name caught Kayden's attention immediately. No one but her sister called Aunt Hollyn that. It was against her better judgment, but she surprised both of her friends by blurting out, "Sure, I'll take that ride home Mr. Ramsey."

Drake and Shades turned to her in complete confusion. Shades went into a quick tizzy. "This is exactly how police get people to confess to things they didn't do. It's one-on-one coercion. Didn't you see those episodes on Netflix? The Making of a Murderer?"

"The second one," clarified Drake. "Even Dr. Phil recently had that episode on his show and agreed about the officers coercing the poor kid in the office by himself."

"Relax," replied Kayden. "Don't worry, anything said is 'off the record' right, Mr. Ramsey?"

Deputy Ramsey smiled, despite himself at the lingo used by Kayden. Ramsey responded light-heartedly. "Of course, miss." He motioned towards his squad car and escorted her to the front passenger's side. He opened the door for Kayden. She stopped before getting in and looked back at the two stunned boys watching.

"Don't worry guys," she said reassuringly. "I'll text you once I get home, Drake."

"Promise?" he replied instantly.

"Yes, I promise." With that, she sat down and the

deputy closed the door. He walked around the other side of the car, tipped his hat at the boys. "Gentlemen," he addressed them and drove off.

****

The drive from school to her house was less than 15 minutes by Kayden's estimate. She had timed it for the last two days of driving with Drake. Officer Ramsey pulled out of the school parking lot and headed toward the business district.

"I take it moving here hasn't exactly been easy, huh?" Ramsey asked Kayden. He was apparently starting small talk to make Kayden more relaxed.

She wasn't about to let her guard down. Kayden was a more direct to the point kind of gal and didn't really like small talk.

"No," she replied. "Let's just get to the meat and potatoes of why you asked me to ride with you home, okay?"

Ramsey kept driving without so much as an inkling to if her comment bothered him or not.

"So much like Hollyn. Never one to mince words nor able to be congealed to people she was around who she wasn't close to. Alright, Kayden," he responded. "Let's get to it."

Kayden was all ears. She couldn't know what was coming next from Deputy Ramsey, but she was on her guard.

Ramsey reached up to the recording device on his cruiser and turned it off. Kayden knew he intentionally did that for her benefit.

"Now that we are truly talking without hidden ears," he began. "How much has Hollyn told you about me?"

A little taken aback at the question, Kayden responded honestly. "To be frank, nothing. In fact, the first time I knew anything about you was the night Aunt Hollyn called and you came to the house."

Ramsey nodded in understanding. "Well, we've been associated with each other now for over 10 years."

"Associated?" repeated Kayden, not understanding what that really meant.

"Hollyn saw me today and we had a little chat. She said she was going to educate you about the family business, starting today."

"What do you know about our 'family business'?" questioned Kayden suspiciously.

"I know what she does behind the scenes when things go bump in the night," answered Ramsey cryptically.

This shocked Kayden. She had thought only their family was involved in such matters. Aunt Hollyn or her mom never mentioned others.

"How are you involved, then?" she fired back.

"I grew up with Hollyn. We have a history together, so to speak. She likes to keep her relationships on the down low."

Down low? Kayden thought. *Poor thing is trying to talk in teen lingo.*

"I was accidentally involved in one of her early efforts at cleaning a family home in Shawneetown. It's where I'm originally from before we moved closer to the Burg," he informed her. "They did something to clean the house of things that go bump in the night that couldn't be explained logically," he informed her.

"Must have been dirty to need two people to

clean a house. Maybe the family needed more brooms," Kayden said sarcastically.

Ramsey looked over at her with a disapproving stare. Kayden's hard exterior melted quickly and she curtly said sorry. He continued, "After that, I started seeing her around more when we moved. Eventually, I started following her until she caught me. She was mad as a hornet's nest."

"Really?" commented Kayden. "How did she respond?"

Ramsey unconsciously rubbed his chin. "She popped me in the jaw."

Kayden laughed out loud despite herself. He frowned again. "It's not really that funny. Hollyn can hit really hard."

Smiling, Kayden replied, "I bet she can."

Ramsey looked back at the road and kept talking. "Anyway, over the years, we became friends. One issue the Toths have always had is balancing out their behind-the-scenes affairs without getting the police involved. Your dad knew Whip pretty good, so they worked together, so to speak. When needed, Whip would run interference to help your family stay in the shadows. What he couldn't do though was assist them with how the surrounding communities felt about them. Lots of rumors, unsolved events and reclusive behavior just added fuel to the fire. Now, I help Hollyn and Whip with your family business. Although I'm more directly involved, since it has only been Hollyn. I'm glad her sister came back. In the end, though, your family legacy to those few of us who know is legendary."

The police deputy said this with true respect. It wasn't lost on Kayden.

The Hungarian Cemetery Secrets Within Backup

"You are probably wondering why I'm the one telling you this?" inquired the deputy. Kayden wondered about that along with a ton of other stuff. She just raised her eyebrows, awaiting a response to his somewhat redundant question.

"The event which happened on Saturday wasn't some lunatic who was out for kicks that night. Hollyn straight up said it was a high level vengeful ghost. Maybe even borderline demonic. She also said it involved your ancestor who seemed to protect, not attack. What do you think 'save them' meant?" he asked out of the blue.

Kayden shrugged, honestly. "I don't know, but to be frank I was scared and supremely curious at the same time. My initial reaction wasn't to run, but to listen and watch. Those dark, scary forms got my attention. They were the real menace. As for the ghost of my great-great whatever, it was not like those others."

Ramsey nodded in understanding and drove into Kayden's driveway, putting the car in park. He looked over at Kayden, showing he wasn't finished talking yet. Ramsey rubbed his finger over his top lip in contemplation.

"It would stand to reason some of those other things manifested from the graveyard as well. Perhaps I'll do some archive digging to find out the surrounding buried graves. Perhaps there is more of a history there we are not yet comprehending."

He looked at Kayden with compassionate eyes and a soft expression. "Thank you for letting me take you home. Tell Hollyn I said hi and I'm going to do some research on who is buried in the general vicinity of your late family member. In the meantime, stay away from Sadie's dad. He is beyond angry, which is understandable, but he is directing his focus on your family. Don't give him ammunition."

Kayden nodded her understanding and suddenly needed to get out of the car and go process what Deputy Ramsey just told her.

"Okay, Mr. Ramsey. Thanks for the ride," she said, getting out of the car.

The Deputy backed his car out of the drive and sped off. Kayden got inside her house and went to her room to think.

***

Kayden heard her Aunt Hollyn get in with Jackson, but remained in her room. She could hear them talking downstairs, though.

"Okay, so say I actually tried to touch one. What would happen?" Jackson asked.

Hollyn made a bitter beer face at Jackson. He smiled and playfully pushed his aunt.

"C'mon Aunt Hollyn," he pleaded.

She stopped making the face and smiled. "Alright Jackson, let's get to it. Ghosts, spirits, and other such entities can physically strike, snag, shove, kick, lift, and bite you. However, we are talking about ghosts and spirits. They are not overly aggressive or evil by nature. Most are just stuck here or their residual energy is attached to an item, location, or person. Spirits are just people who have died and they are generally at peace with death. They move on to the next stage of life."

Jackson wrinkled his nose.

"The next stage of life? They died, so what life

are you talking about Aunt Hollyn?" he asked confused.

Hollyn saw Kayden standing on the last step of the stairs, having come down during their brief discussion. She nodded at her and looked back at Jackson.

"When we die, it isn't the end of us, but the beginning of another journey. One which takes us all to different places based on the life we lived. Religion calls it heaven, other's call it the afterlife, nirvana, or spirit realm. Regardless of your belief, we are more than just our bodies. Your soul controls and runs your body. Your soul will take on an ethereal form which humans cannot see. Where it goes and what it does is different for all of us."

Kayden walked into the room and sat down next to Jackson at the kitchen table. She understood what her aunt was saying. Although they hadn't been the most practicing Russian Orthodox on the block, she very much believed in heaven and hell.

"So how are spirits and ghosts different, then?" Kayden asked.

Aunt Hollyn had been pouring some tea from the fridge in a glass for the kids. She handed Kayden hers and sat down with them.

"A ghost," Hollyn explained, "is a trapped spirit stuck on this plane of existence. Ghosts can do a lot of different things, not all the same. They can speak, create cold spots, generate sounds, move things and touch people."

"Like in the movies," interrupted Jackson, smiling smugly at his sister.

She rolled her eyes and silently mouthed the words 'shut up.'

"May I continue?" Hollyn said rhetorically. "On

the whole, ghosts have probably died tragically or abruptly. Knowing this, many of the souls taken by death can't really acknowledge that they are dead."

"Whoa," chimed Jackson.

Kayden squirmed a little in her seat and repositioned herself with a look of confusion. "How can they not know they're dead?" she asked.

Shrugging, Hollyn answered. "It happens so fast they get cheated out of what could have been in their lives Kayden. A person who lives a long time knows it's just a matter of time before old age happens. A person taken by death unexpectedly feels cheated, angry, sad or any other emotion we feel as humans. The life and expectations they may have planned for becomes an unfinished business for them and they need to still finish it. Therefore, they get tied to people, items or events they were involved in before or during their deaths."

This revelation gave a quiet pause in the room. Aunt Hollyn took a drink of her tea. Kayden had her hands wrapped around hers, watching the liquid inside it. Jackson's eyes wandered off to the opposite wall across from him in deep reflection. An idea came to his mind and just left his mouth.

"Last Saturday we all had experiences at the cemetery. The ghost we saw of our great-whatever grandfather, he died in a mine accident. If what you are saying is true, it stands to reason his 'unfinished business' had something to do with the accident, right?"

Aunt Holly looked at both of the kids. "Perhaps Jackson," she answered. "It could also be something else he was tied to like his family or conflict with someone?"

"But he said, 'save them'," interjected Kayden. "Why would he say that? Save who? The people in the mine who died with him?"

Hollyn answered quickly. "We don't know Kayden, but we're going to find out."

"How?" responded Jackson.

"Training. Get ready. We leave in thirty minutes." With that, she stood and went upstairs to her room. The siblings sat for a second, looking at each other in confusion. What does one bring with them or prepare themselves for to 'get ready'? Both of them would find out soon enough.

****

The three were driving past Harrisburg toward a tiny place called 'Muddy'. It used to be a trade and mining post area; Hollyn informed the kids. They drove to Muddy, where the location of the original Russian Orthodox Church had recently been torn down. A testament to the times and change. Hollyn explained a brief history of the Russian Orthodox church there.

"They had built the church in 1913. Apparently, Tsar Nicholas II had put up the funds to pay for this church. It was well on its way to growing back then because of the jobs in the coal mines there. However, other coal mines came open with better working conditions (like being able to stand up in the mine) so the workers followed. It had left the town and church bereft of people. The church, which had stood there for over 103 years came under disrepair with no one to fix or pay for it."

Hollyn saw what she was looking for as they came upon the small town. As Hollyn's car turned left into Muddy, the sun was in its beginning throws of dusk. The sun started going down around 5:40ish in the late October fall. The leaves were flying around everywhere and the cornfields were all but empty of its seasonal stalks. It made for a typical late October atmosphere. They pulled up to an empty lot with a lone fence, leaves swirling all around and an empty concrete basement foundation.

"We're here," Hollyn declared.

"We're where?" echoed Kayden. "There's nothing but an empty lot with what I guess was where this church stood, right?"

Hollyn smiled at her and shut off the car.

"Not everything is as it seems Kayden. C'mon," she replied, getting out of the car. Jackson followed her, but Kayden lingered, looking at the steps in front of the car. She had her doubts and really didn't want to be here, but her cemetery experience on Saturday motivated her to get out.

As Hollyn walked to the steps, going down into what they left of the church, she checked to make sure the kids were with her. She looked around the area, checking to make sure they were alone. Satisfied, she went into what they left of the church's foundation. Jackson, excited by the whole adventure followed enthusiastically, but Kayden was her usual, skeptical self.

"Get down here Kayden," echoed Hollyn.

Jackson had followed Hollyn directly, with no preamble. He was always the anxious one. This was the type of adventure he loved taking. Kayden came down to stand beside her family.

"Well?" she asked. "We're all standing down her like idiots. The sun is almost down and we won't be able to see anything."

Jackson looked up at the open sky. His sister was right. He turned to Aunt Hollyn, who was focused on the corner wall, and looked at her. She stood close to where the wall and floor met. With what look like practiced counting, she stopped about two feet above the floor and then pushed.

At first, nothing happened, then a portion of the wall moved to the left, revealing a small doorway. Hollyn pulled out a small flashlight and turned it on.

Chapter Thirteen: Hidden Secret

    The dark entrance lit up with Hollyn's flashlight. The light revealed a shortened passageway. The narrow passage led to another wall. It looked like a dead end. Hollyn stopped in front of the wall. She looked back at the two teens following her. She smiled and turned back to the wall and with her left foot she stepped down hard to reveal another hidden panel to open the wall. It moved to the right, revealing darkness beyond. Hollyn flashed her light into the room and walked through. The kids nervously followed their aunt into the dingy room. The door closed behind them. Hollyn saw their frightened expressions at the door closing and elaborated to calm them.

    "It's on a pulley system. The rumor was this place had been built by free-masons, but who knows? I will say, the Harrisburg Cemetery has several freemasons buried there from the early 1900s," she informed.

    Jackson and Kayden looked at Hollyn who held the flashlight ahead of her. She walked to the other side of the concrete room. She reached down to the middle of the wall and both kids could see an old handle. She grabbed it and pushed up. The room came to life as light bulbs from ancient sockets lit up. The wires, which moved around the walls to where the lights hung, were corroded and ancient.

    "Wow," commented Jackson. "It's so old. I cannot believe they still work?"

    "Yeah," his sister commented, "I'm sure it is just a matter of time before they catch on fire or something." Kayden's comment was laced with disapproval.

    Hollyn ignored their comments and walked to the opposite wall where a great number of things occupied. It looked like a musty, old storage closet with an open cross embedded into the woodwork, allowing a visual of what was inside. It had clothing of different variations hanging in it. There was a large table in front of it with six seats. Another couple of shelves lined the wall as well.

    Jackson made his way over to the shelves. Many unusual things were laying on the shelves. Crosses, jewelry, bottles, etc. Lay scattered on the different ledges. He turned and looked back at his aunt.

    Motioning to the shelves he asked, "What is all this stuff Aunt Hollyn?"

    Hollyn looked at her niece who was staring at her and then back to Jackson.

    "Those are different artifacts to assist us in our

work. You will see some scapular medallions, Saint Benedict medals, holy water, and a few other tools. This place is our family's hidden secret."

"Do we also get wooden stakes, silver bullets, and crucifixes also?" Kayden asked in her sarcastic manner.

Pointing at the table, "both of you sit down." Hollyn ordered.

The two teens made their way to the table and sat, Kayden with a little smugness.

Their aunt's demeanor had changed and both of them could tell she was no longer acting like their aunt, but a teacher. Her body language had become more rigid and her face was serious. The lights worked, but not very well given the limited update from its original placement, creating shadows here and there. It added to their aunt's silhouette.

"This place helped us train and gave sanctuary when we needed time alone. All joking leaves at the door. What we will encounter out there is serious and it isn't in a humorous mood. The things we will interact with require a rational mind, teamwork, practice and faith. Understand Kayden?" their aunt asked.

Kayden's first impulse was to sass back at her aunt, but given the new situation, she nodded instead.

"Good," Hollyn replied. "Let me explain the basics. We are not exorcists. Our job isn't to run around dispelling evil from around the area. We deal with ghosts or entities."

Jackson's face took on one of confusion. "What is the difference between them?" Kayden nodded, agreeing with her brother's question.

"I gave you the basics earlier about ghosts, but let me dig a little deeper. Ghosts break down into categories. Orbs are the most common. They are usually white lights which float around areas they are attached to. Orbs are not too bothersome or cause issues, but they can irritate rational people. You feel cold spots in areas which shouldn't be cold. They can sometimes be called funnel ghosts."

Hollyn was walking around the table as she talked. As she circled the teens, she made eye contact with her new wards.

"Funnel ghosts are another way to describe past loved ones or those who used to live at the location the ghost is at. They are rather simple to get rid of, but every once in a while, it becomes harder than expected."

Jackson raised his hand. Kayden rolled her eyes. "We're not in class dork."

Jackson crossed his eyes at his sister in a quiet retort. Hollyn stopped walking and raised her eyebrows at Jackson.

Her brother continued with his question. "If a funnel ghost haunts a house, then what is it called that haunts a house at night, throwing stuff and scaring people? A family member dying and then getting mean to their family doesn't sound right."

Hollyn nodded her agreement. "We call them poltergeists."

Kayden frowned. "I've heard that term. Those ghosts are not friendly."

Her aunt shrugged. She responded, "some are not friendly. They can trip, pinch, bruise or throw things at the people who live there. They can even make noises like crying, yelling, scratching or growling. They are one of the bad hauntings. Takes a bit to get them out."

Kayden cut straight to the chase. "What kind of

ghost are we dealing with Aunt Hollyn and how do we stop them?"

Hollyn sat down at the table and clasped her hands together on the table. Her face took on a fearful look.

"I fear we are dealing with multiple ghosts. Based solely on your description of what you both encountered it is possible we are seeing an Interactive personality ghost. This is a type of ghost that is friendly or comforting and can speak, touch or even show themselves to you. I think our great-great-grandfather is that ghost."

Jackson nodded his agreement. "That description certainly fits the mold for what I saw," he reflected.

Kayden agreed as well. She saw a definitive person standing there and it spoke. The eyes were scary, but everything else wasn't too, off.

Hollyn continued after Jackson made his comment.

"The other ones, though, are a bit more complicated. They were more darkened forms, which we call a Shadow Person. They don't take full form and have no eyes, but are menacing and seem to have dark intentions."

Kayden shuddered, remembering those things slowly walking towards her and her friends. She responded, "What does a Shadow Person do or want?"

Hollyn answered, "no one ever knows specifically. They are in the wrong place at the wrong time. Often they can be scared away, but once in a while this is not the case. I fear we are dealing with the latter."

A moment of silence settled in among the three as the kids took in the information. They had a basic understanding of ghosts, but what were they to do now?

Aunt Hollyn stood up and signaled to the middle of the room.

"This is where we practice. On the floor is a cross. It helps us to focus our energies on the church and our religious faith."

"I don't mean to sound ignorant or negative Aunt Holly," replied Kayden. "Jackson and I haven't exactly been going to church. Mom said she only took us to get baptized. We really don't know what our faith is or does," she concluded.

Aunt Hollyn nodded. She had suspected as much and was ready for this minor snag.

"Honestly, our faith is within ourselves and is present at birth. We know there's a higher power, purpose, or ultimate good in the universe, we just cannot explain it. There is inherently the other side of that coin we know to exist as well. Religion gives us a structure, tools, and means to explore in a more internal method. As we learn these skills together, you will get a sense of inner understanding and come to understand the basics of our faith and belief system. How far you wish to explore will be up to you."

She looked the kids over with a much more loving face.

Addressing Kayden, "do you ever say brief prayers, like please help or I'm struggling, to no one in particular?"

Kayden nodded. "Sometimes."

"And you?" she asked Jackson.

"Sure," he responded.

"When you do this, do you believe in the questions or emotions you are having at the time you are asking or praying?"

They both nodded.

"Do you hope someone or something will hear and help you find the answer to the issues you might have?"

Again, they both nodded.

"Excellent," she said. "You see, you have faith already and didn't even know it."

The kids walked over to the cross on the floor and looked at Hollyn questioningly.

"Now, the leader of our group will stand at the top of the cross. Our seer will position themselves at the bottom. The other two supporters or prayer summoners will take a stance on the left and right portion of the cross."

Kayden's eyebrows went up in frustration. "We don't have four people Aunt Hollyn."

Hollyn let out a sigh. "Yes, Kayden. I'm aware of that. We will when your mother is with us."

Jackson's eyes got big. "You mean mom is really going to do this stuff too?"

Hollyn smiled at her nephew. "Of course she is. She was one of the best seers in the game. Only time will tell if either of you inherited this gift from her."

Jackson took his position on the right portion of the cross and motioned for his sister to go to the other one. Grudgingly, she moved to her spot on the left. Hollyn took her position at the top and they began training.

Chapter Fourteen: The Truth

The next couple of days were a whirlwind for Kayden and Jackson. Drake and Jeremiah showed up every day to pick Kayden up for school. They had been very interested in Kayden's situation with the police officer. Kayden didn't want to lie to them, but knew she couldn't exactly tell them the truth either. No one was to know about her family's secret along with the individuals who helped them. She explained to them Deputy Ramsey wanted to just check on her because of her aunt. Both of her friends at first didn't accept that reason, but Kayden inferred without actually saying her aunt and the deputy had a thing. Once Drake and Jeremiah picked up on this, both of them accepted her story.

Hollyn took Kayden and Jackson to the secret

training grounds to prepare the teens. The beginning of their routine involved learning prayers, symbols, and the history of scenarios they might see while in the field. Their focus right now was preparing to go back to the cemetery and deal with the supernatural roaming the location. Tonight, Deputy Ramsey was coming over to debrief Hollyn on the information he found in the town's historical archives. Hollyn had been working late at night with Kailynn to refresh her abilities as a seer. Their mom was getting exhausted from her new job and late night work.

    They weren't superheroes, but Kayden and her family fought against things that most people didn't believe were real. The unexplained bothered people who couldn't understand or rationalize the nature of it. The whispers and looks at school hadn't ceased. With no explanation for Sadie's death, the town made up their own story. Rumors had run rampant. It didn't help that the newspaper had written a couple of stories about the event. None of the group had heard from Brooklyn and Gage. Their absence from school only fueled the whispers. A couple of rumors kept pointing to Gage being involved because of a ridiculous love triangle. Other whispers spoke about a group prank gone wrong. They centered the constant rumors on Kayden, though no one could really say how or why Kayden was involved. Those who talked about her claimed she moved to Harrisburg because she'd been kicked out of her old school. Others said her religion was witchcraft and Sadie had been caught in the crossfire.

    Owen and Rolland were having indirect encounters at school. The senior bully put his lackeys to work harassing Owen by staring, whispering or accidentally bumping into him in the hallway. Rolland was always around, but smart enough to distance himself from being involved. They would stop once Ayelyn showed up. The boys didn't want the image of stooping to bullying a girl, but Owen alone was fair game. Braelyn would take Ayelyn's place, but Owen being the prideful kid had no issue standing up for himself. Shay and Olivia were left alone. Since classmates had always labeled Shay as the chill kid, no one would engage in a conflict with him. Olivia was more than enough protection for him, anyway. Since she was one of the school's star female athletes, her clout around campus was secure from random harassment. The student's body did not hold her or her boyfriend accountable as involved in Sadie's demise. They just were unlucky to be there.

    Shades, on the other hand, loved the negative and positive attention. Despite his slim build, his connection to the group gave students a chance to engage with an insider. He was a non-threat, but had potential information and insight into his group's inner workings. He loved it. His best friend Drake who everyone considered the group leader was an altogether different matter. Drake had a true blue persona at the school. He mixed and matched with all the different stereotypes. He played JV football, but didn't dress varsity. Worked a part-time job with Owen on his grand-pa's farm. He made good grades, but had no problem hanging out with the outcasts of the school. Those were the kids who just didn't fit in with the distinct clicks. Drake was an excellent judge of character. He was the guy who broke up fights. He didn't start them. If he was defending Kayden, then something wasn't adding up.

For Kayden, the training wasn't as hard or difficult as she had imagined. Jackson imagined they would train like Batman, doing tough exercises and learning combat skills. It was quite the opposite. They started learning how to relax their minds and find focus. They were being taught to observe elements of ghost manifestations, hauntings, and people. They were not exorcists like in the movies who removed demons from people. They truly dealt with ghosts or manifestations of residual energy left from the past. You truly only needed one person to clean, but they had to be very knowledgeable, trained, unwavering in their beliefs and prepared. Hollyn had made that crystal clear. Never go at it alone. It is how family members ended up meeting their own demise earlier in life than what mother nature intended.

   Kayden's bloodline seemed to have a sensitivity to the supernatural and those elements, like ghosts were drawn to them; at least once they opened themselves up to the idea of the supernatural and being trained. Kayden had been distant the whole week from Drake and the others. She was hanging with them, but more tied into her own thoughts. She was reflecting on her new education after school with Aunt Hollyn.

   Friday came and with it, Kayden needed a good weekend away from school and the stares. It was the week of Halloween. Play-offs were looming in the school's air for football and tonight was the school's final regular season game. The scheduled opponent for them was the Benton Rangers. It would decide Harrisburg's rankings and home games. The 7th period bell rang, ending school class time, but starting a pep rally in the gym. Classes had been shortened all day to make room for the rally. All the kids left their last class and slowly made their way to the gym to raise the anticipation level of tonight's game. Kayden needed to get some rest was already relaxing after the bell. Unfortunately for her, relaxation was not in the cards.

***

As the middle of the afternoon continued on a crisp autumn Friday, the anticipation at Harrisburg High School was palpable. It was no ordinary Friday; it was the day of the much-awaited pep rally and senior night for the Bulldog's football team. The student body buzzed with excitement as they gathered in the school's gymnasium, where the initial rally was set to take place.

The gym was a sea of school spirit. Students were decked out in their school colors. Purple and white were everywhere. Some kids donned spirit faces covered in purple and white paint. Other teens held handmade posters, while many chanted along with the cheerleaders. Out came the marching band, playing catchy tunes that filled the air with an infectious energy. The cheerleaders executed flawless routines to the band's school song. The school's mascot, a fierce bulldog, pumped up the crowd with its antics. The atmosphere was electric as the student body came together, united in their support for their football team and to celebrate the seniors who were playing their last regular season home game on the gridiron.

Kayden had found her seat alongside Shades and Drake. Shades was styling some 80's sunglasses. He had informed Kayden they were replicas from a character named Hollywood from the movie 'Mannequin.' He told her Hollywood had an eclectic array of sunglasses in the movie and he thought the actor's style was before his time.

The highlight of the pep rally began when the football team, led by the head coach, made a dramatic entrance onto the basketball court. They emerged from the locker room area hidden by the bleachers. The coach introduced each senior player with a short, heartfelt speech. The booster club honored this year's seniors by awarding them with personalized jerseys as a token of appreciation for their dedication to the team and school. Some players were emotional as they waved goodbye to the crowd, aware this was one of their last moments as high school football athlete.

The head coach delivered an impassioned speech, reminding the entire student body of the importance of unity and school spirit after honoring the seniors. He emphasized that the Harrisburg High School community was not just a school; it was a family. The team was going to dedicate this game to Sadie and her family. The speech resonated deeply with the students, and they responded with resounding applause and cheers. Unfortunately, it also got Kayden and her friends some dirty looks.

To make matters worse for Kayden, instead of things quieting down over the terrible incident, they actually ratcheted up. Sadie had been a bright and spirited sophomore at Harrisburg High School, known for her contagious laughter and her passion for dance. Her sudden and tragic death sent shock-waves through the close-knit community of Harrisburg. The news spread like wildfire, infecting the fears of students, teachers, and parents alike.

The first reaction, upon hearing about Sadie's passing, was disbelief. She was only 15 years old, a life full of promise and potential, cut short by an unforeseen accident. The community couldn't fathom the idea that someone so young, so full of life, could be gone. As the news began to sink in, sadness and grief enveloped the community. The high school, usually bustling with youthful energy, was suddenly subdued and suspicious. Students who knew Sadie shared their memories, as their laughter now tinged with tears. Teachers, too, had found it challenging to concentrate on their lesson planning. They had known Sadie as a diligent and enthusiastic student, always eager to take part in class.

    The community was rallying together in their grief by holding a candlelight vigil that evening. It would occur after the senior football game. Administration voted to host the event at the school's football field, which was sure to see an overwhelming turnout. Kayden could only imagine the future tearful eulogies, stories, and heartfelt tributes that were sure to take place. Given the current situation with her and her friends being in the spotlight, it would not be a good idea for them to be present there.

    The community's overall attitude toward Sadie's death was growing from shock and sadness to a determination to celebrate her life. The Harrisburg community was coming together in the wake of Sadie's death, both to grieve and to find answers about her killer or cause of death. Kayden could feel the negative energy focused on her from the other kids around her. The training her aunt was orchestrating to her and her brother was a kind of reprieve from the current climate at school. It helped move her focus away from the scandal. When she wasn't training or at school, she tried to communicate with Drake. He had been wonderful and protective. He simply had an air about him which demanded others to at the very least respect his presence or word.

As the pep rally finally came to a close, Shades looked over at his two friends. He took his retro sunglasses off and had a serious expression on his face.

"Drake, man. It might be a smart move to not go to tonight's game, dude."

Drake shifted his gaze from Shades to the departing student body, who was making their way to the parking lot and cars. Kayden could tell he was struggling with his thoughts. His brow knit tightly together.

"I hear ya Jeremiah." Drake used his friend's first name, so Kayden could tell he was in serious mode right now.

"We have just as much a right to be there for Sadie, as well as anyone in this damn town! I feel like we owe it to her."

Jeremiah shook his head up and down in understanding, but he wouldn't relent his position.

"I get it, man. We were her close friends, but no one would believe the truth we know. At least, they wouldn't believe who is at fault. Listen buddy, maybe we can just stream a movie tonight and hammer some popcorn or something?" he weakly suggested.

"I'm down for that," came a voice, startling them.

Owen came walking up with his girlfriend, holding his hand.

The group took a relaxing breath, seeing trusted friends instead of angry teens.

"So you are okay with skipping the senior night game then, Owen?" questioned Drake.

The country boy shrugged and looked at Ayelyn when he replied.

"Yeah. Me and Ayelyn had been discussing this and she is a little worried I'll get into a scrap there." He looked up at Drake with frustration showing on his face. "Rolland and I have been doing this little dance of ours all week at school. He's itching for some payback over our minor altercation. This candle light vigil would be the perfect place for him to start some shit with me."

Drake nodded in agreement. He knew how shifty the larger senior boy could be and this wouldn't be beneath him to ruin the vigil just to get payback.

Kayden broke the tension.

"Look guys, I know I don't really know all of you too well, but I'd be willing to invite you guys over tonight and skip the game. We should call Brooklyn, Braelyn, Gage, Olivia and Shay as well. I'm sure my aunt won't care. She might even think it's for the best, you know?"

With that suggestion in mind, Jeremiah put his silly glasses back on, knowing that Drake would be better persuaded to stay away from the game if Kayden made the offer to hang at her house.

Ayelyn replied to Kayden's suggestion. "That sounds pretty cool Kayden. Owen could load his truck up with some firewood and we could cook s'mores or something outside. You have a back yard right?"

Kayden nodded. "Yes, it's a pretty decent size one and secluded from prying eyes."

Shades elbowed his buddy in the ribs. "Sounds like my kind of shin dig, right, man?"

Drake closed his eyes and the features on his face relaxed. When he opened them, everyone was staring at him. He broke into a smile.

"Okay, why not? A little down time away from all this drama and just hanging together seems like a smart move. Besides, we haven't done that since the incident."

They all nodded soberly at this statement.

Kayden broke the tension again.

"Great! We'll meet around 7:00 tonight."

Shades interjected. "We can listen to the game on the radio or YouTube where the high school's sports broadcasting class does home games. Ayelyn you get a hold of Braelyn and Brooklyn. I'll call Shay. Drake, you have Gage. Offer to pick him up since he doesn't have a vehicle."

They all agreed. The rest of the day was just getting started.

*****

When Kayden, Jackson and Aunt Hollyn made it home after school, Kayden called her mom to ask if her friends could come over that evening. Aunt Hollyn had been talking to Jackson about the varsity football game and the candle vigil afterwards. Jackson was engrossed in relaying the information he had gleaned today while at school to his aunt. On the flip side, Kayden had a contrasting idea about a backyard gathering by the fire-pit. That had a unique appeal to her.

Waiting for her mom to respond via text, she decided to run it by her brother and aunt.

"Guys," she said with a hopeful grin, interrupting them, "I was thinking it would be nice to invite some of my friends over tonight. We wanted to hang out by the fire-pit, toast some s'mores, and just unwind after this long week."

Aunt Hollyn and Jackson exchanged concerned glances. It hadn't been two weeks since Sadie's tragic passing in the cemetery, and the concerns were still fresh.

Aunt Hollyn gently spoke up, "Kayden, I know you want to hang out with your new friends, but maybe we should give it a little more time. You know, out of respect for Sadie."

Jackson nodded in agreement. "Aunt Hollyn is right. It just feels too soon, especially on a night like this, when everyone is remembering Sadie at the game to have a small party."

Kayden sighed, her shoulders slumping with disappointment. "I understand your concerns, but I think it could be a way for all of us to find some solace in each other's company, a way to honor Sadie's memory by being together. Besides, neither of you two have seen what it is like at the high school. Every time they bring up Sadie, my friends and I get more dirty looks and veiled threats."

Aunt Hollyn considered Kayden's words, her expression softening. "How about this, Kayden? We can still go to the game tonight, show our support for Sadie and the team, and maybe afterward, if you still want to have a small gathering, we can do it in a way that pays tribute to her."

Jackson nodded in agreement with Aunt Hollyn's compromise. "That sounds like a good idea. We can make it a special evening in Sadie's memory."

Kayden frowned. "You don't get it do you? We all want to go to the game and the candle vigil. The town doesn't want us to go. At least a few of the trouble making kids who keep causing a stir at school feel that way. If we go, it might get ugly. It only takes one of those kids to start something and then who knows how fast it will blow up?"

The evening sun was casting long shadows across the room from the windows. The air had become tense with the ongoing topic. Kayden stood near the fireplace, her arms crossed defiantly, while Aunt Hollyn paced back and forth, her face etched with worry.

Kayden's phone dinged. It was a response from her mom. Just as she was going to look at it, her aunt answered.

"I'm telling you, Kayden, it's just not a good time for friends over right now," Aunt Hollyn said, her voice tinged with frustration. "There's too much tension in town after Sadie's passing. It doesn't look good that everyone involved in the cemetery incident will be partying it up over here while the candlelight vigil is going on. People are upset, and we don't want to get involved in any more trouble."

Kayden's eyes blazed with defiance. "But Aunt Hollyn, no one wants us there at senior night. We have lives too and all this shit that's happened is unfairly affecting them. Having some friends over to chill by the fire who are hurting just as much as our family in the backyard won't hurt anyone."

Jackson sat down on the couch. His shoulders slumped inward. Aunt Hollyn saw his posture and raised an eyebrow.

"Well?" she asked.

Jackson grimaced in frustration. "I was going to ask if a new friend I made could come over and hang out tonight, too. Not a party," he clarified, "just gaming in my room."

Before Aunt Hollyn could respond, there was a

sharp knock on the front door. Startled, they exchanged glances, and Jackson got up to answer it. Deputy Ramsey stood on their doorstep, his stern expression reflecting the seriousness of his visit.

"Deputy Ramsey, what brings you here?" Jackson asked, concern etched on his face as he let the deputy in the house.

Ramsey cleared his throat and stepped inside. "I've got some news that concerns your family," he said, glancing at Aunt Hollyn, Jackson, and Kayden.

Kayden's defiant stance softened as she turned her attention to the deputy.

Hollyn responded, "What's going on, Ramsey?"

Ramsey took a deep breath. "I've been digging through the town's archives, trying to uncover some old records about the mining companies that operated here in the past. I stumbled upon something quite significant."

Aunt Hollyn and Jackson exchanged puzzled glances. "What did you find?" Aunt Hollyn asked, her voice full of apprehension.

Ramsey took out a yellowed, weathered document from his bag and handed it to Aunt Hollyn. She carefully opened it and read. Her eyes widened in disbelief as she scanned the words on the paper.

"This document," she said, her voice trembling, "it reveals a cover-up by one of the mining companies. They knew about the unsafe conditions in the mines where our great-grandfather worked. They hid the dangers and sacrificed the lives of many workers, including him."

Jackson's jaw dropped as he processed the revelation. "How is this even possible?"

Ramsey nodded gravely. "I'm not sure, but I

intend to look further into it. This might change the town's history and bring some justice to your family. I haven't showed Whip yet, but I'm sure he will find it very interesting."

Aunt Hollyn handed the document back to Ramsey, her hands shaking. "Thank you, Ramsey. Our family will need some time to process all of this."

"Do you think it ties into the incident at the cemetery?" Ramsey inquired.

Jackson answered before Hollyn could answer.

"I think it does." They all looked at him. "Think about it. Our great-great-whatever shows up and tells me to help them. He says the same thing to Kayden. Now what could 'them' refer to?"

"The other miners who died in the accident?" Kayden answered without thinking.

Jackson was nodding, "Precisely, sis. The town has blamed him for the accident all these years. What if the other miners who died are angry at the fact they died and the truth of their death went unknown?"

"Or unpunished," echoed the Deputy in deep thought. "Maybe they are lashing out at the town for not discovering the truth?"

"If the mining company covered the deaths up, they needed a scapegoat. Why choose our family to blame it on?" asked Aunt Hollyn.

"I need to dig a little more into the affairs of your great-great-grandfather with Whip. We need to see if we can get some clarification on any altercations he might have had with the mining company," Ramsey announced.

As Ramsey prepared to leave, he turned to the family once more, a look of concern in his eyes.

"There's something else I need to warn you

about. The candlelight vigil for Sadie is coming up, and I'd strongly advise against attending. The town is still reeling from her death, and there's a risk of retaliation from some of the community members, particularly Sadie's father."

Kayden looked at her aunt with a mix of sadness and 'I told you so' written on her face.

Hollyn rolled her eyes and ignored her niece. "We appreciate your concern, Ramsey," Hollyn replied.

Ramsey nodded, understanding the family's resolve. "Just be cautious and stay safe. If you need anything or if you have any more questions about the documents, don't hesitate to reach out." He paused before leaving the house. Looking back at the three of them, he said, "Don't go back to the cemetery before we know more." He specifically looked at Holly, "if and when you go, Whip and I will go with you. Understood?"

Hollyn's body language took a defensive stance over this last statement. She took a step towards Ramsey.

"Are you saying we can't handle the situation, Byron?"

Ramsey came back inside, but stayed only at the entrance of the door.

"Hollyn, I can't have you freelancing this on your own with no police presence. The cemetery is a damn crime scene right now. You show up there doing your thing and anyone sees it... How the hell can we rationally explain that in a police report?"

"You don't," Hollyn retorted.

"Sadie's father is beyond rational right now Hollyn," Ramsey challenged. "He's waiting for you or anyone in your family to mess up and give him a reason to make allegations towards you. We've done our due diligence, but if you go out there and he gets just a sniff of it...Let's just say he will make a dangerous enemy to have."

Jackson got up off the couch and stood by his aunt. Looking at Ramsey, he addressed his aunt softly.

"He's right Aunt Hollyn. You've been doing this all your life. Kayden and I are newbies. Can we just play this one safe?"

She looked at her nephew and her demeanor softened. She ruffled Jackson's hair playfully.

"Okay rat." She looked back at the deputy. "Alright Byron, we'll play it your way. Besides, once I talk to Kailynn we're going to need her to do some seer stuff. Thanks for coming out. As soon as you get a fix on the situation with Whip, you let me know. Okay?"

Ramsey smiled. He turned and stepped out. As Deputy Ramsey left their home, Aunt Hollyn, Jackson, and Kayden were left with a mix of emotions—shock at the uncovered family secret, determination to seek justice, and a somber awareness of the risks they faced in their tight-knit community. Despite the challenges, they were determined to face the past and present with strength and unity.

Kayden read her mom's text. She looked at her aunt. "Mom says it's okay to have friends over."

Hollyn looked at her niece. "Well, guess I'm outvoted. Let's get ready for tonight's home adventures in the yard then."

The siblings smiled and began texting their friends to head over later.

Chapter Fifteen: Egg Splatter

Deputy Ramsey had spent the better part of the morning sifting through old files and dusty archives. It was located in the cramped basement of the Courthouse vault. His fingers were smudged with ink, and his eyes ached from hours of poring over faded newspapers and yellowing documents.

Once Ramsey had left the Toth family, he made quickly for the police station. He parked in the building's rear and went into the back entrance. As he emerged from the dimly lit staircase, a sense of anticipation gnawed at him. He clutched a tattered manila envelope tightly, his findings from the depths of the archives. Deputy Ramsey knew that what he held inside could change the history of their little town forever. He also knew it could shake the foundations of a few locals who held grudges against the Toth family. Those kinds of grudges went generations deep.

Sheriff Warren "Whip" Anderson, a veteran of law enforcement and a respected figure, sat in his office. He had been investigating the mining accident of 1930 since Sadie's death. He knew there had to be some kind of link between the mining 'ghosts' the kids claim to have seen and the Toth family. Ever since he could remember, the Toth family had been the target of so many locals for events occurring in the past. He knew better.

According to most of the findings he could come up with at the station, there was no actual link. The company had blamed Joe Toth, a miner of Hungarian descent, for the deaths of eight of his colleagues. The town had ostracized Toth; shunned as a scapegoat. Unknown to Whip, Deputy Ramsey's recent discoveries promised to shed new light on that fateful day.

Ramsey arrived at Sheriff Anderson's office. Whip was sitting behind a cluttered desk, poring over a collection of weathered maps and documents. Whip looked up as Ramsey entered, his piercing gray eyes narrowing with curiosity. The tension in the room was palpable as Deputy Ramsey laid out the contents of the manila envelope on Whip's desk.

"These documents are like buried treasure, Whip," Ramsey said, his voice hushed. "I found these hidden away, deep in the archives. They paint a different picture of that mining accident. If I'm reading them right, they set Joe Toth up, Sheriff."

Whip Anderson leaned forward, studying the papers spread before him. His fingers traced the yellowed pages, each one a piece of the puzzle. "How did you come across these, Ramsey?"

The Hungarian Cemetery Secrets Within Backup

Deputy Ramsey explained the serendipitous discovery of the documents. He went to explain how they linked the mining accident to a scandal involving the mining company, one that went far beyond mere negligence. As Whip read through the evidence, his face grew increasingly grim. The weight of the revelation settled in, and they both realized that justice was long overdue for Joe Toth and the families of the eight miners who had perished.

"You know what this could mean Bryon?" Whip asked his deputy.

Ramsey turned around and shut the door, making sure they both were alone before he answered. Sitting across from the sheriff, he responded in a low voice.

"The mining company no longer exists, Warren. There will be no one to refute the evidence except any locals who still have a grudge against the Toth family. They may not accept the evidence lightly. With Sadie's recent death, the town wants another scape goat. We both know her death goes way outside our pay grade. We don't deal with the supernatural."

The sheriff sat back and put both hands behind his head, thinking. "Agreed. The supernatural is the Toth's department. It will be tough protecting them and their secret if we have townsfolk intentionally following and harassing them. Keep in mind the voters who elected me want answers."

The room grew quiet as both men sat reflecting. Each of them had their reasons for helping the Toths. They both had seen things while helping the family, which were unexplainable. People didn't want to hear about ghosts or supernatural occurrences. The only time people were willing to engage in spectral speculation was if they were being affected directly. Even then, they kept quiet for fear of what their neighbors or community would think.

Ramsey broke the silence first. "Warren, we are going to need more information before we go public with this," he said, pointing at the fresh evidence.

Whip nodded his agreement. This information would typically help the investigation progress. Unfortunately, they were exploring a case from several decades ago. Further, it didn't connect Sadie's death to anyone because her death had been supernatural.

Grabbing his keys and standing up, Whip replied, "Let's go pay our local historian a visit. Perhaps we can get better acquainted with who some of the key players back then were and how this whole mess got started. I'll give her a quick call, letting her know we're on our way."

Sheriff Anderson and Ramsey sought the town's local historian, Sarah Munroe. She had spent years delving into Southern Illinois' past, and her knowledge was second to none. Whip needed her help to piece together the full story of Joe Toth and the scandal that had remained hidden for over ninety years.

The two lawmen set out from the sheriff's office and made their way through Harrisburg's remaining brick streets. The moon was now sitting high in the night, casting an orange glow over the town's historic buildings. They arrived at Sarah Munroe's quaint little home, which at one time had served as Harrisburg's local library, its windows adorned with lace curtains and shelves overflowing with books and dusty tomes.

When they arrived, Sheriff and Ramsey went upstairs to level two, where Sarah's office was located. Whip didn't bother knocking. He went right in and found Sarah poring over some old maps on her table in the middle of the room. Sarah greeted them warmly, her gray hair neatly tied back in a bun, and her glasses perched on the tip of her nose. Whip gave her a quick summary of Ramsey's discovery. Her eyes widened with intrigue.

"Joe Toth's story has been an old wound in our town's history," she mused. "But what you've uncovered sets a precedence that events of the past are not what they seem. Let's dig deeper into the past and unravel the truth behind that mining accident."

She grabbed her keys and went to the small closet door. Opening it, she took out three rechargeable modern lanterns. She passed one to each of the men. "We're going to head downstairs to the basement where all of my archives are located. The building we're in is super old, as both of you know. The lighting really sucks down there, so I have a few of these babies here to help with the research," she informed them.

Both of the officers nodded their understanding and followed Sarah down to the basement.

Ramsey, Anderson, and Munroe gathered in the dimly lit archives room of the large open basement. Dust motes danced in the feeble shafts of the flickering fluorescent bulbs that pierced the dark confines of the room. The unreliable bulbs cast an antique, almost mystical atmosphere over the area. The air was heavy with the musty scent of old papers and aged leather-bound books.

Whip had embarked on a quest to uncover the long-forgotten story of a mining accident that had occurred in 1930. A story which now had since become shrouded in mystery and scandal. Sheriff Anderson, a force known for his no-nonsense approach, had a personal connection to the case. The Toth's grandfather had been a miner in those fateful tunnels who now appeared framed for the accident.

Deputy Ramsey, who was also known for his keen investigative skills, meticulously sorted through stacks of dusty, yellowed documents, while Sarah Munroe, the town's resident historian, flipped through a stack of well-worn journals. Whip felt lucky to have such a stalwart companion on his side. He also knew Sarah had dedicated her life to preserving the town's history, and her expertise was indispensable in unlocking the secrets of the past.

"Sarah, do you think we'll ever find out what really happened down there?" Sheriff Anderson asked, his voice filled with a mix of determination and uncertainty.

Sarah looked up from her reading, her eyes gleaming with a combination of excitement and trepidation. "We're about to find out, Sheriff," she replied, pushing her round spectacles up on her nose. "I've come across something intriguing about Joe Toth, the man blamed for the accident."

Sarah recounted the background of Joe Toth, a miner who had become the scapegoat for the tragic event. She explained how the town's mining company had a history of exploiting its workers, paying them meager wages and subjecting them to dangerous working conditions. Joe Toth, it seemed, had had his fair share of run-ins with the company over unfair labor practices.

"In these old reports," Sarah continued, "I found evidence that suggests Joe was a thorn in the mining company's side. He'd been trying to organize the miners, advocating for better safety regulations and fairer wages. But what's most intriguing is that Joe mentioned something in his personal journal I found; something that may have sealed his fate."

Whip's ears perked up, but he had questions. "Personal journal?"

Sarah stopped her reading and pulled down her glasses to look at Warren. "In the past, Sheriff, workers kept journals when or if they needed to document issues occurring at their job. They didn't have computers or smart phones. His journal or log book has some pretty interesting things in it. Unfortunately for Joe, because the company, as we have recently discovered, was potentially covering up the accident. They used the journal as evidence against Toth by painting him as angry and out for payback against his employer."

This line of logic made perfect sense to Whip. It was not like the police back then couldn't be swayed easily enough by an influential industry such as the coal mine to see things their way.

Deputy Ramsey leaned in, his curiosity piqued. "What did he mention, Sarah?"

Sarah lowered her voice, as if sharing a long-buried secret. "It appears that Joe Toth stumbled upon a hidden secret within the mine, something the company desperately wanted to keep under wraps. According to his journal, he believed there was a vast underground cavern filled with valuable minerals the company didn't want anyone to discover. It also was leaking elements of pocketed gas in the mine shafts which could cause asphyxiation or worse an explosion."

Sheriff Anderson and Deputy Ramsey exchanged glances, their eyes reflecting a growing sense of unease. "So, are you saying that the mining company might have been willing to kill to protect their secret?" the sheriff asked, his voice filled with a mix of anger and disbelief.

    Sarah nodded gravely. "It's a possibility, Sheriff. Joe's notes imply that the company might have gone to great lengths to ensure the cavern's existence remained concealed, even if it meant endangering the lives of the miners. If we can find more evidence to support this, it could change the entire narrative of that 1930 mining accident."

    As they delved deeper into the archives, the trio of dedicated investigators realized they were not just unearthing history; they were unraveling a web of deception, greed, and tragedy. With each passing page, the truth behind the mining accident of 1930 was slowly coming to light, and it promised to be a scandal that would forever alter the town's perception of its past.

    ****

    Kayden and her friends gathered around a crackling fire-pit amid a sprawling, moonlit backyard. The flames danced, casting flickering shadows that stretched and swayed across their faces. They were becoming a quickly tight-knit group, each one bringing their unique personalities to the circle.

    Shades, the group's resident storyteller, had a way with words that could transport everyone to the past with his vivid tales. Drake always kept the atmosphere flowing, while Braelyn, with her calming presence, was the one to turn to for advice and solace. Owen, the country boy, was known for his spontaneous ideas, and Shay, the philosophical artist, was often lost in thought, just enjoying the surrounding beauty.

Olivia, Gage, Ayelyn, and Brooklyn were the friends who rounded out the circle, each contributing their own energy and laughter to the mix. They all reveled in the fire's warmth and the delectable scent of marshmallows roasting over the flames.

As the Bluetooth speaker filled the air with the distant sounds of a football game, the group's conversation shifted to the uncomfortable topic of Sadie. Sadie had met a tragic and inexplicable end at the nearby Hungarian cemetery. It had become an eerie place. The location held its fair share of ghost stories, but nothing like what happened to Sadie. The atmosphere grew tense as they spoke of her death, with many theories and suspicions. But now, they found themselves trapped in a shadowy web of secrets and grief after the tragic death of their friend Sadie.

The mood was instantly changed when Aunt Hollyn came out of the house holding a large plate. As she approached, the smell of recently cooked chocolate chip cookies hit the group's nostrils.

The cookies hit the spot. Hollyn let a tray of them out and went back into the house. She had other plans tonight, which included her sister.

Just as the game was about to end, playing from the speaker, the night was shattered by the sudden pelting of eggs. The gooey missiles rained down upon the group from the cover of the trees, their laughter turning to surprise and annoyance. Gage and Owen, quick to react, recognized the culprits hiding in the shadows and sprang into action.

"It's that asshole Olson who I got into a fight with at school," cried Gage.

Owen added, "He's also with Dickerson. I'd

recognize that fat dip-shits' laugh anywhere."

Drake stood in front of Kayden protectively with his back getting pelted by the eggs. "Looks like they didn't go to the game," he observed to his classmates.

Shay had lifted the lid off the cooler of soda he brought, using it as a shield. If he was worried, angry or upset, it wasn't showing. Olivia got behind him.

The eggs were random and hit everywhere, splattering on contact. Shades had simply dropped to the ground in a kneeling position, putting his hands over the back of his head.

Brooklyn and Braelyn grabbed onto each other in a hug, trying to hide from the falling meteoric missiles flying in the air.

Gage had turned his back to where the eggs were coming from just in time to see one hit Braelyn square in the face. She let out an angry scream. Gage rushed over to her and Brooklyn, now standing in front of them to block anymore oncoming objects. It was too late. They all had gotten splattered; some more than others. Braelyn looked at Gage with a red mark on her face from where the egg had made contact. It was all in her hair. She saw Gage's face and knew he was going to ignite. He growled.

"Gage, it's okay. They're just eggs..." Braelyn said, trying to calm Gage down, but all Gage could see was red.

"The bastard's going to pay," he said in a dark voice. "I'm going to WAFFLE STOMP HIS SACK..." He turned and ran toward the egg throwers. Owen was hot on his trail. Both lit out so fast, no one else had time to think or react.

Ayelyn squealed Owen's name, telling him to stop, but Owen was already gone into the tree line.

Looking at each other, they went into action. The rest of the group, fueled by a mixture of indignation and excitement, joined in the pursuit. The chase was a wild one, filled with shouts. As they navigated through the dark woods, the moonlight cast eerie silhouettes on the towering trees.

As they raced through the dense undergrowth, their adventure led them to a familiar place on the other side—the cemetery.

The very location where Sadie had met her mysterious and untimely end. The group paused, their breaths visible in the chilly night air, and a somber hush fell over them as they realized where they had ended up. The gravestones stood like silent sentinels, each one holding secrets and stories from long ago. Up ahead, they could see Owen surrounded by Dickerson and his two lackeys from the last party, punching at each other. Gage and Olson were wrestling around on the ground.

It was seniors versus sophomores and the odds were not in their favor. Drake made a hard dash towards Owen. Brooklyn, seeing the very boy who had antagonized her at school, ran over to him and jumped on his back. Brooklyn started pulling at Olson's hair and scratching at his face with her fingernails. Olson immediately stopped fighting with Gage. He now was trying to dislodge one furious girl off his back.

At that moment, their carefree evening took an unexpected turn. The combination of their pursuit of the egg-throwers and their accidental return to the cemetery stirred an uneasy feeling in the group. Shades ran to Brooklyn and worked to peel her off of Olson before he threw her off. He got her detached as she kicked toward Olson, while Shades pulled her back.

Shay helped him subdue Brooklyn. Olivia was also helping Shay.

Owen was trading punches with Dickerson, while Drake was taking on his two henchmen, Vargo and Silas. The two boys were about the same size as Drake, but not really fighters. They were more crowd support for bullies. Neither really had the stomach for fighting, but with their 'noble' leader, Rolland, fighting against Owen, neither had the stomach to leave him. They knew it would have consequences later for them, so the teen melee continued around the tombstones.

Kayden was at a complete loss of thought. She didn't know what to do. The scene before here was something out of the Cobra Kai series on Netflix. She and Ayelyn stood there yelling at the boys to stop. Feeling helpless, she could only stand there and watch them play it out. She watched Drake knock Vargo off his feet onto the ground by kicking him in the groin. He was being held from behind by Silas. When Vargo went down, she caught a quick movement from something a short way away from them. It was a light shining from...

She froze in fear. It was her great-great-grandfather looking towards her from a ways off. The eyes glowed in the night and the little candle light from his work hat flickered back and forth.

"Oh, my God!" she stammered.

Ayelyn standing next to her had been paying attention to Owen. The words from Kayden brought her eyes away from Owen and to her friend.

"What is it?" she asked Kayden.

"Look," pointed Kayden to the ghostly miner.

Ayelyn grabbed Kayden's arm and froze in fear. She had enough wits about her to scream at Owen.

"Owen, they are coming back!"

Owen had Rolland in a headlock and was applying pressure on his fat neck when his girlfriend's words got his attention. Looking around at what she was pointing at, he saw the ghostly apparition as well.

"Shit," he gasped, letting go of Dickerson, who collapsed coughing on the ground.

Owen backed away from Rolland and walked backwards towards the two girls. He stopped in front of them and both girls peeked around each of his shoulders. Owen looked towards Drake.

Drake was still stuck in a bear hug. He popped his head back into Silas' nose. Silas let go immediately and Drake spun, landing an elbow upside Silas' face, knocking him to the ground. Drake backed away, putting both boys on the ground in front of him instead of being between them. He was panting.

Kayden yelled to Drake. "Drake, look!" pointing behind him.

Drake spun and saw the ghostly miner who was walking towards him and the others slowly. Drake turned and saw Gage getting pummeled by the senior who was on top of him punching away. Drake sprinted up on Olson and grabbed him from behind. The adrenaline of the ghost gave him new reserves of energy and he slung the senior off Gage away to the side. Reaching down, he grabbed Gage by the shirt and pulled him up. Gage's face was swollen around the eyes and his nose had blood pouring out it.

"C'mon Gage. We have to go. Those damn ghosts are coming back."

Gage didn't respond verbally, but put his arm around Drake's shoulders, using him as a crutch to walk. Drake to his credit grabbed Gage around the waist and helped him.

Olson got up from the ground and looked at the two boys trying to walk back to their friends standing in a clump together. He noticed Rolland was still on the ground, trying to get back to breathing without coughing. Silas and Vargo were both kneeling on the ground. Vargo was still holding his crotch and Silas looked to have a possible broken nose as he held his face. He shook his head.

What a bunch of pussies, he thought.

However, his thoughts were quickly broken by unfamiliar noises erupting from the darkness. They were of a whining mix. To Olson, it sounded close to the noises walkers made like in The Walking Dead Series he watched on television. Those sounds were eerie and all around him.

Kayden and the group huddled together away from the four bullies who stood at various places among the grave markers. The familiar sounds were now becoming more solidified in the air and everyone knew what was getting ready to follow.

Kayden looked at Drake.

"What are we going to do? We can't just leave these guys here. You know what will happen to them."

Gage interrupted, "Why not? Piss on these guys," he spat.

Drake, holding Gage up immediately disagreed. "Those guys are ass-clowns, but they don't deserve what is coming, Gage," he said disapprovingly. "Sometimes I wonder about you, man."

"Besides," Shades followed, "if those guys disappear, they are going to blame everything on all of us. We all are back out here while this is going on? How the heck can we explain that to the police and town?"

Everyone nodded. Jeremiah was right. They had to do something. Brooklyn yelled at the boys.

"Olson! Rolland! Silas! Vargo! Get out of there. Come over to us now!"

All four of them looked at her, confused. She pointed behind them and they looked as one to where the noises were filtering in from. The specter was still moving forward by the glow of the moonlight. Now something else appeared. The blackened forms of the mangled and wretched remains of the former miners who had burned to death so long ago. They moaned as they closed in on the four boys who stood among the tombstones. Fear consumed Silas and Vargo. They started making their way towards the group. Olson wasn't so intimidated by the appearance of the ragged masses moving slowly.

He looked back at the group standing together, waving him to run. "This is how you guys killed Sadie isn't it? You lure her here and dress in these costumes to scare her," he spat at them. "I won't be fooled by this horseshit," he declared to them.

"I don't know, man," answered Rolland, standing up and nervously moving slowly towards Drake's group. "If they are all over there standing, who the hell is dressed up in those black outfits? I can't even see their faces."

Olson looked hard too at them and then it happened. The candle-lights lit up on the heads of these things. At once he became concerned, but then the lights seemed calming and that initial emotion of worry disappeared. It was replaced by a calm easiness. All that existed was the candlelight. He thought he could hear voices around him, but they were far away and muffled.

Rolland yelled again at Olson. He had no intention of sticking around. He turned to the group behind him and began running. Just as he took his third step, he tripped on a hidden tombstone marker sticking in the ground. He fell hard and his large body jiggled forward, knocking the breath out of him.

Kayden knew both of them would not get out by themselves without help. She grabbed Drake by the arm and spun him away from the sight.

"I've got an idea," she blurted. She turned to face the rest of the group. "Who has their cell phones with them?" she asked.

They all pulled them out. No one went anywhere without a cell phone anymore. She smiled. "Okay, we only have one shot at this. Those things displace when light is directly shined on them, but it won't last. They'll short out our phones once we use them."

Just then, a yell went out. Some of the blackened figures were upon Olson. They started melting back into the ground and Olson with them. Olson himself sank slowly down into the earth. It had knocked him out of his stupor, but his feet had already sunk.

Kayden turned back around to the others. The training over the last week took over. Aunt Hollyn had instructed her on how do deal with a large group of entities. She didn't have any of the tools, but she knew most of the rules surrounding them.

"Shay and Olivia, take Gage out of here," she order. "Shades, Ayelyn, Brooklyn and Owen get Rolland on his feet and out of here. They haven't got to him yet. Head immediately to my house. Avoid looking at their little candlelights." They nodded. "Go now!" she exclaimed loudly, kicking everyone into motion. She looked at Drake.

"Give me your phone," she commanded. "You grab Olson and I'll take care of the specters." Drake nodded and turned. They saw Olson was now up to his knees, pounding at the ground, but to no avail. Drake looked back at Kayden.

"You ready?" he asked weakly.

She nodded. "Let's go," she said as she took off at a run towards Olson. Drake darted past her. Olson saw them coming to help. He reached out to Drake's approaching form, yelling for help. Panic and sheer terror were plastered on his face. His face was all Drake focused on. He would not get pulled in by those things again. He reached Olson and wrapped both arms around him.

"Don't let me go down there, man," pleaded Olson to Drake.

Drake replied, "Grab onto me hard, Olson. Get ready to kick your feet out while I pull."

The specters started coming back up at the unexpected newcomer coming to their prey's rescue. They began to rise and proceed to take Drake as well. Drake kept his eyes closed and commanded Olson to do the same.

Suddenly, Kayden was there and immediately flashed the cell phones flashlights directly at the four supernatural beings in front of her. The light penetrated the ghostly beings and they shrieked in pain.

"NOW!" yelled Kayden. Drake heaved with all his might. Olson used every muscle he had in his legs to yank them upward. The ground gave and both of them fell backwards hard. Just then, the lights on the phones went out. The batteries drained as the ghostly candlelights' flames grew larger.

Kayden didn't waste any time. She backed off, bent over and helped Drake get up. Drake pulled Olson up as well. He had lost both his shoes, but his feet seemed perfectly fine.

"Run," said Drake.

They all three saw ahead of them the other group helping the very large Dickerson towards Kayden's house. They were almost on top of them when the group ahead simply stopped. Kayden couldn't believe they would just stop running. She and the other two boys almost ran smack into them.

"What in the hell are you guys doing?" questioned a panicked Drake.

Shades responded, "There are two more of those damn things standing between us and the wooded area leading back to Kayden's house."

"Dammit," exclaimed Kayden. "Take your phones and directly shine it on them," she commanded.

"No good," responded Brooklyn. "Mine is dead."

"So is mine," Ayelyn confirmed in a terrified voice. Owen had his arm around her protectively.

"What do we do now?" Shades asked, turning to Kayden.

She was out of options. "Seems only bright lights faze these things and we're out of those," she said resignation oozing out of her mouth.

"We could rush them," suggested Drake.

"I'm not running anywhere near them," Rolland responded, backing away from the approaching two figures. He pushed his way through the group back towards the cemetery.

"Are you crazy, fat-ass?" yelled Owen. "You wanna go back to the cemetery?"

"Beats staying here waiting for those other two things coming towards us," retorted Dickerson.

"They've flanked behind us too," Jeremiah observed, looking past Dickerson. The senior turned around and took a brief glimpse of the other figures.

"They've regrouped," Drake informed the group.

Just then, two bright lights emerged from behind the two approaching figures. The figures shrieked in pain and faded away immediately. In their place stood Aunt Hollyn and Deputy Ramsey. Both were waving around ignited roadside flares. The light was intense and none of the entities seem to want any part of the flares.

Flairs? thought Kayden. The ghostly beings could manipulate electricity, batteries, or anything of tech worthiness, but fire or natural chemicals were immune to their ability. At least, that is what Aunt Hollyn had taught her and Jackson.

"You guys," commanded Deputy Ramsey, "get going over here now!" None of the kids needed any prompting. They all made a hasty retreat towards their rescuers. As they all united, Ramsey told them to follow him. Hollyn followed up the rear. As Kayden went past her, she could see the displeasure in her aunt's face.

Great, Kayden thought. *Aunt Hollyn is going to rip me a new one for this.*

Chapter Sixteen: Riddles in the Dark

Upon clearing the tree line, Kayden found herself back to their original fire-pit. Broken eggs laid everywhere on the ground and splatter from them decorated the grass, trees, gravel and anywhere else they exploded. Everyone was sitting or huddled around each other in different pockets around the fire. Deputy Ramsey was looking at Gage, who was sitting on Shay's cooler. Olivia was applying ice to his face from the cooler. From a squatting position, he looked up at Kayden when she and Drake came up. Aunt Hollyn wasn't far behind. Her flare was still going, but she calmly walked over to the fire-pit and dropped it in with the logs.

Putting her hands on her hips indignantly, she turned to Kayden.

"Okay," she began, "whose idea was it to go back into that cemetery after you had all been warned not to? Huh?" she prodded.

Kayden opened her mouth, but another voice beat her to it.

"It was my fault, ma'am." Olson had collapsed to his knees on the ground and tears were streaming down his face. His body was exhausted and all the energy he had earlier had played itself out. "Me and a few of those guys," he continued, pointing at Dickerson and his lackeys, "came out here to play a joke on everyone. We thought it would be funny to pelt them with eggs and run off." He held his head down dejectedly.

Hollyn raised an eyebrow at the admission from the older teen.

"How did that turn out for you?" another voice answered, coming from the house.

Everyone turned to see whose voice it was coming from behind them. Whip and Kailynn had exited from the back door and were walking towards the kids. Whip had a very serious expression on his face. It definitely wasn't one of tolerance right now.

"It was a mistake, sir," Olson replied weakly.

"Damn right it was, son," Whip curtly replied. "From what I have gathered in the last few minutes upon arriving here with Deputy Ramsey, you and your so-called pals and their hazing effort may have some serious consequences. First," he said, showing one finger as he counted the issues, "you were trespassing. Second, you assaulted everyone here by hitting them with foreign objects, even if they were eggs. Third, you four are all high school seniors and probably every bit 18 years old. You engaged in a physical altercation with these under age teens and put a hell of a beating on this young man right here."

Whip patted Gage on the shoulder reassuringly. Deputy Ramsey stood up besides Whip and looked over at Hollyn.

"You would be in your rights to press charges against these young men, Miss Toth."

Kailynn walked over to her sister and responded to Ramsey.

"I think tonight's events were more effective in learning lessons than perhaps arresting anyone Deputy Ramsey. Whip," she said, looking to the Sheriff. "If these young men promise to stop harassing our kids here as well as spreading rumors at school about Sadie's passing, then I'm willing to not press any charges."

Whip tipped his hat to Kailynn respectfully. He nodded to Ramsey. The deputy walked over and grabbed Olson by the arm and helped him stand. He then pointed at the other three boys who had crashed the party. "You three and this one here," he said, shaking Olson's arm, "will come with me. I'll be taking you home tonight and speaking to each of your parents about tonight's little stunt."

"What about the cemetery?" cried Rolland. "What about those things running around out there? They almost got Olson," he whimpered, pointing at Olson. "They came after all of us. How you going to explain that to our parents?"

Whip immediately stepped in and addressed everyone.

"The cemetery was supposed to be off limits right now. It is an active crime scene and you dumb-asses went right in there and trampled shit all over the place. It disturbed the scene and contaminated potential evidence. The Deputy and I will have to start all over again. That alone is a punishable offense which would get you certain jail-time and suspicion of Sadie's death."

"You can't be serious," retorted Rolland.

Whip got right up into Rolland's face. "Oh, I'm deadly serious Dickerson. So, I'm going to give you and your buddies some FRIENDLY advice." Whip put strong emphasis on the word, friendly. "The events you saw in the cemetery might have been the moonlight casting weird shadows around and perhaps with all the fighting going on, it just seemed there was something there, but in fact it was just the adrenaline. Understand?"

Rolland swallowed hard as Whip was almost nose to nose with him. Silas and Vargo began nodding and agreeing immediately.

Dickerson nodded as well. "Okay, I got it Sheriff. Tonight was just a prank gone bad and we all got carried away fighting in the cemetery. Nothing else happened."

"Make sure you remember that, Rolland. If I hear a bunch of shit being spouted out about tonight's events from the grapevine, I'm coming straight to you. He looked at all four of them.

He nodded to Ramsey. Ramsey took his cue and escorted all four of the boys to his police car and got them situated inside. He came back to the fire and the rest of the group. He moved closer to Hollyn and Kailynn.

"You guys need to figure out how you are going to handle these kids here when we leave. I'll take care of the dip shits in the car and their families, but given the recent events we've uncovered tonight along with another romp in the cemetery, it might be important to think about possibly leveling with these kids."

Hollyn shook her head on that last part. "You take care of the bully's Ramsey. We'll deal with our kiddos here. Telling the truth may not be the right solution tonight."

Ramsey shifted his weight uncomfortably and looked at Kailynn. "You were always more reasonable than Hollyn," ignoring Hollyn's glare and arms crossing defiantly. "Perhaps you can talk some good sense into her."

Hollyn took a step towards Ramsey, but Kailynn butted in front of her.

"Thank you for your help, Deputy. I'm sure we will manage. We'll talk more tomorrow."

Ramsey tipped his hat at Kailynn. "Ma'am," he replied respectfully as he turned around and headed for his car. Whip grabbed him by the arm and they both moved out of earshot of everyone. Everyone could see Whip was instructing something to his deputy. When Whip had finished his quick conversation, Ramsey went to the car and drove off.

Once Ramsey drove off, Whip came back to the group and stood over by the fire. He put both his hands out to warm them up, rubbing them together. Everyone watched expectantly. Whip took a deep breath and exhaled slowly.

He looked around at everyone. "Well, it has been quite a night, guys. I guess we need to have a quick chat about tonight's events."

The teens nodded in agreement. The first time at the cemetery had been but a blur, but this time it was definitive. There was something bad in that place and beyond explanation.

"Given the things you've seen already, I won't blow sunshine up your asses," the Sheriff said bluntly. "Those two over there," he said, pointing at Hollyn and Kailynn will be more knowledgeable of the things you've been seeing and can explain it better than I can. Here's what I know." He cleared his throat. Looking at Gage, "son, you definitely got in a fight with the young men we just hauled out of here. All of you did," he clarified to everyone. "Now, given the fact no one was harmed who went back into the cemetery, we will leave all that out of the story. I know you will want to discuss it some amongst yourselves and Kayden's family there," he said again, pointing to them.

"Just note, I nor the deputy are blind or ignorant to the events you have seen. However, it isn't something we go spouting out to the locals. There's no telling what kind of hornet's nest it will cause and it can only get worse for you guys around school and in our community. I'd like to keep a lid on what you've seen, so we can deal with it quietly before things get out of hand."

The sheriff looked around at everyone sitting there to make sure they understood what he was saying. When no one answered, he nodded his head in acceptance of their quiet response.

"We will get this taken care of and none of you need to worry about the cemetery or events that happened there involving Miss Sadie."

There was a collective sigh of relief from the teens, especially on that last part.

Hollyn walked over to the sheriff and thanked him while escorting him back to his squad car. Once he had pulled out of the drive, she made her way back to the group. Concern was laced all over her face, but Kayden could see there was more frustration than anything hiding behind her facade.

"Ms. Toth?" came Drake's voice. "I was hoping maybe you could shed some light on what we have been dealing with here?" Drake's voice was one of respect and Hollyn could truly see the concern on the boy's face.

Hollyn took a deep breath and let her shoulders slump in resignation a little. Looking at her niece and then sister, she responded to Drake.

"I was going to simply try to dismiss some events or down play them to a degree, but given the current status of your direct interaction with the paranormal in the cemetery, it would be insulting." Hollyn frowned and hesitated for a moment before continuing.

She bit her bottom lip, then said, "What you have seen twice now in the cemetery are ghosts. You can call them specters, dark figures, or anything else you'd like. The fact is, they are ghosts of the souls from the past, still trapped here on our mortal plane of existence."

"Trapped?" echoed Shades from his sitting spot. "What traps a ghost?"

Kailynn spoke up in response. "They do it to themselves to a degree."

"Why would any person intentionally become a ghost who just stays in the same place scaring or hurting anyone?" Olivia chided in disbelief. "I mean, what could they possibly gain by doing something like that?"

Hollyn stepped toward the fire and looked down on Olivia who was standing behind her boyfriend. Shay was now sitting on the cooler again and her arms were draped around his neck.

"Trust me, Olivia, they do not want to be here, nor had they intentionally planned on the situation they find themselves in now," Hollyn responded.

Braelyn snickered a bit, "Well, they are in it now and don't seem to have a problem hurting people."

Many of the group nodded their agreement.

Kayden who was standing next to Drake, shifted her weight on the other foot. "The situation depends on their manner of death and what life was like for them." Everyone turned their faces towards Kayden. She couldn't read exactly what each of them was thinking about her based on her response to Braelyn. Owen had raised an eyebrow at her response and put his arm around Braelyn.

"How do you know that?" Owen asked earnestly.

Aunt Hollyn beat her to the punch. "I taught her that," Hollyn responded to Owen. He closed his mouth and nodded.

Gage who had been quiet this whole time after slowly recovering from the beating he took from Olson broke his silence.

"And who taught you?"

Hollyn looked him squarely in the eye when she answered. "The family business."

"Hollyn," chided Kailynn.

"What?" she retorted.

"Guys," interrupted Kayden. "Can we please argue another time when it is not in front of my friends?"

Both sisters looked at each other, emotions

seething under the surface. They managed to at least calm down enough to put on a good front. The other teens knew there was tension there, but politely ignored the minor confrontation.

"Without saying too much guys, let's just say our family comes from generational experience passed down. Trust me."

"I trust you," Drake responded immediately.

Shades stood up next to his buddy. "I will second that thought," he said to support Drake, lowering his sunglasses and wiggling his eyebrows for effect.

Brooklyn gave a huge eye-roll and gave a little huff. "So then, what is this cemetery's issue then?"

Kayden smiled at Shades and Drake for their support. She looked at Brooklyn who was still holding ice on Gage's face.

"The ghosts we are seeing were once the miners who worked in the mines here in Ledford. I don't think they are actually buried in the cemetery's part you've been at. They are located somewhere in the original Hungarian Cemetery to the left of the one you have been at," answered Hollyn.

Owen frowned. "We already know as much about the miners. Remember Jeremiah's storytelling at the fire?" he questioned rhetorically. "What we want to know is why are they terrorizing us and there's another actual cemetery out there?"

Kayden looked at everyone and then at her aunt. Hollyn nodded in understanding. Kayden stepped forward. Everyone's eyes were on her.

"The accident in the mines killed those men and my great, you know, grandfather. Their souls are at unrest from the accident. They may be mad or feel there is some message they want to impart to others here on the earthly plane. They need to be helped into the next life. They haunt the area we think until justice can be served on their behalf."

The response was eerily quiet. Only the crackling of the fire could be heard along with the occasional rustling of leaves from the wind. A response came from an unlikely voice.

Shay responded, "Do you actually know where they are buried in the older cemetery part we haven't been to? I mean, how do we help them go into the next life without getting hurt by them?"

"Who said anything about helping them?" Gage replied sharply.

Shay looked at his friend with a kind expression and shrugged his shoulders. "You don't have to help them, Gage. It's okay dude. I know if I was stuck here and couldn't get free, I'd hope someone from somewhere would help me."

"You being too naive, baby," said Olivia. "We never have to go into that cemetery again. Why help those things at all after what they did to our friend?" Olivia, standing behind Shay, squatted down and threw her arms protectively around her boyfriend. Shay reached up and patted her arms lovingly.

He looked to the side of her face was and answered. "It's not that I think what they did to Sadie was right or justified, however do we really want that to happen to anyone else in our town?"

Shades stood up and addressed Kayden. "You still haven't said what 'we' actually need to do to help stop them." Jeremiah had taken his glasses off and the serious expression on his face showed his concern.

Before Kayden could respond, her aunt chimed in.

"None of you are going to help. We'll deal with this issue. The situation is out of your scope of experience. I admire your willingness to hear Kayden out and even some of you are open to helping, but this calls for experts." Hollyn walked over to Kayden and stood next to her. Drake was on the other side.

"What exactly makes you guys experts?" Owen asked skeptically. "It's not like there is a manual for things like this nor do you have some business in town that people hire to get rid of ghosts."

Kailynn asked for everyone to calm down. Once they did, she decided tonight was over for the group and things needed to be put to bed.

"We are not really at liberty to discuss the 'family business' kids. Just know we will take care of things quietly and with no one else getting hurt. I think the night is getting late and we are all exhausted from tonight's events. All we ask is that you keep things quiet." She looked around at everyone's reaction.

"We won't say anything," Drake answered. "It's not like anyone would believe us anyway and we don't want to get into the Sheriff's cross-hairs, right, guys?"

The group nodded and Kailynn relaxed a bit. "Okay, then Hollyn and I will head inside. We need to see how your brother is doing, anyway. You guys wrap things up here, please." She and Hollyn left the kids to go inside. She had almost forgotten Jackson was inside with his sleep-over friend. She hoped they hadn't been affected too much by things tonight.

Once they were inside, Kayden looked at everyone. They were looking at her expectantly.

"Well, Caviar? What is the deal here?" Brooklyn inquired, not waiting for anyone else to start up the conversation. "Just telling us you'll take care of things doesn't sit well with me."

Braelyn nodded her agreement with her friend. "Yeah Kayden. You know a lot more than what has been said. Spill it," she demanded.

Drake put his arm around Kayden for reassurance. "Hey, it's okay if you don't want to say more, but we would appreciate a little more understanding. We're in this together. Keeping each other in the dark with unspoken riddles isn't really helping us cope with things better."

Kayden frowned. She knew Drake was right and her new friends deserved some explanation. Her Aunt Hollyn told her when they helped people who were being plagued by the dead, there wasn't much to hide from them about their family experience. Weren't her friends classified as those people now? Internally, she made a choice. It was time to reveal a little more to them regardless of her aunt's instructions.

"Look guys, I can't explain everything. I don't even understand if I actually know all of it. Here's what I know. Apparently, my family has a long history of dealing with spirits who still roam around, disturbing the living. The Russian Orthodox Church recruited my family a long time ago to protect those around this area from the supernatural. My family has been continually trained down through the generations to deal with this kind of stuff."

"Whoa," said Jeremiah to himself, but loud enough for everyone to hear.

Gage sat taller, pushing the cold compress Brooklyn was holding away from his face. "So you are saying your family is like the Ghostbusters?" He stood up.

Kayden just nodded slowly. "In a manner, yes."

"How long have you known this?" asked Drake.

Kayden looked at him. Shame was covered all over her face.

"Not until after all that stuff happened to Sadie."

She turned to the rest of the group.

"Look, I don't like any of this stuff, nor asked to be a part of this family legacy shit. I just wanted to fit in at school and find friends." Her shoulders slumped down in a dejected position.

"Hey," Drake spun her to him. He grabbed her by both shoulders reassuringly. "We're not mad or disappointed at you Kayden. It just would be nice to be on the same team instead of on the sideline when things are happening, you know?"

"I wouldn't go that far, Caviar," replied Brooklyn. "However, I can see your minor dilemma. I'm not sure how I personally would have handled it, but I agree with Drake. We are on the same team."

Gage, standing, nodded his agreement with Brooklyn.

She nodded. She also knew they couldn't really understand what she was going through and the seriousness of her family's legacy.

"My family is important to me, guys. Aunt Hollyn ordered me to keep things quiet. If people knew anything about what we did outside the public's eyes, we'd not only be shunned, but life for our family in this town would be done. Can you please try to understand the difficult position I'm in?"

Shades lowered his glasses and put an arm around Kayden, big brother style. Squeezing her to him playfully he said, "No problem, Kayden. We all can keep this secret between us, right guys?" he motioned to the group.

Everyone agreed with him.

Drake took the reins as always, following his buddy's lead. "Okay guys, Kayden's aunt probably is ready for us to head out. We'll stay in touch over the weekend with our cells and keep a low profile." He looked at Kayden. "You can update us on Monday once your family does their thing, right?"

She smiled back at him. "I promise."

Chapter Seventeen: Never a Dull Moment

Once the group left, Kayden went into the house. She heard low whispering coming from the study. It was next to the kitchen. She went to find out who was talking and about what.

"It has to be tomorrow," hissed Aunt Hollyn.

"None of us are ready, Hollybear," Kailynn replied.

"This is getting worse. We know what is going on now and how to deal with the issue. Let's just get it done," her sister retorted.

Just then, the door opened and Kayden stepped in. The two sisters looked like they were just caught trying to sneak out of their parent's house at night without permission. Aunt Hollyn, upon seeing Kayden, took a deep breath and lowered her shoulders to a more relaxed position. Kailynn who had been standing on the left of the desk in the den, walked toward her daughter and gave her a loving hug.

"I'm so relieved you and the other kids are okay," she murmured into her daughter's ear.

Kayden squeezed back this time to her mom's embrace. She didn't realize how much she appreciated having her family around. Kailynn released her daughter and stepped back, looking at Hollyn.

"Okay, so we all need to talk a little about tonight and the issue we're going to have to deal with."

Just then, an excited shout came from upstairs, interrupting the moment. Kayden looked at her mom questioningly. Picking up on her daughter's stare, she explained.

"Jackson and his friend are playing online and they get excited once in a while."

Kayden rolled her eyes.

"Kayden, I get tonight wasn't your fault and based on what I saw once Ramsey and I got to the cemetery, you handled yourself well. Had you not been there, I'm afraid we would have had more potential deaths on her hands," Hollyn acknowledged to her niece.

Kayden's face showed surprise at her aunt's compliment. She hadn't expected that reaction to the events in the cemetery.

"But it doesn't excuse the situation to begin with," interrupted her mother.

Right on cue, Kayden thought.

Deflecting the moment, Kayden questioned. "How did Ramsey and the Sheriff get to our house so fast, anyway?"

    This definitely deflected Kailynn's admonishment of her daughter's recent exploits. Luckily, Hollyn answered the question.

    "Looks like Ramsey and Whip have been doing a little digging of their own and found out some very interesting information thanks to our town's historian." A look of satisfaction was etched all over Hollyn's face.

    Kayden eyed her mother, who also seemed to have a bit of a smirk on her face as well. Both sisters explained to Kayden the information they uncovered in the town's archives about their family along with the long forgotten mining company of Ledford. As they relayed the information to Kayden, she listened. Her eyes kept getting bigger and bigger. Turns out Joe Toth had actually been lobbying for better work conditions and fighting against the mining company all along. His efforts were drawing too much attention to the company and then the accident happened. An accident which he had been arguing with the company eventually would happen. Instead, the company created a cover up, not only of the accident, but what they were actually doing.

    Once Whip and Ramsey had the information, they paid Kayden's family a visit to at the very least let them know what could be in the works. Upon getting there, the kids were gone. Ramsey and Hollyn went into action with Whip and Kailynn staying behind as contingency help. The kids had lucked out, with Aunt Hollyn showing up when things seemed lost. Since Whip now had another issue with unwanted eyes seeing even more of the events happening, he knew shutting down the rumor mill and prying eyes just got that much harder.

Kayden had to sit down and absorb all the recent events. Her aunt and mom completely understood the overwhelming set of events which were now in motion. They had to stop the cemetery from hurting anyone else in the community and keep the rest of the kids involved safe. Their family's reputation was now set to undergo another shift in perception to the community and her family was going to engage in the family business. All within the next 24 hours, it would seem.

Kayden looked at her aunt and mom. "Well, now what happens?"

Kailynn looked at her sister. They shared a common understanding. She looked back at her daughter with a serious yet resolute expression.

"Now, we plan for tomorrow and get ready."

*****

Friday evening in the small town of Ledford was usually a quiet affair, but for Jackson and Boyd, this night was about to take an unexpected turn.

Jackson had invited Boyd over to his house to play online games after the whole incident with the Geek Squad had unfolded. The new friend seemed overly enthusiastic about hanging with Jackson, which actually baffled him. The rumors around school over Sadie's passing and how his family was involved didn't faze this kid.

Boyd was a skinny African-American kid. He had a lighter, almost bronze skin tone. Up close, his appearance looked as if he had a fantastic sun tan. He had really intense blue eyes, which really really stood out. Jackson and Boyd had really hit it off. Turns out they had a lot of common interests. The most recent, of course, was online gaming.

The two teens were engrossed in a fierce Clash Royale battle, the glow of their screens lighting up Jackson's room as they strategically plotted against opponents from around the world online.

As the digital war raged on, a sudden commotion outside grabbed Jackson's attention. Laughter mixed with shouts echoed through the air, prompting Jackson and Boyd to exchange puzzled glances. They abandoned their virtual battlefield and peered out the window, curious to find the source of the disturbance.

To their surprise, they spotted Jackson's older sister, Kayden, and her friends gathered around a fire-pit in the backyard. The glow of the flames revealed their faces, illuminated with excitement. However, the joy was short-lived as a barrage of eggs came hurtling towards them, courtesy of a group of bullies who had emerged from the shadows. Jackson was told in no uncertain terms by his sister to be invisible tonight. Kayden didn't want her younger brother embarrassing her in front of her new friends.

More like being embarrassed around Drake, Jackson thought smugly.

Jackson was seeing something completely unscripted. Jerks hurling eggs at everyone. He smiled despite himself as the entire scene being played out from his window had a certain sense of humor to it. Boyd woke Jackson from his thoughts.

"Dude, who is chucking eggs at your sister and her posse?" he asked curiously.

"I don't know, but I'm pretty sure that dude Gage who is with them won't take it lying down. He has a bit of a temper from what my sis has told me," answered Jackson.

The Hungarian Cemetery Secrets Within Backup

The pelting shortly stopped and the two boys could hear laughing in the distance from kids hiding out in the brush. Just as Jackson predicted, Gage shot out into the tree-line.

Kayden and her friends scattered, following the bullies in hot pursuit. To Jackson's horror, they sprinted toward the nearby cemetery, disappearing into the darkness. Jackson knew they would quickly be in the cemetery among the tombstones.

Great, he thought. *This is exactly what Aunt Hollyn didn't want to happen. The cemetery was dangerous and now Kayden and her friends had gone smack back into it. I have to tell Aunt Hollyn and mom.*

The air was thick with tension, and Boyd, who was still processing the surreal scene, turned to Jackson with wide eyes.

"Is this normal around here?" Boyd asked, the unease clear in his voice.

Jackson hesitated, torn between the desire to protect his sister and the weight of the rumors swirling around his family at school.

"Not exactly," he replied vaguely, trying to downplay the situation.

Boyd was loving it. This is exactly the kind of action he had hoped for by coming over to hang with Jackson. Whether the rumors being spread at school were true or not didn't matter to Boyd. The thrill of getting out of the normalcy of a small town and seeking random adventure was happening right now!

Just as Jackson contemplated whether to intervene or stay put, the unmistakable sound of a car pulling into the driveway reached their ears. Jackson's heart skipped a beat. It was the police. He glanced at Boyd, concern etched across his face. Boyd's face though was lit up in excitement.

"Dude, the police just pulled up! Wow, that was fast. Your mom or aunt must have called and saw the egging too," he surmised.

Jackson wasn't so sure. "C'mon, let's go spy on things downstairs," Jackson suggested. Boyd was eager to follow his new friend.

The doorbell rang, and Jackson's mom, Kailynn, and Aunt Hollyn got up from the couch to answer it. The flickering lights from two patrol cars outside revealed the stern faces of Sheriff Whip and Deputy Ramsey.

Boyd's curiosity intensified. His eyes darted between Jackson and the unfolding scene at the door. He whispered, "What's happening, man?"

"I... I don't know," Jackson stammered, torn between loyalty to his family and the urge to confide in his new friend.

As Kailynn and Hollyn spoke with the law officers, Hollyn's expression changed from polite confusion to sudden realization. Panic flickered in her eyes as she noticed Kayden's absence.

"They're missing," Hollyn gasped, catching Jackson off guard. His mind raced as he grappled with the dilemma of choosing between his sister's safety, the family secrets, and Boyd's growing curiosity.

Jackson intervened. "Aunt Hollyn," he yelled, running down the staircase. "Kayden and her friends just got hit by people throwing eggs outside," he informed them.

"Yeah," corroborated Boyd. "They chased them into the tree-line," he added, pointing to the trees in the back of the yard.

Now all faces got serious and worried.

"You mean that way," the deputy pointed, "towards the cemetery?" he questioned.

Jackson nodded.

Kailynn turned to her son. "You and Boyd get back upstairs right now and let the grown-ups handle this. Understand Jackson?"

Kailynn put an emphasis on 'Understand.' Jackson knew exactly what his mom was saying without being told.

"C'mon Boyd, they got this. We'll just get in the way." Boyd shrugged and followed Jackson back upstairs to his bedroom. The night that begun with online battles had now transformed into a real-life mystery, with Jackson caught in the crossfire of family troubles and unexpected police visits. Add the fact his new friend Boyd, which Jackson didn't know if he could trust or not was also witnessing things as well.

The atmosphere in Jackson's room had grown tense as Boyd and Jackson went back to the window. They watched as Deputy Ramsey and Aunt Hollyn moved urgently around the trunk of the police car. Jackson's curiosity intensified, and he shot Boyd a glance, silently acknowledging the shared need to understand the unfolding events.

"What do you think they are looking? Jackson asked.

Boyd inched closer to the window, peering through the blinds. His eyes widened as he whispered, "They found something. What's going on?"

Jackson joined him, squinting to catch a glimpse of the mysterious contents being carried from the police car. The two figures, Ramsey and Hollyn, swiftly took off towards the cemetery, leaving the dark silhouette of the tree-line as their destination.

The window had been slightly opened all night to Jackson's room to let in the cool night air. It was how they had heard things from outside to begin with. The minutes felt like an eternity, accentuated by distant shouts and muffled screams.

Boyd's brow furrowed with worry, mirroring the concern etched across Jackson's face. The anticipation was unbearable as they strained to discern the chaos unfolding beyond the window.

"Dude," Boyd said to his friend. "Screaming and shouting? You think they are fighting or something? If so, why are there screams? They sound more scared than angry. Don't you think?"

Finally, from the depths of the trees, Kayden's friends and a group of boys emerged, running towards the fire-pit. Among them was someone being assisted, struggling to keep pace. Jackson's heart pounded in his chest as he scanned the group for his sister. Relief washed over him when he spotted Kayden with Drake, accompanied by Deputy Ramsey and Aunt Hollyn.

The duo looked worn out, their faces etched with a mixture of fear and exhaustion. Ramsey and Hollyn held a couple of road flares, their eerie glow casting an unsettling light on the solemn gathering. The teens huddled around the fire-pit, their expressions a mixture of guilt, fear, and confusion.

"Looks like we have our answer," Jackson stated.

Boyd nodded his head in agreement. "Yep, road flares. They make bright light to see by at night. Makes sense, I guess," Boyd pondered, "but wouldn't you think a law officer possessed a flashlight? I mean, they have spotlights to search for people who runaway during arrests."

Jackson thought he knew the answer to that

question given the place they were headed to and what his Aunt Hollyn said about what could happen at the cemetery. He wasn't about to tell Boyd about it, though. Intentionally deflecting his new friend's question he responded.

"They probably used them for more effect. You know, kids who might fight and then see a cop with a red flare blowing all over the place coming at them might add a bit of shock factor, you know?"

Boyd shrugged, "I guess."

As the tension peaked, Sheriff Whip materialized from the shadows of the house. His stern gaze surveyed the group, and his voice carried the weight of authority.

"The cemetery was supposed to be off limits right now. It is an active crime scene and you dumb-asses went right in there and trampled shit all over the place. It disturbed the scene and contaminated potential evidence. The Deputy and I will have to start all over again?" he thundered, his disappointment palpable.

Jackson saw the Deputy looking up at them and immediately backed away from the window. Boyd, seeing what Jackson saw, also did the same. They didn't want to get in trouble for eavesdropping.

After a little time passed, both of them went back to the window strategically avoiding detection by the participants down in the yard. The scene unfolded as Ramsey, with a no-nonsense demeanor, began directing some boys towards the waiting police car. The squad car door opened, swallowing them in darkness before driving off into the night.

Jackson's family and friends stood subdued by the fire-pit, the gravity of their actions sinking in. The sheriff continued to lecture them, his words a stern reminder of the consequences they faced. Boyd, still processing the whirlwind of events, glanced at Jackson, silently seeking an explanation.

"Seems like never a dull moment at the Toth house, huh?" Jackson murmured to Boyd, a heavy weight on his chest. The secrets that had shrouded his family were on the verge of unraveling.

Boyd smiled at Jackson. "Dude, this has been one of the best nights for fun I can remember. If it is like this all the time, we're going to have to be best friends."

Jackson's face took on the look of confusion. "You actually like this kind of stuff?" he asked.

Boyd grinned even bigger. "Like this stuff?" he repeated. "I love this stuff."

Chapter Eighteen: Hatching a Plan

Saturday morning was anything but lazy. Jackson had been woken up by his mom banging on the door. He checked his phone.

8 o'clock in the morning? Had the woman gone crazy? It's the weekend, thought Jackson.

Kailynn got the boys up and treated them to some early morning doughnuts. She then explained to them there was some family stuff planned early and apologized for not telling Jackson earlier. After driving Boyd home, she came right back to their house and explained the facts to Jackson.

Jackson sat on the couch and his mom was pacing the floor as she talked. She informed him about last night's events in full. Kailynn had decided there would be no more secrets or protecting her kids' innocence, since they would be engaging in their first cleansing. She needed to be up front with them, so they could prepare as best as possible for the upcoming trials. She knew they had only been practicing for just over a week. This put her and Hollyn at odds. Hollyn said they could handle their part as long as both she and Kailynn were there. Kailynn wasn't so sure, but circumstances had forced their hand to deal with the cemetery. After going over the exploits of the teens, she then revealed what she, Kayden and Hollyn had been doing last night.

"We decided to put an end to this cemetery nonsense tonight. Sheriff Whip and Deputy Ramsey came by and had some recent revelations to reveal to us," she explained.

Turns out their family history wasn't as to blame for the mining accident as previously thought. Evidence from the archives threw new light into the mining company's cover up. It also explained the issue with the miners and their great...grandfather. Now that they had the pieces of the puzzle, it all made sense. Kailynn explained the souls of these poor miners were trapped on this plane to plague the living at night until the truth of their deaths had been settled.

Jackson's eyes kept getting larger and larger. It was a lot to take in for an 8th grader, but he took it in stride. Once she had finished explaining, Jackson sat there dumbfounded. Kayden came down from her room and saw Jackson and her mom.

As she approached them, a smirk displayed across her face.

"Mom, tell you?" she asked Jackson.

His eyes slowly met hers and he merely nodded.

"Don't sweat it little brother," she said sincerely.

"I went through it last night and can barely process it now." She shrugged, "All that's left it seems is to actually do what Aunt Hollyn has been teaching us."

Kailynn nodded.

"Which is why we are heading to Muddy," came a voice from down the hall.

Aunt Hollyn emerged into the living room with a cheerful smile on her face.

I am beginning to think she is rather enjoying this too much, thought Kayden with a frown.

"What's with the sour face, Kayden? This will be over by tonight," she said with full certainty.

"Regardless," interrupted Kailynn. "We need a few final practice runs before we set out after it tonight."

Hollyn nodded.

Everyone left the house and packed in Hollyn's car. They were headed for Muddy.

***

The family practiced in their hidden cove underground in Muddy. They were at it for hours. Hollyn finally felt the kids knew their part. Her sister took to it like riding a bike. She started at it a little rusty, but overall sharpened up as they routinely rehearsed.

Hollyn knew they might need a little more help on this one. Too many people were asking questions. The town was in a state of unrest. Last night's events were a tremendous example of that. More people would get bolder and venture out into the cemetery seeking answers or cheap thrills. They wouldn't be able to keep a lid on things much longer. The police were also dealing with the aftermath. This was the best time to hit the cemetery.

They headed into town. Hollyn had texted Ramsey to meet her and the kids. It was going to be a chance encounter, at least, to the locals.

The family parked by the statue of the Big Muddy Monster and walked towards the courthouse. As they walked, Sheriff Whip and Deputy Ramsey just happened to be strolling towards them on the sidewalk in front of the town square. A sense of tension hung in the air. The kids, Jackson and Kayden, fidgeted nervously, their eyes wide with curiosity and a hint of fear.

Hollyn walked up to the two and began the conversation.

"Sheriff Whip, Deputy Ramsey, we appreciate you meeting with us. We believe it's time to confront the mining specters at the Hungarian Cemetery," her expression deadly serious.

Sheriff Whip raised an eyebrow. "Mining specters? You're saying we've 100% got ghost miners haunting our cemetery?" He looked at Ramsey.

Kailynn nodded in response to Whip's question. "It's a long story, but yes. They've been causing disturbances, and they are what we've been dealing with for the past few weeks now."

"Ghost miners? You now feel that is what I was seeing last night at the cemetery?" Deputy Ramsey replied, crossing his arms.

"I understand it sounds unusual, but over the years, we've witnessed strange occurrences firsthand," Hollyn responded seriously. "With what you two found out last night in the archives, it makes the most sense. We have a plan to cleanse the cemetery and put an end to this haunting."

Jackson whispered to Kayden, "Do you think they'll believe us?"

"I don't know, but Mom and Hollyn seem sure about this," she responded to her brother quietly.

Sheriff Whip stepped back and leaned on the building. They were in front of the local bar. He readjusted his hat.

"Alright, lay it out for us. What's your plan?"

Kailynn unfolded a piece of paper she and Hollyn had been working on.

"We've gathered information on the specters' patterns. They're most active around midnight. We aim to go into the original, old cemetery armed with protective artifacts and perform a ritual to cleanse the area."

Deputy Ramsey raised an eyebrow over the response. "Rituals? Are we talking about some kind of occult stuff? Doesn't sound like your usual cup of tea Hollyn," he reasoned.

Hollyn calmly smiled back at the deputy. They had gone on several past 'adventures' together, so it made sense why Ramsey was a bit confused.

"I actually have family members to assist me this time, Ramsey. It's not a solo mission like we've engaged in; in the past. It's more about positive energy and religious methods passed down through generations. We want you two to come with us, be on standby, and use road flares to blind the specters if things go south."

Sheriff Whip looked skeptical. "Are you sure road flares against ghost miners will work? This is unconventional, to say the least."

Ramsey agreed with Hollyn on this. He and she had successfully pushed the ghosts away from the kids in the cemetery using the flares. He whispered to Whip, probably openly agreeing with Hollyn quietly.

Kailynn interrupted him by pleadingly answering.

"We wouldn't ask if it weren't necessary. My kids are involved in this. I don't feel great putting them in harm's way, but having you two there would help. Harrisburg's history is at stake here."

Deputy Ramsey nodded. Kailynn knew he'd come, regardless. His feelings for Hollyn were too strong not too.

Those two need to sort out their relationship better, she thought.

"Sheriff, what do you think?" Ramsey asked his superior respectfully, knowing the order of rank.

Sheriff Whip rubbed his chin in dramatic fashion.

"It's bizarre, but I've seen stranger things." He looked at the two sisters. "Alright, we'll be there. But I want everything laid out clearly before we go traipsing into a haunted cemetery."

Hollyn nodded respectfully. "Agreed. We appreciate your support. Let's make a plan and get ready for tonight. Time is of the essence and it is already 4 pm. It will get dark soon."

"Let's meet at the house around ten tonight and outline the details of our plan," Hollyn instructed them.

The parties separated in different directions when Ramsey turned around and posed a question.

"Hollyn," he called, "you know it's Halloween tonight, right?"

Kayden and Jackson had been so wrapped up in the events of the last 24 hours that the date marking an eerie evening of trick-or-treaters had flown right over the top of their heads. Their mom seemed equally surprised.

"Oh my," Kailynn expressed. "We need to head to Aldi's right now and grab candy."

Hollyn simply smiled back at Ramsey with a flirtatious manner. "Naturally Byron; you're not scared are you?"

The deputy straightened up tall, as if caught slouching. Hollyn turned around thinking she got one over on her friend. As they began walking again, Ramsey's voice caught her off guard.

"Not when a beautiful woman needs my help," he responded teasingly.

Hollyn mis-stepped at the response, but didn't turn around to acknowledge Ramsey. Her sister snickered, but Hollyn let that go, too. Internally, she was smiling ear to ear.

Ramsey turned around and caught up to Whip who had kept walking. Once he fell in line with Whip, the sheriff muttered.

"Real cute deputy."

Ramsey outwardly smiled. "I thought so."

***

As the sun dipped below the horizon, casting long shadows across the quiet town of Ledford, Hollyn and Kailynn prepared for the daunting task that lay ahead. The air at the house was thick with anticipation as they gathered their supplies for the midnight showdown at the Hungarian Cemetery.

Halloween had ensued. Oddly enough, very few trick or treaters came to the Toth's home for candy. Kayden chalked it up to being in a small town with little to no population. She also felt their name was tied to the latest series of events.

Time passed quickly for the kids. They had texted their friends and down played their plans for the evening. Everyone who had been there last night had also kept a low profile in the evening by staying home. Drake had told Kayden Halloween was a cool event in Harrisburg. Trick or treating began at 5 pm and ended at 9 pm. The police were usually out, making sure no shenanigans were taking place.

Kayden had asked what 'shenanigans' he was talking about. Drake informed her that here in the Southern Illinois area, kids liked to go soaping car windows, throwing toilet paper all over people's trees and front lawns, or even more bizarre was corning. The term corning confused Kayden, so Drake had elaborated. Since corn was one crop grown in the area, once it was harvested, kids would grab left over cobs in the field. They would shuck the kernels into socks and then go around throwing corn at houses or cars to scare people at night.

Kayden laughed out loud at this.

What a weird way to add 'trick' to the night, she reflected.

The moon hung low in the sky, casting an eerie glow on the gravestones that awaited them.

Hollyn had a determined look in her eyes as she double-checked her equipment. She wore a pendant passed down through generations, believed to protect its wearer from malevolent spirits. It was the Saint Benedict medal. Hollyn's religious object was a Christian symbol of opening doors and opening up hard paths.

Orthodox tradition held that it could help protect

the wearer from curses, evil and vices. She had several of them which were blessed by the church. She had given each of her family members one to wear in their efforts tonight.

While one side had Saint Benedict and the cross on it, the reverse side of the medal carried the Latin phrase, 'Vade retro satana.' In our English tongue, it meant 'Begone, Satan.'

Kailynn clutched a bag filled with an assortment of herbs and charms, passed on to her by her grandmother, who had a reputation for being a wise woman in matters of the supernatural. These were more for her state of mind and ability to channel her own energy. She was given the gift of sight. It allowed entities to commune with her and her with them.

It was sort of like Tyler Henry, but in Kailynn's case she geared to those spirits causing problems to the living.

The kids heard a car pull up in the drive and saw their back-up to tonight's events come to the door. The sisters met with Sheriff Whip and Deputy Ramsey in the kitchen. The law enforcement officers exchanged skeptical glances, unsure of what they were getting themselves into. Jackson and Kayden peeked out from the side of the living room, excitement mixed with trepidation evident in their youthful faces.

Hollyn took charge, laying out the details of their plan. The mining specters were said to be most active around midnight, and the Hungarian Cemetery, with its dark history, was the epicenter of their haunting. The group would venture into the heart of the old forsaken cemetery armed with an array of supernatural deterrents, aiming to cleanse the grounds of the lingering spirits. Hollyn would lead the cleansing, but warned that because it was Halloween, the rift between the land of the living and dead would be stronger. In other words, more open to the dead.

Sheriff Whip listened intently, his eyes narrowing as Hollyn recounted the tales of the spectral miners who had met tragic fates in the Ledford mines of long ago. Deputy Ramsey crossed his arms and exchanged glances with the sheriff. Despite their reservations, the officers agreed to provide backup, armed with road flares to blind the specters if the need arose.

With the plan in place, the group dispersed to make final preparations. Hollyn and Kailynn lit candles and set up a makeshift altar to harness positive energy. Meanwhile, Sheriff Whip and Deputy Ramsey unloaded their patrol car of road flares, flashlights, and a hopeful prayer the spectral occupants of the cemetery cooperated with the Toth family.

As their cell phones showed around midnight, the unlikely team converged on the dirt path leading to the Hungarian Cemetery. Tonight differed from the other nights when Kayden was at the other cemetery. The air was colder, and an otherworldly hush settled over the path to the graveyard. Uncharacteristic of the late fall weather, not a wisp of wind was present in the old cemetery. The darkness among the trees and broken cemetery made their present situation seem even more perilous.

Armed with determination and a mix of ancient and modern tools, the kids stepped into the realm of the unknown, ready to confront the spectral forces that lurked in the shadows. The stage was set for a midnight showdown that would test their courage and unravel the mysteries that haunted Ledford.

Chapter Nineteen: Spectral Showdown

The Toth family didn't just carry a few trinkets with them for protection. The kids adorned what was called in the Orthodox Church as scapulars. A scapular was most often referred to as a sacramental object. It was essentially composed of small pieces of wool cloth (usually only an inch or two square) and thin connecting strips.

Jackson thought they were cool. He remembered seeing monks wearing a similar type of vestiges on the history channel and these exact images were seen on certain video game avatars. Kayden felt silly, but any advantage she had over these spectral miners was okay with her. Besides, no one she was with looked any different. There were four of them walking out to the graveyard dressed in the religious garbs like ancient warriors. Kailynn and Hollyn had on black scapulars. Aunt Hollyn had told them these were no longer used in the church. They were the colors of St. Benedict. The church now allowed the medals of St. Benedict, which everyone had on as well to represent, however Hollyn said she and her mom were old school and still used the scapular as well.

Kayden and Jackson had on a dual color: black and dark blue woolen fabric. The black piece had the image of St. Michael, God's Archangel who most Christians called upon when going into spiritual battle. The police officers, on the other hand, felt a little out-of-place walking among the four of them dressed in such a manner. Hollyn had just shrugged and told them it was Halloween, so no one would really think much of it if they were seen. No one could really argue with that logic.

As they proceeded to the outskirts of the cemetery, Ramsey was walking close to Hollyn. Whip was bringing up the rear with Kailynn.

Ramsey, without taking his eyes away from what lie ahead of him quietly asked Hollyn, "What's with these garbs?"

Hollyn smiled despite herself. She answered quietly, "their scapulars. The point of the garment is to protect the body by defending against anything which might represent evil, sin, Satan, hell, etc."

"Oh," responded Ramsey with an eye-brow raise.

"The kids' scapular is a sign of devotion to St. Michael the Archangel," continued Hollyn.

"I know who that is," interrupted Ramsey.

"Of course you do. Everyone knows God's greatest warrior archangel. It's more than that."

"Really?" responded the deputy. "Please

enlighten me."

Hollyn wrinkled up her nose in frustration at the man. He got under her skin so easily with his seemingly arrogant nature. He always was trying to protect her and asking a million questions.

Sheesh, she thought. *He always managed to peel back my layers though, frustrating man!*

"The garment helps protect the wearer against vices, addictions, false teachings, blasphemy and the conversion of all sinners. It also brings an increase in love, hope, faith, humility, affirmation of God and the grace of a proper Christian or saintly death," she concluded.

"Death?" repeated Ramsey in a shocked voice. "Good Lord Hollyn, bringing these kids here to something like that?" His tone was reprimanding.

She looked at him disapprovingly. "Who are you to pass judgment on me, Byron? I was indoctrinated into this life much earlier than they were. Society may have become more civil on the surface, but the negative elements of evil still exist underneath. Those facts haven't changed. You, a police officer should know that better than anyone," she finished in a chiding voice.

Ramsey was glad it was dark out. He didn't want Hollyn of all people to see how red in the face he was from blushing. She had a point, but it still didn't make him feel any better.

They had finally come to the spot of their family member's grave site. Hollyn turned and motioned to the kids and her sister.

"Line up in our designated formation." She motioned to Ramsey and Whip. "You two will remain inside our four points. Remember, keep your eyes down.

Do not look into the eyes or lights of these spirits. It is how they overwhelm you."

Whip looked around. Nothing was there yet. He and Ramsey moved to the center, pulling the flares out and sitting them at their feet. Next, they kept their flashlights on, but pointed outward.

Once ready, Whip reviewed verbally again with Ramsey.

"Right. Once things start, we'll either see the shadows emerge or our flashlights go out. That will indicate they are coming to us. We drop the flashlights, grab the flares." His voice sounded nervous.

Deputy Ramsey nodded his agreement. "Exactly. We keep our heads focused on the ground, we don't look up."

"Just like that scene in Indiana Jones and Raiders of the Lost Ark," quipped Jackson. "When the Germans opened the Ark and all those spirits flew out and killed everyone looking." Jackson's energy was at an all-time high at the events which were getting ready to start.

"Thanks Jackson. Made me feel a lot better," responded Ramsey dryly.

"Do not light those flares unless I or Kailynn yell to," interjected Hollyn.

The wind picked up, causing the leaves to rustle eerily. The air felt thick with anticipation as the Toth family and the two police officers stood in their designated formation, ready for whatever might transpire. The atmosphere was charged with a sense of otherworldly energy.

Hollyn began the ritual by invoking the troubled spirits of the miners. Raising her hands out with her palms upward toward the sky, she said, "My Lord, you are all powerful. You are God, you are Father. We beg you through the intercession and help of the archangels Michael, Raphael and Gabriel, for the deliverance of our brothers and sisters who are enslaved by the evil one. All saints of Heaven, come to our aid!"

    Kailynn, Jackson, and Kayden mirrored her actions. In response to her initial prayer, the kids and Kailynn recited the litany Hollyn had made them memorize. Together, they responded, "Holy God, Holy Mighty, Holy Immortal, have mercy on us."

    Ramsey and Whip stayed quiet while the family engaged in the bvprayer ritual. Each shining their flashlights around the perimeter searching for any sign of movement.

    The kids and Kailynn continued repeating their prayer, slowly and together as one voice. Kayden relaxed more and fell into the chant. Jackson too, seemed more in sync as well.

    Suddenly, a low hum filled the air, and a faint, bluish light flickered around the grave of their deceased family member. Where once nothing stood, now the spirit of their former ancestor. His light bore a remarkable blue tint, which emanated from the candle perched on his hat.

    Hollyn, seeing him fully for the first time, gave a loving smile and respectfully nodded her head to him. His eyes were little lights of which no human eyes reflected. His face, covered in dark soot returned her nod. Hollyn knew they were ready and so was he.

    The spirits were approaching. Ramsey felt a chill run down his spine as the shadows emerged, casting an ethereal glow around them. The flashlights flickered momentarily, causing everyone to hold their breath.

    Hollyn, standing at the forefront, raised her

hand, signaling for everyone to remain steady. The battle of wills had begun.

Both officers dropped their flashlights and kneeled down to grab the flares.

The spirits had come as they were summoned. Kayden and Jackson closed their eyes as their aunt had instructed. They used only their ears and sense of touch to guide them. Kailynn too followed her children's example. She raised her hands up to mimic her sister.

The spirits of the dead miners surrounded the group, their presence felt more than seen. The scapulars worn by the Toth family had a very faint glow. It was a soft glow in response to the spectral energy, creating a protective barrier around them. None of them knew this, nor the law officers who were staring at their feet.

The air became charged with an otherworldly tension, and the spirits seemed to hesitate. Ramsey, despite his skepticism, couldn't deny the palpable energy enveloping them. He tightened his grip on the flares, ready for whatever might come.

Hollyn continued her prayer, ramping up the intensity. "From anxiety, sadness and obsessions, we beg You. Free us, O Lord. From hatred and envy, we beg You, Free us, O Lord."

Moans of anguish and pain came from all around them. The intensity of the prayer was inflicting a new form of pain on these tortured souls. Anger and rage from their decades of self-imprisonment over their wrongful deaths were not easily let go of. They wanted revenge for their deaths.

"From thoughts of jealousy, rage, and death, we beg You, Free us, O Lord. From every form of sinful acts, we beg You, Free us, O Lord," Hollyn beat on with her prayer.

The others continued their own litany: "Holy God, Holy Mighty, Holy Immortal..."

Ramsey didn't move his eyes or head, but knew his boss could hear him.

"Do you think it's working?" he ventured the question.

Whip, hearing his deputy frowned. "I do not know, but there's no doubt something is happening."

Hollyn heard them and wanted to throttle Ramsey for interrupting, but she continued to focus and concentrate on her own part in this ritual.

"From every division in our family, and every harmful friendship, we beg You, Free us, O Lord. From every sort of spell, malefic, witchcraft, and every form of the occult, we beg You, Free us, O Lord!"

The energy from the former miners was weakening, but the will of these men from a former life taken fought to remain. Kayden could sense their hesitation and felt an urge she couldn't explain or overcome. Without thought or warning, she broke ranks in her group.

"We're here to honor Joe Toth and the honorable men who died with him. We pay our respects in peace and know your deaths were caused by the mining company. Your legacy and truth will be told to the entire community," she exclaimed in an assertive voice.

Hollyn, looking back at her niece in shock, turned back toward Joe's tombstone. He stood there smiling and nodded to her to continue. She closed her eyes and finished the prayer.

"Lord, You Who said, "I leave you peace, My peace I give you, grant that, through the intercession of the Virgin Mary, we may be liberated from every evil spell and enjoy your peace always. In the name of Christ, our Lord. Amen!"

"Amen," the teens and Kailynn echoed.

As if in response, the spirits who were now upon them all swirled around, creating a mesmerizing dance of light and shadow. The air was filled with a mix of emotions reaching out to the living everywhere. The Toth family held their ground, their scapulars glow dimmed. Everyone felt a sense of ease fill the void and ventured to look out around them.

Ramsey, initially unsure about the whole situation, looked as well. He saw Whip next to him, captivated by the ethereal display. It was as if the spirits were acknowledging their presence rather than confronting them.

Just like in Indiana Jones, thought Ramsey. He looked back at Jackson. Jackson ventured a look at Ramsey, smiled and nodded his head.

"Told you so," he said to the deputy as if reading his mind.

After a moment that felt like an eternity, the spirits faded away, their luminous forms dissipating into the night. The wind carried their whispers, a mixture of sorrow and acceptance.

Thinking it all over they relaxed, only to see one spirit left. It was Joe Toth. Only this time, he wasn't in an old mining outfit. He had on a pair of blue jean overalls with a red shirt tucked underneath. His eyes still had the bright orbs in the sockets, but everything else about him was plain as day.

He walked toward what was left of his living family and stopped short of Hollyn. She had never experienced this sort of ending to a cleansing. She was dumbfounded standing there with her arms still up, looking at Joe.

"Thank you child," he said in a very loving voice. "May God shine His light on you all, always."

Joe's form slowly dissipated upwards and out; breaking away into tiny pieces, which eventually turned to nothing.

Hollyn lowered her hands, and the family exhaled collectively, realizing they had successfully navigated the encounter. The flashlights flickered back to life, and the Toth family, along with Ramsey and Whip, stood there, awestruck by the experience.

"That's it?" asked Whip, standing up and slapping his hat on his leg. "I start back to church tomorrow."

A grunt of agreement circulated around the group. Ramsey looked around at everyone. He motioned to Hollyn.

"That was pretty incredible. You are definitely special Hollybear."

Hollyn walked over to Ramsey and threw her arms around him in a heartfelt hug. When she pulled away, Ramsey pulled her back and kissed her.

Hollyn initially tried to retreat, but then gave up immediately and enjoyed the kiss.

"About time," said Whip from the side, watching them in disgust. "I've been sick of seeing all this flirtatious banter from you two over the years. Maybe you two can figure things out without acting like you don't like each other."

Kailynn laughed out loud at that as she walked up behind her kids and hugged them.

"Don't bet on it, Sheriff," she replied.

"Yeah, she's pretty hardheaded," acknowledged Kayden.

Breaking from their kiss, "look who's talking. What was it they called you? Caviar?" retorted her aunt.

Kayden's face turned red from embarrassment.

"Caviar?" repeated Jackson. "Oh, I bet you love that sis," he said playfully.

"Shut up, Jackson," Kayden steamed.

They turned and left the graveyard. Ramsey couldn't help but reflect on the events of the night. He might not fully understand the mystical beliefs of the Toth family, but one thing was certain–there were forces beyond the realm of his understanding.

Ramsey and Whip said their goodbyes for the evening and made their way to the squad car. The scapulars, once symbols of ancient devotion, now carried an extra layer of significance for them.

Little did either of them know that this Halloween night would forever alter their perception of the supernatural, leaving them with a lingering sense of awe and respect for the mysteries that coexisted with the tangible reality they patrolled as police officers.

The four family members made it inside to their house exhausted, but unable to come down off the night's intensity level. Jackson went to play some late night online gaming to lower his excitement. Kayden went to her room and laid down. She thought of Drake. Looking at her phone, she had twenty missed texts. Looks like the group wanted a check-in. As she was getting ready to respond to them, her aunt and mom came in.

Kayden couldn't tell if this was an inquisition or lynching. She prepared for the worse, after all she went out of the circle and put them all in danger.

Hollyn spoke first. "What you did tonight was reckless. Breaking our protective circle could have allowed those spirits to attack us. It left us vulnerable Kayden," she stated with disdain coming off her tongue.

Kailynn put a hand on her sister's shoulder to calm her down. She grabbed Hollyn and pulled her back a step. She stepped forward and with a stern voice agreed with her sister.

"Hollyn is right Kayden. You could have hurt us."

"Or worse," interrupted Hollyn.

"Relax Hollyn," Kailynn defended.

"I'm sorry, guys," Kayden said, in a very apologetic voice. She meant it. She knew based on what her aunt had drilled into her head, what could have happened. "I don't know why I did it. I felt compelled for reasons I cannot explain," she whined.

"Compelled?" questioned her mom, prompting Kayden to explain more specifically what she meant.

Kayden shrugged her shoulders. "You know, instinctively I felt an emotional pull to act. I could feel the miner's grip loosening while we were praying, but their will to stay was keeping them from leaving. It was like I knew what they needed to hear or feel to let go. You know?" she asked, looking for some kind of understanding.

Kailynn stood looking at her daughter dumbfounded. Hollyn to her credit wasn't much better, but still had a disapproving look on her face. They both stood there staring at each other for what seemed an eternity. Finally, Kayden couldn't stand the stare off so she broke the silence.

"Well?" she said to both of them, hoping for some kind of response to their weird reaction to her explanation.

"Well," echoed her mom. "If what you are saying is true, you are a lot like Hollyn. You feel not only their energy, but emotions."

Kayden's eyebrows raised in confusion. "What does that even mean?" she responded.

"It means," interjected her aunt, "you have an ability to talk to them without actually speaking. You can understand their emotional state and interpret their need or desire, causing them to stay or act on the mortal plane."

Kayden's eyes about bulged out of her head. She had heard them talking through her emotions?

"Just because you heard them and felt the need for action, still doesn't free you from breaking rank, kid. Remember that next time we have to go through this," Hollyn instructed and strutted out of the room, shutting the door behind her.

Her niece looked back at her mother confused and a bit dejected. She helped the family succeed tonight and with minimal training compared to what her aunt said she had growing up. Looking back at her mom, Kailynn could see the hurt in her daughter's eyes. She moved to sit next to her and hug her. Kayden didn't resist. Quietly, she whispered to her daughter.

"She's just mad because you can do it better than she could back at your age," Kailynn said.

"Really?" Kayden responded.

From outside the door, somewhere down the hallway, Hollyn yelled, "I heard that!"

Kailynn giggled next to her daughter. Kayden looked at her mom as if to ask, 'how did she hear that?'

Her mom shook her head. "She didn't hear us. She just knows her sister too well."

Chapter Twenty: Tying Up Loose Ends

On Monday, Aunt Hollyn informed the kids she would take them to school and pick them up. After the events over the weekend, she felt an escort might be in their best interest.

Kayden had spent much of Sunday texting the group. She said she would fill them in on her Halloween night's exploits in person. It's not that she didn't trust them, but she didn't trust texting information which might implicate her and her family over the cemetery issue. It was good enough for Drake, Owen, and Shay. The others were skeptical, since she had chosen not to tell them about things until everything blew up on Friday. However, with those three behind her, she felt pretty safe that things would be okay. Technically, Shades was with her all the way, but his insatiable need to be in on the gossip led him to go begging and pleading with her to throw him a bone. All she would tip off was things were over. He finally relented.

They would meet up after school and head to the park. Drake promised to drive her home afterward. Aunt Hollyn was okay with that plan. She liked Drake and felt he and his friends were great for Kayden. The Harrisburg Park was a nice place which had a strong family atmosphere to it. Drake said they would meet under a pavilion by the lagoon. Kayden really didn't know what he meant by a lagoon. It sounded ominous, but he had sent the laugh emoji along with all her new friends.

Brooklyn had texted, "relax Caviar. It's a pond."

***

Jackson, on the other hand seemed to have found himself a possible best friend. Boyd Baker had taken on the role of his side-kick and relished the attention it was bringing to him at school. Jackson was not someone who desired being put in the spotlight, but given the events of the last three weeks since he came to this school; it was hard to avoid. Boyd didn't make it any better. However, there were perks to having a side-kick. Boyd started introducing Jackson to a few of his friends and even a few cool girls who he referred to as 'fire.' Things were getting interesting to Jackson. New school, friends, and he was fitting in nicely.

Boyd couldn't wait to see what the next big surprise adventure from hanging around Jackson would be, but he was ready.

The Hungarian Cemetery Secrets Within Backup

* * *

***

Ramsey and Whip met with Hollyn in the morning after she dropped off the kids at school. Bringing the mining company's cover up to light was the major topic of concern. They met at the BBQ Barn for coffee and breakfast. Whip was a biscuit and gravy guy and had been ordering that breakfast dish for years. He had been coming to this location since he could remember. They were famous for their pies, especially the raisin. While waiting for the server to seat them, Ramsey insisted on picking up Hollyn's tab. This immediately started an argument for at least five minutes, but she relented once Whip cleared his throat harshly. Hollyn stopped and looked around at the other patrons who had stopped eating to watch them make a spectacle of themselves. Her face turned red instantly and zipped up.

Whip shook his head. "Well, you two put yourselves in the spotlight."

Ramsey chuckled quietly and made a public apology to the customers. This put them at ease and everyone went back to their own business. Early morning crowd catered to the older, retired generation who frequented the business. Coffee was good and the service was spot on.

When they got to their table, Ramsey ordered the hickory smoked Kentuckian ham & eggs, while Hollyn went with the chicken and waffles. Once coffee was poured for a second round, Whip addressed the issue.

"Okay Hollyn," he started, "here's how we're going to play this out. I had a professional landscaper, who I know pretty well check out the cemetery. He was 'fairly' certain the death of Sadie was an accident. Apparently, some of these older cemeteries can have sinkholes which over time develop through natural stages of erosion, land shifts, minor earthquakes, and even critters like groundhogs. Poor Sadie, that night, simply stumbled into one in the dark. She tried to claw her way back up through it, but unfortunately succumbed to asphyxiation," he finished solemnly.

Hollyn liked the cover-up story. It would explain the series of events which corresponded with testimony that night. No one was really going to refute it and it took the heat off of the kids.

"The story connects dots logically," she responded. "It gives the town a proper explanation for the events leading up to that night. The town is all about supernatural rumors and ghost tales from the past regarding the place. It might just be accepted by everyone," she surmised.

Ramsey blew on his coffee. "It will also allow us to introduce the mining cover-up," he commented from his cup.

"How so?" asked Hollyn, clearly confused.

Whip took the reins to her question. "Since we had to open up an investigation into the cemetery because of the teen's unfortunate accident, our team accidentally stumbled onto the cover-up in the archives. We let the press run with it. We're fairly certain with the press digging into the archives, which are free to the public they will see for themselves. We will be fully supported by the locals on our assessment of events," he concluded confidently.

Ramsey nodded his agreement.

Hollyn raised her eyebrows in a little disbelief.

She knew there would eventually be some kind of release to the information, but not so soon after the cemetery debacle. She looked around the tables at the patrons eating. They had got a corner table away from anyone trying to listen to their conversation. When she was satisfied she could speak with no one 'accidentally hearing her', she addressed the sheriff quietly.

"What about Sadie's dad? He was really torn up and fully blames our family. He ripped into poor Kailynn while she was at work," she informed him.

Whip put down his coffee and sat back in his chair. A look of serious contemplation shown on his face.

"I'm planning on addressing the situation with him personally before I release the statement."

That caught Hollyn off-guard. "Are you sure that is a good idea?" she challenged.

"We do," responded Ramsey, cutting off Whip. "He needs a little different attention than most of the family member's victims we deal with. Chris Stone's standing in the community and business status makes him a little different to deal with. He can cause a large stink for many people, especially you guys, if he pushes things. With us giving him the common courtesy of revealing things, before we 'officially' go to the press, well; it might calm the storm and satiate Chris," the deputy concluded.

"Let me make sure I have this right," Hollyn replied. "Accident at Ledford because of a sinkhole and cover-up revealed in investigation. Our family name gets cleared along with the unfortunate souls who were victims of the mining accident and Sadie's death gets an official report as 'accidental asphyxiation?'" she summed up.

Warren nodded. "Bottom line," he answered, "case closed for both incidents."

Ramsey stood up. "The morning is getting on Sheriff. I'll meet you at the station."

He walked over to Hollyn. She looked up at the deputy. He bent down and kissed her cheek. "May I call you later?" he asked sheepishly.

Hollyn surprised by the gesture, blushed. She coughed a little at her words.

"Sure Byron, I'd like that."

He nodded and left the restaurant.

Silence passed between Warren and Hollyn. Finally, he stood up after paying the server for his breakfast. Putting on his hat, he tipped the front to Hollyn.

"Until our next meeting Ms. Toth."

Warren left Hollyn to finish her food.

***

Kayden finished telling the group about the series of events which completed the chapter on the Hungarian Cemetery. All of them sat stunned at the unfolding of the story. None of them had dreamed Kayden's family along with the Sheriff and Deputy would have worked together in the manner she had retold. It left them with many questions, but Kayden had been up front with them before she started revealing the story. She couldn't really get in depth on some things her family were practicing in nor the police's involvement in the incident. None of it technically happened and everyone there would deny being a part of it. They would have to just accept it at face value.

Drake, as always, found his voice in the group and was the first to speak after Kayden's tale.

"Kayden," he started quietly. "That all sounded dangerous."

She nodded her agreement with his assessment.

"Yeah," added Shades, "but totally bad-ass!"

Gage smiled at Shade's comment along with the others.

Owen gave a playful punch into Kayden's shoulder. "No one should mess with you, girl," he joked. His girlfriend came up to Kayden and gave her a hug, but said nothing.

Brooklyn asked, "So what happens now?"

"Good question," Gage echoed, looking back at Kayden.

Kayden shrugged her shoulders in uncertainty. "All I know is Aunt Hollyn was supposed to talk to the Sheriff after she dropped us off at school. I haven't been home yet, but she thought the police would make some kind of announcement on the whole unsolved case today," she revealed.

Olivia put her arm around Shay. She was sitting on his lap. "Does this mean that the entire issue is going to be put to bed, then?" Shay sat holding her, content as a puppy.

"If what Aunt Hollyn says is true, the police will end Sadie's case, yeah," she responded. "As far as it being put to bed?" she continued. "I am not familiar with how this town fully works yet, but given the short time I've been here, I'd say memories are long."

Gage answered, "Damn right they are," he spat with an edge to his voice.

"Well, we're in the clear, man," Drake said specifically to Gage. "The only ass-clowns who will be an issue are those who just want attention at school," he said.

"The world's full of them," replied Shades jovially.

Everyone chuckled.

Once the mood had relaxed, Kayden stood up from the picnic table as they were sitting around under a pavilion. She addressed the entire group.

"Thank you guys for helping me through all this stuff. You do not know how much I needed your support." Her face was serious and appreciative.

"Well Caviar," Brooklyn responded. "Your welcome, but we're going to have to help you next on your hair," she said, looking concerned.

"Oh, I know," Braelyn agreed, picking up where Brooklyn was going.

Ayelyn left Owen's side and went over to Kayden and ran her fingers through her friend's raven hair. "Are we talking make-over ladies?" she asked out loud to no one specifically.

"Basketball is starting up girls," Olivia barked. "It will have to be a Saturday night event, if it's going to happen," she cooed.

Kayden looked at the girls and then at Drake confused.

"Don't look at me, kid," Drake said. "Chicks secrets are not my area of expertise, but if you want me to shoo them off, just say the word," he challenged in a humorous tone.

"Good luck with that," Owen replied with sarcasm. "Make-overs are a big deal, man."

"Does that mean there will be a girl pillow fight in pajamas later in the night?" asked Shades seriously.

"Jeremiah," cried Brooklyn, "you are always

taking things too far."

"I told you not to call me Jeremiah, Brooky," he retorted.

Gage laughed. "Well, Shades," he quipped, "that certainly wasn't a no."

***

Later that night, at the Toth family home, everyone was sitting in the living room watching television quietly, enjoying an uneventful evening. Kayden was on her phone texting, Jackson was playing a game on one of his apps, Kailynn was nodding off in the recliner and Hollyn was actually watching Yellowstone Season 2. Hollyn really liked Beth Dutton's character in the show. Sure, she could be a little over the top and down right mean as a gar, but she was always dedicated to family, especially her dad. Hollyn could relate.

For a Monday night, it was relaxing.

A knock at the door startled everyone out of their lazy stupor. Kailynn jerked up out of the recliner and Hollyn stood, moving up beside her. From the silhouette standing outside the door, Hollyn knew right away it was Ramsey.

"I've got this," she said, putting a reassuring hand on Kailynn's shoulder.

"You sure?" Kailynn said, just a touch of concern in her voice.

"Oh yeah. My boy toy can't get enough of me," she responded in a cocky voice.

Shaking her head at Hollyn, Kailynn told the kids she was calling it a night and went upstairs to go to bed.

As she was heading up the flight of steps, Hollyn answered the door.

Before Ramsey could say anything, Hollyn beat him to the punch.

"I said you could call me, not show up here like a dog in heat, Ramsey," she touted to the Deputy.

He gave her a wry look at the comment.

She reached out to straighten his collar. "Well, since you're already here..." she let the comment hang in the air.

His eyes got big at her statement. Hollyn loved catching him off-guard.

"Ummm, I'm here on official police business Hollyn," he stammered.

"Well, get to it then," she said in a disappointing pout.

Ramsey regained his composure. "The case has been officially closed and listed as an accidental death. It was announced this afternoon. We convinced the Stone family not to sue the City of Ledford for the hazardous hole, as no one could predict it was even there."

"How did Chris take the news?" asked Hollyn, curious about their interaction.

"As well as he could, I expect," replied Ramsey. "He's hurting and having someone to focus his pain on is one thing, but an accident...well, he and his family will begin focusing on healing from it."

Hollyn understood what he was getting at. She could relate to that a lot based on her experiences over the years.

"Alls well, that ends well I guess," she quipped.

"We also revealed to the press the evidence recently found in our archives. I expect you'll have some reporters hawking around the house soon asking questions. I just wanted to make you aware, so you don't do something rash before knowing what was going on," he stated.

"Rash? Me?" she answered indignantly.

"Who would believe you capable of that?" he answered with sarcasm.

She gave him a disapproving look.

"Well, that's about it," he said with finality.

She smiled. "Thanks for coming by Byron," she replied a bit disappointed.

He turned around and she began to close the door, already looking back into the living room. Suddenly, the door stopped short of shutting. It hit something. She turned to look; it was Ramsey's foot. Her face showed total confusion.

"Something else, Deputy?" she asked uncertainly.

Ramsey smiled and pulled the door open. "You said since I was already here," he said in a seductive tone.

Now it was Hollyn's turn to stammer.

"Ummm, you said you were doing official business," she responded, caught off her guard.

"Yep," he replied. "Now it's complete, so I'm off the clock," he clarified, reaching around Hollyn's waist and pulling her to him. It all happened so fast, Hollyn's mind could barely register what her lips were already telling her as Ramsey kissed her deeply.

Jackson and Kayden both watched the entire spectacle unfold.

"That's live entertainment," murmured Jackson with a huge grin on his face.

"First time I ever seen her speechless. Let's see if we can keep it going," Kayden said mischievously.

She grabbed Jackson's arm and pulled him with her. They stepped up behind the two as they kissed.

"So," Kayden's voice interrupted their moment. Both of them broke off their kiss.

"Will we be calling you Uncle Ramsey soon?" Kayden asked innocently.

Jackson loved the orneriness of his sister and played on her move. "Do we get to ride in the police car and flash the siren Uncle Ramsey?"

Ramsey laughed, but Hollyn pushed away from him.

"I've heard enough from you two," she said in a frustrated voice. It was also mixed with embarrassment. "It's a school night. Get your butt's upstairs and ready for bed," she ordered, pointing up the steps.

Kayden and Jackson put on the disappointed faces, but turned to go up the stairs. They walked dejectedly up to add extra drama to the scene. However, they were both smiling as they went. Upon getting to the top, their mom was standing on the landing, waiting for them. Both paused, thinking they were going to get into trouble.

Kailynn smiled at her kids and motioned them to keep going. When both of them reached the top with her, Kailynn hugged them both at the same time. She then commented, "bout time she found someone who can handle her."

"No one can handle her mom," Kayden said.

"Same could be said about you," smirked Jackson.

"Ouch!" he yelled. Kayden punched him in the arm and walked straight to her room, grinning the entire time.

About the Author

Joshua Banks was raised in Southern Illinois. Initially, he started working in sales/marketing for Coca-Cola out of college, but transitioned into teaching high school English. He's been in education for over 22+ years. Recently he is taking a swing on another path part-time, while continuing to teach. He released his first Indie novel, High School Basketball: Establishing a Program. Joshua has also tried his luck at audiobook narration with ACX and Findawayvoices. He has been lucky enough to work with authors Holly and Ryan Garcia, Jaxon Reed, Frank Wood, Shana Gorian, David Owain Hughes, Kevin Candela, Robert Barlow Jr, and many others. It was getting to know Holly that he submitted his work to the editor of CloseToTheBone Publishing. Now, his Sci/Fi novel, Event Horizon released in the winter of 2021. As an Indie publisher, he has followed up with his second novel in his Event Horizon Series called Dark Sentinel the following year.

Thank you for reading. To learn more about Joshua Banks, go to: officialjoshuabankswebsite.com

Other Books by Author:

Event Horizon… Released Nov 2021
High School Basketball: Establishing a Program… Released Dec 2021
Dark Sentinel: Event Horizon Series…Released November 2022

Joshua Banks

Short Story from the excerpts of **The Hungarian Cemetery: Secrets Within the Muddy Waters Series** found in **TRICK-OR-TREAT THRILLERS** edited by Roma Gray…Released February 2024

Audiobooks Narrated/Produced by Joshua Banks

The Longest Halloween, Book Three: Gabbie Del Toro and the Mystery of the Warlock's Urn by Frank Wood
Ethinium's Vault: Steam & Aether, Book 1 by Jaxon Reed
Welcome to Spirit County: Trick-or-Treat Thrillers, Paranormal Westerns: Kevin Candela (Author), Roma Gray (Author), John Bruni (Author), Dona Fox (Author), Essel Pratt (Author), Raymond Johnson (Author), Night Sky Book Services (Publisher)
The Complete Exoskeleton Chronicles by Chad Descoteaux
Santa: An Interview by Meaghan Hurn
Playing With Reality by Kevin Candela
Bow-Legged Buccaneers from Outer Space by David Owain Hughes
The Easton Falls Massacre: Bigfoot's Revenge by Holly Rae Garcia & Ryan Prentice Garcia
The Haunted Lighthouse, The Legend of Creepy Hollow, and The Curse of Pirate's Cove from Tales of the Lost and Found by Shana Gorian
Time Passed by Robert Barlow Jr.
D.O.G. Executive Order by Robert Barlow Jr.
In Search of the Perfect Buzz: An 80's Metal Memoir by Tommy Schenker
My Backpack is Heavier Than Yours by Dr. Edwin Garcia Jr.

To Learn More

Listed below are images captured of what is left of the original Hungarian Cemetery (2024).

Joshua Banks

HUNGARIAN CEMETERY

HUNGARIAN CEMETERY

Made in the USA
Monee, IL
09 March 2024

54723103R00164